THE HEIGHT OF THE SCREAM

Ramsey Campbell lives in Liverpool, and has been a full-time writer since 1973. He also reviews films for BBC Radio Merseyside.

Acclaim for his novel THE DOLL WHO ATE HIS MOTHER:

'It's superb. Grand Guignol in the grand manner. This is the chilling best!' Robert Bloch

'At once beautiful, shocking and thoroughly terrifying: we see and hear, we smell and feel the acid stench and spider touch of fear. An outstanding achievement' Fritz Lieber

'The climax of the hunt is one of the most effective sequences in modern horror fiction' Stephen King

Also by Ramsey Campbell in Star:

**THE DOLL WHO ATE HIS MOTHER
THE FACE THAT MUST DIE
THE FAR REACHES OF FEAR
SUPERHORROR**

THE HEIGHT OF THE SCREAM

Ramsey Campbell

A STAR BOOK

published by
the Paperback Division of
W. H. ALLEN & Co. Ltd

A Star Book
Published in 1981
by the Paperback Division of
W. H. Allen & Co. Ltd
A Howard and Wyndham Company
44 Hill Street, London W1X 8LB

First published in Great Britain by
Millington Books Ltd, 1978

Copyright © 1976 by Ramsey Campbell

Printed in Great Britain by
Hunt Barnard Printing Ltd., Aylesbury, Bucks.

ISBN 0 352 30803 6

This one is for
Lin Carter, Richard Davis, Hugh Lamb
Robert A. W. Lowndes, Michel Parry, David Sutton
good men all

Sport. Thou nib, thou quill, thou more than porcupine!
Go, get thee hence; and scribe us such a tale
As may unfix the brain within its cage,
Unfix the locks, and start the soul to flee.

The Schemer's Stratagem

This book is sold subject to the condition that it shall
not, by way of trade or otherwise, be lent,
re-sold, hired out or otherwise circulated without the
publisher's prior consent in any form of
binding or cover other than that in which it is published
and without a similar condition including this
condition being imposed on the subsequent purchaser.

Contents

The Scar	6
The Whining	25
Missing	34
Reply Guaranteed	51
Jack's Little Friend	68
Beside the Seaside	80
The Cellars	88
The Height of the Scream	105
Litter	123
Cyril	135
Smoke Kiss	144
The Words that Count	153
Ash	164
The Telephones	175
In the Shadows	183
Horror House of Blood	192

The Scar

"It was most odd on the bus today," Lindsay Rice said.

Jack Rossiter threw his cigarette into the fire and lit another. His wife Harriet glanced at him uneasily; she could see he was in no mood for her brother's circumlocutions.

"Most odd," said Lindsay. "Rather upsetting, in fact. It reminded me, the Germans—now was it the Germans? Yes, I think it was the Germans—used to have this thing about *doppelgängers*, the idea being that if you saw your double it meant you were going to die. But of course you didn't see him. That's right, of course, I should explain."

Jack moved in his armchair. "I'm sorry, Lindsay," he interrupted, "I just don't see where you're tending. I'm sorry."

"It's all right, Lindsay," Harriet said. "Jack's been a bit tired lately. Go on."

But at that moment the children tumbled into the room like pierrots, their striped pajamas bold against the pastel lines of wallpaper. "Douglas tried to throw me into the bath, and he hasn't brushed his teeth!" Elaine shouted triumphantly.

"There'll be spankings for two in a minute," Jack threatened, but he smiled. "Good night, darling. Good night, darling. No, you've had a hard day, darling, I'll put them to bed."

"Not so hard as you," Harriet said, standing up. "You stay and talk to Lindsay."

Jack grimaced inwardly; he had wanted Harriet to rest, but somehow it now appeared as if he'd been trying to escape Lindsay.

"Sorry, Lindsay, you were saying?" he prompted as the thumping on the staircase ceased.

"Oh, yes, on the bus. Well, it was this morning, I saw someone who looked like you. I was going to speak to him until I realized." Rice glanced around the room; although his weekly invitation was of some years' standing, he could never remember exactly where everything was. Not that it mattered: the whole was solid. Armchairs, television, bookcase full of Penguins and book-club editions and Shorrock's *Valuer's Manual*—there it was, on top of the bookcase, the wedding photograph which Jack had carefully framed for Harriet. "Yes, he was as thin as you've been getting, but he had a scar from here to here." Rice encompassed his left temple and jawbone with finger and thumb like dividers.

"So he wasn't really my double. My time hasn't run out after all."

"Well, I hope not!" Rice laughed a little too long; Jack felt his mouth stretching as he forced it to be sociable. "We've been slackening off at the office," Rice said. "How are things at the jeweller's? Nothing stolen yet, I hope?"

"No, everything's under control," Jack replied. Feet ran across the floor above. "Hang on, Lindsay," he said, "sounds like Harriet's having trouble."

Harriet had quelled the rebellion when he arrived; she closed the door of the children's room and regarded him. "Christ, the man's tact!" he exploded.

"Shh, Jack, he'll hear you." She put her arms around him. "Don't be cruel to Lindsay," she pleaded. "You know I always had the best of everything and Lindsay never did—unhappy at school, always being put down by my father, never daring to open his mouth—darling, you know he finds it difficult to talk to people. Now I've got you. Surely we can spare him kindness at least."

"Of course we can." He stroked her hair. "It's just that—damn it, not only does he say I'm losing weight as though I'm being underfed or something, but he asks me if the shop's been broken into yet!"

"Poor darling, don't worry. I'm sure the police will catch them before they raid the shop. And if not, there's always insurance."

"Yes, there's insurance, but it won't rebuild my display! Can't you understand I take as much pride in my shop as you take in the house? Probably some jumped-up little skinheads who throw the loot away once their tarty little teenyboppers have played with it!"

"That doesn't sound like you at all, Jack," Harriet said.

"I'm sorry, love. You know I'm really here. Come on, I'd better fix up tomorrow night with Lindsay."

"If you feel like a rest we could have him round here."

"No, he opens out a bit when he's in a pub. Besides, I like the walk to Lower Brichester."

"Just so long as you come back in one piece, my love."

Rice heard them on the stairs. He hurried back to his chair from the bookcase where he had been inspecting the titles. One of these days he must offer to lend them some books—anything to make them like him more. He knew he'd driven Jack upstairs. Why couldn't he be direct instead of circling the point like a wobbling whirligig? But every time he tried to grasp an intention or a statement it slid out of reach. Even if he hung a sign on his bedroom wall—he'd once thought of one: "I shall act directly"—he would forget it before he left the flat. Even as he forgot his musings when Jack and Harriet entered the room.

"I'd better be off," he said. "You never can tell with the last bus round here."

"I'll see you tomorrow night, then," Jack told him, patting his shoulder. "I'll call round and pick you up."

But he never had the courage to invite them to his flat, Lindsay thought; he knew it wasn't good enough for them. Not that they would show it—rather would they do everything to hide their feelings out of kindness, which would be worse. Tomorrow night as usual he would be downstairs early to wait for Jack in the doorway. He waved to them as they stood linked in their bright frame, then struck off down the empty road. The fields were grey and silent, and above the semi-detached roofs the moon was set in a plush ring of cold November mist. At the bus-stop he thought: I wish I could do something for them so they'd be grateful to me.

Harriet was bending over the cooker; she heard no footsteps—she had no chance to turn before the newspaper was over her face.

"I see the old Jack's back with us," she said, fighting off the *Brichester Herald*.

"You haven't seen it?" He guided her hand to the headline: *Youths Arrested—Admit to Jewel Thefts*. He was beaming; he read the report again with Harriet, the three boys who'd hoped to stockpile jewellery but had been unable to market it without attracting the police. "Maybe now we can all get some sleep," he said. "Maybe I can give up smoking."

"Don't give it up for me, Jack, I know you need it. But if you *did* give it up I'd be very happy."

Douglas and Elaine appeared, pummelling toward their tea. "Now just you sit down and wait," Jack said, "or we'll eat it for you."

After tea he lit a cigarette, then glanced at Harriet. "Don't worry, darling," she advised. "Take things easy for a while. Come on, monsters, you can help clear up." She knew the signs—spilled sugar, dropped knife; Jack would turn hypertense with relief if he didn't rest.

But ten minutes later he was in the kitchen. "Must go," he said. "Give myself time for a stroll before I meet Lindsay. Anyway, the news ought to give the conversation a lift."

"Come back whole, darling," Harriet said, not knowing.

Yes, he liked to walk through Lower Brichester. He'd made the walk, with variations, for almost two years; ever since his night out drinking with Rice had settled into habit. It had been his suggestion, primarily to please Harriet, for he knew she liked to think he and Lindsay were friends; but by now he met Lindsay out of a sense of duty, which was rarely proof against annoyance as the evening wore on. Never mind, there was the walk. If he felt insecure, as he often did when walking—the night, Harriet elsewhere—he gained a paradoxical sense of security from Lower Brichester; the bleared fish-and-chip shop windows, the crowds outside pubs, a drunk punching someone's face with a soft moist sound,—it reassured him to think that here was a level to which he could never be reduced.

Headlights blazed down a side-street, billowing with mist and motorcycle fumes. They spotlighted a broken wall across the street from Rossiter; a group of girls huddled on the shattered bricks, laughing forth fog as the motorcycle gang fondled them roughly with words. Rossiter gazed at them; no doubt the jewel thieves had been of the same mould. He felt a little guilty as he watched the girls, embracing themselves to keep out the cold; but he had his answer ready —nothing would change them, they were fixed; if he had money, it was because he could use it properly. He turned onward; he would have to use the alley on the right if he were not to keep Rice waiting.

Suddenly the shrieks of laughter behind the roaring engines were cut off. A headlight was feeling its way along the walls, finding one house protruding part of a ruined frontage like a piece of jigsaw, the next dismally curtained, its neighbor shuttered with corrugated tin, its makeshift door torn down like an infuriating lid. For a moment the beam followed a figure: a man in a long black coat swaying along the pavement, a grey woollen sock pulled down over his face. The girls huddled closer, silently. Jack shuddered; the exploratory progress of the figure seemed unformed, undirected. Then the light was gone; the girls giggled in the darkness, and beyond a streetlamp the figure fumbled into the tin-shuttered house. Jack turned up his coat collar and hurried into the alley. The engines roared louder.

He was halfway up the alley when he heard the footsteps. The walls

THE SCAR

were narrow; there was barely room for the other, who seemed in a hurry, to pass. Jack pressed against the wall; it was cold and rough beneath his hand. Behind him the footsteps stopped.

He looked back. The entrance to the alley whirled with fumes, against which a figure moved toward him, vaguely outlined. It held something in its hand. Jack felt automatically for his lighter. Then the figure spoke.

"You're Jack Rossiter." The voice was soft and anonymous yet somehow penetrated the crescendi of the motorcycles. "I'll be visiting your shop soon."

For a moment Jack thought he must know the man, though his face was merely a black egg in the shadows; but something in the figure's slow approach warned him. Suddenly he knew what that remark implied. Cold rushed into his stomach, and metal glinted in the figure's hand. Jack retreated along the wall, his fingers searching frantically for a door. His foot tangled with an abandoned tin; he kicked it toward the figure and ran.

The fog boiled round him; metal clattered; a foot hooked his ankle and tripped him. The engines were screaming; as Jack raised his head a car's beam thrust into his eyes. He scrabbled at potato peelings and sardine tins, and struggled to his knees. A foot between his shoulders ground him down. The car's light dimmed and vanished. He struggled onto his back, cold peel sticking to his cheek, and the foot pressed on his heart. The metal closed in the figure's palm. Above him hands displayed the tin which he had kicked. The insidious voice said something. When the words reached him, Rossiter began to tear at the leg in horror and fury. The black egg bent nearer. The foot pressed harder, and the rusty lid of the tin came down toward Jack's face.

Though the bandage was off he could still feel the cut, blazing now and then from his temple to his jawbone. He forced himself to forget; he stuffed fuel into the living-room fire and opened his book. But it failed to soothe him. Don't brood, he told himself savagely, worse is probably happening in Lower Brichester at this moment. If only Harriet hadn't seen him unbandaged at the hospital! He could feel her pain more keenly than his own since he'd come home. He kept thinking of her letting the kettle scream so that he wouldn't hear her sobbing in the kitchen. Then she'd brought him coffee, her face still wet beneath her hair from water to wash away the tears. Why had he told her at the hospital "It's not what he did to me, it's what he said he'd do to Douglas and Elaine"? He cursed himself for spreading more suffering than he himself had had to stand. Even Rice had seemed to feel himself obscurely to blame, although Jack had insisted that it was his own fault for walking through that area.

"Go and say goodnight to Daddy," Harriet called.

The children padded in. "Daddy's face is getting better," Elaine said.

He saw the black egg bearing down on them. God, he swore, if he should lay one finger—! "Daddy's surviving his accident," he told them. "Good night, children."

Presently he heard Harriet slowly descending the stairs, each step a thought. Suddenly she rushed into the room and hid her face on his chest. "Oh, please, please, darling, what did he say about the children?" she cried.

"I won't have you disturbed, my love," he said, holding her as she trembled. "I can worry enough for both of us. And as long as you take them there and back to school, it doesn't matter what the sod said."

"And what about your shop?" she asked through her tears.

"Never mind the shop!" He tried not to think of his dream of the smashed window, of the foul disorder he might find one morning. "The police will find him, don't you worry."

"But you couldn't even describe—" The doorbell rang. "Oh God, it's Lindsay," she said. "Could you go, darling? I can't let him see me like this."

THE SCAR

"Oh, that's good—I mean I'm glad you've got the bandage off," said Lindsay. Behind him the fog swallowed the bedraggled trees and blotted out the fields. He stared at Jack, then muttered "Sorry, better let you close the door."

"Come in and get some fire," Jack said. "Harriet will have the coffee ready in a minute."

Rice plodded round the room, then sat down opposite Jack. He stared at the wedding photograph. He rubbed his hands and gazed at them. He looked up at the ceiling. At last he turned to Jack: "What —" he glanced around wildly—"what's that you're reading?"

"*The Heart of the Matter.* Second time, in fact. You should try it sometime."

Harriet looked in, dabbing at one eye. "Think I rubbed in some soap," she explained. "Hello, Lindsay. If we're talking about books, Jack, you said you'd read *The Lord of the Rings.*"

"Well, I can't now, darling, since I'm working tomorrow. Back to work at last, Lindsay. Heaven knows what sort of a state the shop will be in with Phillips in charge."

"You always said you could rely on him in an emergency," Harriet protested.

"Well, this is the test. Yes, white as usual for me, please, darling."

Harriet withdrew to the kitchen. "I read a book this week," Rice caught at the conversation, "about a man—what's his name, no, I forget—whose friend is in danger from someone, he finds out—and he finally pulls this someone off a cliff and gets killed himself." He was about to add "At least he did something with himself. I don't like books about people failing," but Jack took the cue:

"A little unrealistic for me," he said, "after what happened."

"Oh, I never asked," Rice's hands gripped each other, "where did it?"

"Just off the street parallel to yours, the next but two. In the alley."

"But that's where—" he lost something again—"where there's all sorts of violence."

"You shouldn't live so near it, Lindsay," Harriet said above a tray. "Make the effort. Move soon."

"Depressing night," Jack remarked as he helped Rice don his coat. "Drop that book in sometime, Lindsay. I'd like to read it."

Of course he wouldn't, Rice thought as he breathed in the curling fog and met the trees forming from the murk; he'd been trying to be kind. Rice had failed again. Why had he been unable to speak, to tell Jack that he had seen his double leave the bus and enter an abandoned house opposite that alley? The night of the mutilation Rice had waited in his doorway, feeling forsaken, sure that Jack had decided not to come; ashamed now, he blamed himself—Jack would be whole now if Rice hadn't made him feel it was his duty to meet him. Something was going to happen; he sensed it looming. If he could only warn them, prevent it—but prevent what? He saw the figures falling from the cliff-top against the azure sky, the seagulls screaming around him— but the mist hung about him miserably, stifling his intentions. He began to hurry to the bus-stop.

The week unfolded wearily. It was as formless in Rice's mind as the obscured fields when he walked up the Rossiters' street again, his book collecting droplets in his hand. He rang the bell and waited, shivering; the windows were blurred by mist.

"Oh, Lindsay," said Harriet. She had run to the door; it was clear she had been crying. "I don't know whether—"

Jack appeared in the hall, one hand possessively gripping the living-room doorframe, the cigarette upon his lip flaking down his shirt. "Is it your night already?" he demanded of Rice. "I thought it'd be early to bed for us. Come in for God's sake, don't freeze us to death."

Harriet threw Lindsay a pleading look which he could not interpret.

"Sorry," he said. "I didn't know you were tired."

"Who said tired? Come on, man, start thinking! God, I give up." Jack threw up his hands and whirled into the living-room.

"Lindsay, Jack's been having a terrible time. The shop was broken into last night."

"What's all that whispering?" a voice shouted. "Aren't I one of the family any more?"

"Jack, don't be illogical. Surely Lindsay and I can talk." But she motioned Lindsay into the living-room.

"Treating me like a stranger in my own house!"

Lindsay dropped the book. Suddenly he realized what he'd seen: Jack's face was paler, thinner than last week; the scar looked older than seemed possible. He bent for the book. No, what he was thinking was absurd; Harriet would have noticed. Jack was simply worried. It must be worry.

"Brought me a book, have you? Let's see it, then. Oh, for God's sake, Lindsay, I can't waste my time with this sort of thing!"

"Jack!" cried Harriet. "Lindsay brought it specially."

"Don't pity Lindsay, he won't thank you for it. You think we're patronizing you, don't you Lindsay? Inviting you up the posh end of town?"

This couldn't be, Rice thought; not in this pastel living-room, not with the wedding photograph fixed forever; their lives were solid, not ephemeral like his own. "I—don't know what you mean," he faltered.

"Jack, I won't have you speaking to Lindsay like that," Harriet said. "Lindsay, would you help me make the coffee?"

"Siding with your brother now," Jack accused. "I don't need him at a time like this, I need you. You've forgotten the shop already, but I haven't. I suppose I needn't expect any comfort tonight."

"Oh, Jack, try and get a grip on yourself," but now her voice was softer. Don't! Lindsay warned her frantically. That's exactly what he wants!

"Take your book, Lindsay," Jack said through his fingers, "and make sure you're invited in future." Harriet glanced at him in anguish and hurried Lindsay out.

"I'm sorry you've been hurt, Lindsay," she said. "Of course you're always welcome here. You know we love you. Jack didn't mean it. I knew something would happen when I heard about the shop. Jack just ran out of it and didn't come back for hours. But I didn't know it would be like this—" Her voice broke. "Maybe you'd better not come again until Jack's more stable. I'll tell you when it's over. You do understand, don't you?"

"Of course, it doesn't matter," Lindsay said, trembling with formless thoughts. On the hall table a newspaper had been crumpled furiously; he saw the headline—*Jeweller's Raided—Displays Destroyed*. "Can I have the paper?" he asked.

"Take it, please. I'll get in touch with you, I promise. Don't lose heart."

As the door closed Rice heard Jack call "Harriet!" in what sounded like despair. Above, the children were silhouetted on their bedroom window; as Rice trudged away the fog engulfed them. At the bus-stop he read the report; a window broken, destruction everywhere. He gazed ahead blindly. Shafts of bilious yellow pierced the fog, then the grey returned. "Start thinking," was it? Oh yes, he could think—think how easy it would be to fake a raid, knowing the insurance would rebuild what had been destroyed—but he didn't want the implications; the idea was insane, anyway. Who would destroy simply in order to have an excuse for appearing emaciated, unstable? But his thoughts returned to Harriet; he avoided thinking what might be happening in that house. You're jealous! he tried to tell himself. He's her husband! He has the right! Rice became aware that he was holding the book which he had brought for Jack. He stared at the tangled figures falling through blue drops of condensation, then thrust the book into the litter-bin between empty tins and a sherry bottle. He stood waiting in the fog.

The fog trickled through Rice's kitchen window. He leaned his weight on the sash, but again it refused to shut. He shrugged helplessly and tipped the beans into the saucepan. The tap dripped once; he gripped it and screwed it down. Below the window someone came out coughing and shattered something in the dustbin. The tap dripped. He moved toward it, and the bell rang.

It was Harriet in a headscarf. "Oh, don't come in," he said. "It's not fit, I mean—"

"Don't be silly, Lindsay," she told him edgily. "Let me in." Her eyes gathered details: the twig-like crack in one corner of the ceiling, the alarm clock whose hand had been amputated, the cobweb supporting the lamp-flex from the ceiling like a bracket. "But this is so depressing," she said. "Don't stay here, Lindsay. You must move."

"It's just the bed's not made," he tried to explain, but he could see her despairing. He had to turn the subject. "Jack all right?" he asked, then remembered, but too late.

She pulled off her headscarf. "Lindsay, he hasn't been himself since they wrecked the shop," she said with determined calm. "Rows all the time, breaking things—he broke our photograph. He goes out and gets drunk half the evenings. I've never seen him so irrational." Her voice faded. "And there are other things—that I can't tell you about—"

"That's awful. That's terrible." He couldn't bear to see Harriet like this; she was the only one he had ever loved. "Couldn't you get him to see someone, I mean—"

"We've already had a row about that. That was when he broke our photograph."

"How about the children? How's he been to them?" Instantly two pieces fitted together; he waited, chill with horror, for her answer.

"He tells them off for playing, but I can protect them."

How could she be so blind? "Suppose he should do something to them," he said. "You'll have to get out."

"That's one thing I won't do. He's my husband, Lindsay. It's up to me to look after him."

She can't believe that! Lindsay cried. He tottered on the edge of revelation, and fought with his tongue. "Don't you think he's acting as if he was a different person?" He could not be more explicit.

"After what happened that's not so surprising." She drew her headscarf through her fingers and pulled it back, drew and pulled, drew and pulled; Lindsay looked away. "He's left all the displays in Phillips' hands. He's breaking down, Lindsay. I've got to nurse him back. He'll survive, I know he will."

Survive! Lindsay thought with bitterness and horror. And suddenly he remembered that Harriet had been upstairs when he'd described his encounter on the bus; she would never realize, and his tongue would never allow him to tell her. Behind her compassion he sensed a terrible devotion to Jack which he could not break. She was as trapped as he was in this flat. Yet if he could not speak, he must act. The plan against him was clear: he'd been banished from the Rossiters' home, he was unable to protest, Harriet would be alone. There was only one false assumption in the plan, and it concerned himself. It must be false. He could help. He gazed at Harriet; she would never understand, but perhaps she needn't suspect.

The beans sputtered and smouldered in the pan. "Oh, Lindsay, I'm awfully sorry," Harriet said. "You must have your tea. I've got to get back before he comes home. I only called to tell you not to come round for a while. Please don't, I'll be all right."

"I'll stay away until you tell me," Lindsay lied. As she reached the hall he called out; he felt bound to make what would happen as easy as he could for her. "If anything should happen—" he fumbled—"you know, while Jack's—disturbed—I can always help to look after the children."

Rice could hear the children screaming from the end of the street. He began to walk toward the cries. He hadn't meant to go near the house; if his plan were to succeed, Harriet must not see him. Harriet —why wasn't she protecting the children? It couldn't be the Rossiters' house, he argued desperately; sounds like that couldn't reach the length of the street. But the cries continued, piercing with terror and pain; they dragged his footsteps nearer. He reached the house and could no longer doubt. The bedrooms were curtained, the house was impossibly impassive, reflecting no part of the horror within; the fog clung greyly to the grass like scum on reeds. He could hear Elaine sobbing something and then screaming. Rice wanted to break in, to stop the sounds, to discover what was holding Harriet back; but if he went in his plan would be destroyed. His palms prickled; he wavered miserably, and the silver pavement slithered beneath him.

The front door of the next house opened and a man—portly, red-faced, bespectacled, grey hair, black overcoat, valise clenched in his hand like a weapon—strode down the path, grinning at the screams. He passed Rice and turned at his aghast expression: "What's the matter, friend," he asked with amusement in his voice, "never have your behind tanned when you were a kid?"

"But listen to them!" Rice said unevenly. "They're *screaming!*"

"And I should damn well think so, too," the other retorted. "You know Jack Rossiter? Decent chap. About as much of a sadist as I am, and his kids ran in just now when we were having breakfast with some nonsense about their father doing something dreadful to them. I grabbed them by the scruff of their necks and dragged them back. One thing wrong with Rossiter—he was too soft with those kids, and I'm glad he seems to have learned some sense. Listen, you know who taught kids to tell tales on their parents? The bloody Nazis, that's who. There'll be no kids turning into bloody Nazis in this country if *I* can help it!"

He moved away, glancing back at Rice as if suspicious of him. The cries had faded; perhaps a door had closed. Stunned, Rice realized that he had been seen near the house; his plan was in danger. "Well, I mustn't waste any more time," he called, trying to sound casual, and hurried after the man. "I've got to catch my bus."

At the bus-stop, next to the man who was scanning the headlines and swearing, Rice watched the street for the figure he awaited, shivering with cold and indecision, his nostrils smarting with the faint stench of wet smoke. A bus arrived; his companion boarded. Rice stamped his feet and stared into the distance as if awaiting another; an inner critic told him he was overacting. When the bus had darkened and merged with the fog, he retraced his steps. At the corner of the street he saw the fog solidify into a striding shape. The mist pulled back like web from the scarred face.

"Oh, Jack, can you spare a few minutes?" he said.

"Why, it's the prodigal brother-in-law!" came in a mist steaming from the mouth beside the scar. "I thought Harriet had warned you off? I'm in a hurry."

Again Rice was caught by a compulsion to rush into the house, to discover what had happened to Harriet. But there were the children to protect; he must make sure they would never scream again. "I thought I saw you—I mean, I did see you in Lower Brichester a few weeks ago," he said, feeling the fog obscuring security. "You were going into a ruined house."

"Who, me? It must have been my—" But the voice stopped; breath hung before the face.

Rice let his hatred drive out the words. "Your double? But then where did he go? Come on, I'll show you the house."

For a moment Rice doubted; perhaps the figure would laugh and stride into the mist. Ice sliced through his toes; he tottered and then plunged. "How did you make sure there was nobody about?" he forced through swollen lips. "When you got rid of him?"

The eyes flickered; the scar shifted. "Who, Phillips? God, man, I never did know what you meant half the time. He'll be wondering where I am—I'll have to think up a story to satisfy him."

"I think you'll be able to do that." Cold with fear as he was, Rice was still warmed by fulfillment as he sensed that he had the upper hand, that he was able to taunt as had the man on the cliff-top before the plunge. He plunged into the fog, knowing that now he would be followed.

The grey fields were abruptly blocked by a more solid anonymity, the streets of Lower Brichester, suffocating individuality, erasing it through generations. Whenever he'd walked through these streets with Jack on the short route to the pub each glance of Jack's had reminded him that he was part of this anonymity, this inertia. But no longer, he told himself. Signs of life were sparse; a postman cycled creaking by; beyond a window a radio announcer laughed; a cat curled among milk-bottles. The door was rolled down on a pinball arcade, and a girl in a cheap fur coat was leaping about in the doorway of a boutique to keep herself warm until the keys arrived. Rice felt eyes finger the girl, then revert to him; they had watched him since the beginning of the journey, although the figure seemed to face always forward. Rice glanced at the other; he was gazing in the direction of his stride, and the scar wrinkled with a faint sneer. Soon now, Rice thought, and a block of ice grew in his stomach while the glazing of the pavement cracked beneath his feet.

They passed a square foundation enshrining a rusty pram; here a bomb had blown a house asunder. The next street, Rice realized, and dug his nails into the rubber of the torch in his pocket. The blitz had almost bypassed Brichester; here and there one passed from curtained windows to a gaping house, eventually rebuilt if in the town, neglected in Lower Brichester. Was this the key? Had someone been driven underground by blitz conditions, or had something been released by bombing? In either case, what form of camouflage would they have had to adopt to live? Rice thought he knew, but he didn't want to think it through; he wanted to put an end to it. And round a corner the abandoned house focused into view.

A car purred somewhere; the pavement was faintly numbered for hopscotch. Rice gazed about covertly; there must be nobody in sight. And at his side the figure did the same. Terrified, Rice yet had to repress a nervous giggle. "There's the house," he said. "I suppose you'll want to go in."

"If you've got something to show me." The scar wrinkled again.

Bricks were heaped in what had been the garden; ice glistened in their pores. Rice could see nothing through the windows, which were shuttered with tin. A grey corrugated sheet had been peeled back from the doorway; it scraped at Rice's ankle as he entered.

The light was dim; he gripped his torch. Above him a shattered skylight illuminated a staircase full of holes through which moist dust fell. To his right a door, one panel gouged out, still hung from a hinge. He hurried into the room, kicking a stray brick.

The fireplace gaped, half curtained by a hanging strip of wallpaper. Otherwise the room was bare, deserted probably for years. Of course the people of the neighborhood didn't have to know exactly what was here to avoid it. In the hall tin rasped.

Rice ran into the kitchen, ahead on the left. Fog had penetrated a broken window; it filled his mouth as he panted. Opposite the cloven sink he saw a door. He wrenched it open, and in the other room the brick clattered.

Rice's hands were gloved in frozen iron; his nails were shards of ice thrust into the fingertips, melting into his blood. One hand clutched toward the back door. He tottered forward and heard the children scream, thought once of Harriet, saw the figures on the cliff. I'm not a hero! he mouthed. How in God's name did I get here? And the answer came: because he'd never really believed what he'd suspected. But the torch was shining, and he swung it down the steps beyond the open door.

They led into a cellar; bricks were scattered on the floor, bent knives and forks, soiled plates leading the torch-beam to tattered blankets huddled against the walls, hints of others in the shadows. And in one corner lay a man, surrounded by tins and a strip of corrugated metal.

The body glistened. Trembling, his mouth gaping at the stench which thickened the air, Rice descended, and the torch's circle shrank. The man in the corner was dressed in red. Rice moved nearer. With a shock he realized that the man was naked, shining with red paint which also marked the tins and strip of metal. Suddenly he wrenched away and retched.

For a moment he was engulfed by nausea; then he heard footsteps in the kitchen. His fingers burned like wax and blushed at their clumsiness, but he caught up a brick. "You've found what you expected, have you?" the voice called.

Rice reached the steps, and a figure loomed above him, blotting out the light. With studied calm it felt about in the kitchen and produced a strip of corrugated tin. "Fancy," it said, "I thought I'd have to bring you here to see Harriet. Now it'll have to be the other way round." Rice had no time to think; focusing his horror, fear and disgust with his lifetime of inaction, he threw the brick.

Rice was shaking by the time he had finished. He picked up the torch from the bottom step and as if compelled turned its beam on the two corpses. Yes, they were of the same stature—they would have been identical, except that the face of the first was an abstract crimson oval. Rice shuddered away from his fascination. He must see Harriet—it didn't matter what excuse he gave, illness or anything, so long as he saw her. He shone the beam toward the steps to light his way, and the torch was wrested from his hand.

He didn't think; he threw himself up the steps and into the kitchen. The bolts and lock on the back door had been rusted shut for years. Footsteps padded up the steps. He fell into the other room. Outside an ambulance howled its way to hospital. Almost tripping on the brick, he reached the hall. The ambulance's blue light flashed in the doorway and passed, and a figure with a grey sock covering its face blocked the doorway.

Rice backed away. No, he thought in despair, he couldn't fail now; the fall from the cliff had ended the menace. But already he knew. He backed into something soft, and a hand closed over his mouth. The figure plodded toward him; the grey wool sucked in and out. The figure was his height, his build. He heard himself saying: "I can always help to look after the children." And as the figure grasped a brick he knew what face waited beneath the wool.

The Whining

When Bentinck first saw the dog he thought it was a patch of mud. He was staring from his window into Princes Park, watching the snow heap itself against folds of earth and slip softly from branches. Against the black trees on the far side of the park, flakes shimmered like light within the eyelids. Bentinck gazed, trying to calm himself, and his eye was caught by a brown heap on the gradual slope of the whitened green.

It lanced his mood. He sighed and began to gather his coffee-cup, smashed in a momentary rage. At least he hadn't allowed his fury to touch the Radio Merseyside tape-recorder, which contained its source. He opened the French windows and hurried around the corner of the house to his bin, almost tripping over the half-buried handle of an axe. As he returned he saw that the brown heap was shaking snow from its plastered fur and staring at him. It freed its legs from the snow and struggled toward him, half-engulfed at each weak leap.

Bentinck hesitated, then he shrugged flakes from his shoulders and closed the windows. After mopping the carpet he played back the tape. He'd worked at Radio Merseyside only a month, and already here he was, allowing a councillor to feed him answers which begged specific questions, the ones the councillor was prepared to answer. And off the tape Bentinck was absolutely and articulately opposed to capital punishment, in fact to any violence: that was what infuriated him. Well, he might as well be calm; the incident was beyond resolution. He might as well enjoy his free afternoon. He bundled his coat about him and emerged into the park.

Small cold flakes licked his cheeks. He crossed to the lake, his footsteps squeaking. Ducks creaked throatily across the silver sky, and a flurry of gulls detached themselves from the white with rusty squawks. Behind him Bentinck heard a wet slithering. He turned and saw the dog.

As soon as he met its eyes the dog changed direction. It began to sidle around him, a few feet away, curving its body into a shape like a ballerina's expression of shame. It circled him crabwise, pointing its nose toward him. It was several shades of mud, with trailing ears like scraps of floorcloth, and large eyes. Its legs were short and bent like roots, and its tail wavered vaguely. "All right, boy," Bentinck said. "Whose are you?"

He stepped toward it. At once it leapt clumsily backwards, rather as an insect might, he thought. "All right," he said, slapping his shin. It skidded to its feet and shook off a dandruff of snow. As it did so he saw that its skin was corrugated with ribs. "Food," he said, remembering a bone he'd intended to use for soup. But the dog stayed where it was, tail quivering. "Food, boy," he said, and began to tramp back to his flat.

Then the dog commenced whining like a gate in a high wind, a reiterated glissando rising across a third. "Food! Food!" shouted Bentinck, almost at the windows, and the couple in the first-floor flat peered out warily. I've been a fool once today, Bentinck thought, and then glared up at them; their hi-fi seemed to need a good deal less sleep than he, and while he wouldn't complain unless it became intolerable he was damned if he would whisper for them. "Here, boy!" he shouted, and hurried to the refrigerator. Over the slight squeal of its door he heard the incessant cry from the park.

He tore a piece of meat from the bone and hurled it toward the dog. The animal made a gulping leap and began to claw up an explosion of snow where the meat had landed. Leaving the bone inside the window, Bentinck found a towel in his laundry-bag. In the living-room he halted, surprised. The dog was sitting in front of the gas fire, gnawing the bone. It snarled.

"Do sit down," Bentinck said. "You don't mind if I close the windows?" Out of the corner of one eye the dog watched him do so. "I don't suppose you'd consider lying on this towel. No, I thought not," he said. "Just so long as we can both have the fire." The dog grumbled as he sat down, but continued chewing. Bentinck gazed at it. Its back legs curled around and its tail followed them, as if to form a pleasing contrast to the sharp straight bone. Somehow, Bentinck thought, the contrast expressed the dog.

Gradually its jaws wound down. Bentinck had been lulled by the sight of its satiety; only the appearance of a pool seeping from beneath the animal startled him alert. Bending closer, he realized that it wasn't the thawing of the dog. "Now wait a minute," he said, springing up. The dog winced back from him, leaving the bone; it began to cringe, and its tongue and tail quivered. "All right, you poor sod, it's not your fault," he said. "I hope you don't object to the *Echo.*"

But when he returned with the newspaper, the dog was scraping at the carpet and worrying the tape-recorder's lead. "I'm tempted to offer you the tape, but on balance I think you've been enough of a good deed for one day," he said. Wrapping his hand in the towel, he fished the bone out of the pool and threw it into the park. With a bark that combined a whoop with its whine, the dog followed.

Later, at Radio Merseyside, he edited the tape and had an unpleasant slow-motion conversation with his producer. As he returned to his flat he thought he saw the dog lapping at the lake, at its encroaching margin of mud and waste paper. "I'm afraid I didn't quite manage to pin him down." "Well, you can't be expected to learn everything at once." "That's true." "But you'll have to work on mastering interviews." "Yes, I will." "Won't you." "Yes, of course." God, thought Bentinck savagely. He filled a soup-bowl with water and set it outside the windows. Under the sill the snow was flecked with blood, and there were claw-marks on the frame.

He was awakened by dull thumps overhead, which his heart imitated and continued. He dragged the alarm clock into view and saw it was four o'clock. Then he became aware of the whining, the cause of the protests resounding through the floor above. Wearily he groped his way to the French windows. As he opened them snowballs hailed down from the first floor, and the dog yelped. Indignant, Bentinck spread newspapers on the carpet and coaxed the dog inside. It slithered through the windows like a timid snake and lay down panting. "That's it, boy," Bentinck said. "Bedtime, what's left of it."

Three hours later the whining prodded him awake. "No, no, boy, shut up," he mumbled—but almost at once the dog clawed open his bedroom door and crawled toward him as if under fire, leaving a snail's trail of melted snow. He stroked its back as it came within reach, and the dog attempted to writhe itself through the carpet. Leaning over to follow his hand, Bentinck saw that the animal had an erection. It peered at him from the corner of its eye, slyly. "You go back to your own bed," Bentinck said and retreated under the blankets.

But the whining prised him forth. He opened the French windows and the dog galloped toward them, halting at his side. "I know, you're scared to go out alone," he said. "I take it I've had my sleep." He shaved, washed and dressed, trying to hush the dog. "A walk will do me the world of good," he said, opening the windows. "Jesus wept."

His feet crunched through the glazed snow and plunged into the mire of the paths. Ducks swam through a grey coating of snow. The dog ran ahead, casting itself in a curve, struggling to its feet and running back toward him. He found a dripping stick and threw it, but it only sank into banked snow with a thud. By the time they'd circled the lake his feet were soaking. He hurried inside, closing out the dog, picked up the telephone and dialled. "Didn't you use that tape? Good," he said. "I'd like to try him again." He changed his boots and left by the front door.

But the councillor had gone to Majorca for a week. When Bentinck neared home that evening, still composing questions, he hesitated at the park gates. He could go round to the front door and avoid the dog. However, he intended to take advantage of the park while its litter and mud were draped. Nothing moved on the dimming slopes. He reached his windows and unlocked them. As he did so the dog scrambled around the corner of the house and shot into his flat.

"Well, I know what *I'm* having for dinner," Bentinck said, cutting cellophane open. The dog lay on the kitchen tiles and watched him; its tail strained to rise and fell back. "You see what that says?" Bentinck said, flourishing the packet. "Dinner for one." But as he ate, his left hand secretively passed scraps of meat beneath the table, where wet teeth snapped them away.

"It's usual for guests to leave when the host shows signs of collapse," Bentinck said, tying his pajama cord. He changed the newspapers by the windows and shivering, unlocked the halves. "The Gents' is outside," he said. But the dog lay down, tearing the top layer of paper. Bentinck closed the windows and his bedroom door. He set the alarm, and the whining started.

"No," he said, opening the door. "No," when the dog refused the invitation of the windows. "*No,*" as it began to gaze sidelong at him. Upstairs he could hear the first rumbles of displeasure. He picked up a newspaper. He'd read that a rolled-up newspaper was the kindest instrument with which to chastise a pup. He rolled the *Echo* and struck the dog's rump with the face of the year's Miss Unilever.

The dog yelped and rolled over. Then it began to fawn, curling itself about the carpet as if all its bones were broken. It stood up in a dislocated way, its hindquarters belatedly regaining an even keel, and came toward him, licking its lips and whining. "Be quiet," he said and struck it again, harder. It spun over, almost somersaulting, and sidled back to him. Its tongue flopped out, dripping; it rubbed against his legs, swinging its tail in a great arc, and whined. "Oh, get out," he said, disgusted. "Come on. Out now." It climbed up his leg, pressing its crotch against him. "Out!" he shouted and opening the windows, picked up the struggling dog and hurled it into the snow. Then he buried himself in bed. Above him the hi-fi began to howl and thump.

For the next week he kept the windows closed. He avoided the couple on the first floor but was ready with an argument should he meet them. Each night he heard the whining and the scrape of claws on wood. On the Sunday afternoon he saw the dog ploughing through the lake in pursuit of a stick thrown by three children, which had lodged beneath a bench overturned into the lake. He watched the animal as it tried to lift the bench on its shoulders, to force itself beneath the seat, and for a moment admired the dog and envied the children. Then his mind shifted, and he wondered whether they would be able to resist the creature's temptation to sadism. He rolled up a newspaper and struck himself on the arm. He was surprised by how much it hurt.

That night the dog attacked the window while he was still reading. Bentinck rolled the paper and flourished it. The dog redoubled its efforts. One of the lower panes was scribbled with crimson, and the animal's left front paw was darker tonight. Bentinck frowned and went to bed, and in the morning called the RSPCA.

When they arrived, two men in a snarling van, the dog had vanished. Bentinck had gone to the edge of the park to entice the dog into the flat, and almost didn't hear their knocking. "Clever dog you've got there," one said, stamping the snow of the search from his boots. "Better not tell him we're coming next time." "It isn't mine," Bentinck said, but it wasn't important, and besides they were already driving away. He collected together his equipment to interview the councillor. He opened the windows, and the dog hurtled out from beneath his bed into the park.

That evening the dog wasn't waiting when he returned. He inched

THE WHINING

his way through the windows and locked them. Then, controlling himself, he made coffee. At last his hand crept forward and switched on the tape. "I'm not concerned with punishing specific criminals. I'm concerned that violence is becoming an everyday fact of life." "Now this is complete nonsense, isn't it?" he heard himself saying angrily, and switched off before his fury surfaced completely. Then the French windows began to shudder.

He stared at them. The dog was hurling itself against them, clawing at the frame. Bentinck leapt to his feet and gestured it away, but it swung its tail and began to dig at the sill. He wrenched open the windows to chase the dog away, but it had already squeezed into the room. "Come on," he said. "I don't want you." He was still trying to drive it out when someone knocked at the door of the flat: a man with a thin frowning face and long grey hair tucked inside a car-coat. Of course, the landlord.

"I'll get my checkbook," Bentinck said, wondering why the man was frowning.

"The people upstairs have been complaining about your dog."

"It's not my dog," Bentinck said, dropping his checkbook. "And in any case I'm surprised they can hear it at all over their hi-fi, which they play till all hours."

"Really? It's odd you haven't complained before. Whose dog is it if it isn't yours?"

"God knows. All I know is I'd like to see the last of it."

"Do you know, I've gone through life convinced that the man's the master of the dog. What is this dog, a hypnotist?"

"No," Bentinck snarled, "a bloody pest."

"Well, I'll tell you what to do with pests, just between us. You get some meat and cook it up with poison. Simple as that. I'll even let you dig in the garden if you do it quietly. There's your rent book. I'll see myself out."

The landlord left, leaving the door ajar. I've tried the RSPCA, Bentinck said furiously, you try them if you're so bothered. I might give them a ring about you. The dog was fawning at his feet. "Stop that," he shouted, stamping, and stood up to close the door.

Behind him there came a thud. The dog was chewing the tape-recorder lead and had pulled the machine to the floor. "Haven't I made myself clear?" Bentinck shouted. He opened the windows and stamped at the dog, urging it toward them. It crawled around the room, cringing back from furniture, trying to climb his leg, and he grasped it by the scruff of its neck and dragged it yelping toward the windows. Still holding the dog, he closed the windows behind him.

"Now go. Just go," he said, kicking slush at it. It ran splashing toward the bins, its tail wagging limply, but when he turned to the windows it began to sidle back. "Go, will you!" he shouted, running at the dog and tripping. He pushed himself to his feet, his hands gloved in ice, as the dog leapt at him and smeared his mouth with its tongue. "Go!" he shouted and fumbling behind him for what he'd tripped over, threw it.

He heard the axe strike. The dog screamed and then began to whine, its cry rising and rising. "Oh Christ," Bentinck said. There was no light from the first floor, and he couldn't see what he'd done, only make out the dog dragging itself by its front paws through the crackling slush toward the park. He couldn't do anything. He couldn't bear to touch the dog. He stumbled toward it and saw the axe cleaving the snow. Closing his eyes, he picked up the axe and killed the dog.

Afterwards he found a spade standing against the house. He had to hold the dog together while he wrapped it in polythene. Shovelling and kicking, he disguised the discolored snow. Then he dug a hole at the edge of the park, filled it in and tried to scatter snow over the disturbed earth. For hours he lay in bed shaking.

Next morning a corner of polythene was protruding from the ground. Bentinck trod it out of sight, shuddering, feeling the ground squelch beneath his heel. When he came home, having successfully edited the tape, he found a whole edge of polythene billowing from a scraped hollow. Several dogs were chasing in the park. He dug the ground over, watching for a face at the first-floor window, as the first flakes of new snow drifted down.

He awoke to the memory of a whining. He sat up, hurling the blanket to the floor. For minutes he listened, then he padded to the French windows. The garden was calm and softened by unbroken snow. A full moon floated in the clear sky, coaxing illumination from the landscape. He returned to his bedroom. Thick darkness lay beneath the bed.

The councillor blustered. Bentinck shrugged him off and turned his back. Before him, dawning from the shadows, lay a dog or a young girl. Bentinck held scissors, a red-hot poker, an axe, a saw. He awoke writhing, soaked in sweat, an eager whining in his ears. His whole body was pounding. He let his breathing ease, and groped for the clock. Before he could reach it, a tongue licked his hand.

The couple on the first floor were awakened by shouts. Groaning, they turned over and sought sleep. At eight o'clock they were eating breakfast when they saw Bentinck staggering about the park. "He's drunk. That explains a lot," the woman said. But something in his manner made them go to his assistance. When they drew near they saw that his trouser legs were covered with dried blood. Around him in the snow the prints of dogs' paws formed wildly fragmented patterns. "Listen," he said desperately. "You realize it's impossible to exorcise an animal? They don't understand English, never mind Latin." They took his arms and began to guide him back to his flat. But they hadn't reached the house when he looked down and started to brush at his shins, and kick, and scream.

Missing

19/5/73: Well, I went to Lis and Pat's party after all, even though Fran couldn't make it. Though it's more a question of my not being able to make it with her, or her not wanting to make it. Anyway.

I nearly didn't go (I have to finish my essay on Camus by next week!) But I was writing by the window, or trying to, and every time I looked across the road I could see the wall of their flat. Looked like a bright blue abstract—they chose the colors while tripping, of course. Besides, upstairs had started arguing and I couldn't write under those conditions. So I bought a party can and went over.

Wasn't bad as parties go, once I stopped myself thinking how I should be reading *L'Étranger*. (Exams next month; must score some speed). Lis asked after Fran, though I've only taken her over there once. Must have ruined part of the party, because I'd had a really fine joint and too much Johnny Walker, and I ended up crying we're damaging each other by not making it and not being able to give each other up, which is probably true. Lis must be used to getting my head together by now, and she knows what it's about because Fran admitted to her she hadn't told her parents in case they disapproved of me, but I could see it was turning off the rest of their guests.

Jim was there, which was nice. He's only been back in Liverpool a few weeks and he's already doing a series for the *Echo* on local murders. I talked to him when I came down. Says he's found a particularly gruesome case which happened a few streets away. He's trying to find a picture of the woman who did it. I said I'd help him look through the newspaper files. Well, it might be useful to get my face known around the *Echo*.

There was one rather strange incident while we were talking. Now I think about it there wasn't anything specifically strange, but it seems to have stayed with me more than the rest of the party. So: Jim was telling me how he's concentrating on this case, the Voodoo Murder as he says it's known locally, when I noticed a girl staring at us from the other side of the room—at least, at Jim. Odd I hadn't noticed her before, because she really was rather beautiful: long black hair, very pale smooth skin like velvet, a kind of controlled grace and watchful stillness that went with her long triangular face. Almost as tall as me and in her early twenties, I'd say. She was watching Jim with a sort of sad eagerness, and I pointed her out to him. "So she is," he said. "That's flattering."

"Aren't you going to introduce me?" I said, though perhaps I was joking or just partying, because she seemed absolutely the opposite of Fran.

"Since I've never seen her before I don't think so. You can always approach her yourself. I don't take my wedding ring off at parties."

The strange thing is that we were whispering and faced away from her as well, so that she couldn't have been lip-reading, yet when we turned back she was gazing at me; didn't spare a glance for Jim. "I'd say that was your cue," he said. I wasn't so sure; I found being the object of her obsession rather disturbing, that sadness and yearning began to affect me until I was sharing them without the least idea why. I actually took a John-Wayne-at-the-saloon gulp of Scotch as if to fortify myself. Then I set out across the room, falling over someone on the way.

I wasn't halfway there before she turned and made for the door. Forget it, I thought. The excitement of the sexual chase isn't my trip. I have enough frustration with Fran. But obviously she wasn't playing at all, because I heard the flat door shut and her hurrying downstairs. I looked out of the window and saw her striding up Princes Avenue, straight through a gang smashing bottles on the pavement. Jim looked dreadfully embarrassed and I had to persuade him it wasn't his fault.

I left soon after. Promised to meet Jim next week. Lis and Pat were arguing as I tried to say goodbye. "You didn't invite her, did you?" Pat was demanding. "No, did you?" "Why the fuck would I be asking you if I invited her?" The strange sad brunette, no doubt. Don't know why they should make an issue of her.

Just thinking how I'll have to hide this from Fran. Not that there's anything very devastating in here, but there's no point in provoking jealousy. I wouldn't mind her requiring so much if she gave me more. Something's got to change. Only last week she was opening my chest of drawers to inspect my clothes: "What's in this silver paper?" and me with a death-grin as I grabbed it: "Oh nothing, just an old half a bar of chocolate, I'll throw it away." Half an ounce of Congo bush, and I had to grope among the bacon rind to retrieve it when she'd gone.

Well, they've stopped screaming at the baby downstairs, so perhaps I can snatch some sleep. Christ, this place looks like a dosshouse. Must clean up.

20/5/73: Shouldn't write things like that. It must have got inside my head and kicked everything else out. When I'd had breakfast this morning I just stood looking at the unmade bed and the dirty dishes. Then I lost patience with myself and threw the bed together and attacked the washing-up and broke a plate. I envy Pat, having Lis.

Fran wasn't at lectures today. Probably her period—maybe that was why she wouldn't go to the party. This is where it feels worst, because I can't ring her at home in case one of her parents answers. Suppose it weren't her period? It's not knowing that screws me up.

Two boys were fighting in the front garden tonight. One had a brick, I think. They'd gone when I went down, but there was blood on the path. I came back upstairs, thinking how I know nobody in the building. I can hear them shouting and hitting each other sometimes, but I never speak to them—I don't think I really want to find out any more about them.

I can't read *L'Étranger* under these circumstances. It just makes them seem inevitable. I'll have to take it to the library and read it there.

Must try and get some sleep. Trying makes it harder, of course. I didn't sleep too well last night. There was a reason but I can't remember.

21/5/73: At least now I know why I couldn't sleep. It may help, although I don't see quite how. It was that the bed felt cut in half. When I turned over and came face to face with the wall it was enough of a shock to wake me up. I felt as if the wall had been thrust between me and the other side of the bed. Maybe I should buy a double bed (just like that, write a check, ha ha) with Fran in it. Or someone.

Fran wasn't in again. I could write her a letter, if her parents don't open her mail.

My day was made, to some extent, tonight. I'd gone to the library in Lodge Lane to read Camus. That wasn't one of my more brilliant ideas. The place smells of old cloth, and there's a dull stench of fish and chips clinging to everything. Old men asleep at the tables or fighting over the newspapers, brandishing their sticks—women wrangling over romances or bringing them back, complaining that they've read them (how can they tell?)—only the kids seem at all alive, and how long can they stay that way? I don't know how the staff fend off suicide. So I was trying to read *L'Étranger* amid all this, trying to ignore it all, and I looked up and saw the sad girl from the party sitting at the next table.

She didn't look at me. She was watching the staff at the desk, and when their *Echo* arrived she went over and asked for it. She moved like a steady flame through the murk of the library. Christ, I've got poetry. But it did seem like that. I was going to look at her and smile as she returned to her table, but at the last moment I retreated to Camus, feeling somehow ashamed. (Of what?) I watched her for a while, wanting her not to change, not to succumb to the surrounding despair. Another bit of romantic style; I'll have to watch that, especially when discussing Camus. At last I gave up, because I knew I'd feel guilty if she caught me watching, and left.

So it wasn't altogether a pleasant trip, but a good one nevertheless. Still I find myself wondering about her. She's too young to sit in libraries in the evening, waiting for the papers to arrive. All right, I was in there too, but students aren't human after all, you don't lodge them where they can work at their best. What bitterness and passion. But that girl—she shouldn't have been in there. It's bloody wrong, that's all.

22/5/73: Fran's back. I think it must have been her period, because she said "You know when my last one was. Please, you don't have to ask." Obviously I don't want to embarrass her. She's going to make us dinner here on Friday, so that's something. It could be more than that.

I met the sad girl in the laundrette tonight. What a conversationalist she is. No, that's unfair, it was really my fault. I'd taken Camus with me (my god, I must be getting desperate) but she came in just after I did. I was putting my washing in the machine, throwing the powder on the floor and dropping the coin under people's feet. She didn't help, just watched sadly. But she was watching, which I suppose is some sort of progress. (Oh come on, progress toward what?)

Two girls were bullying a couple of little boys, so I chased them out. Real hairy-chested stuff. She smiled sadly at me and I felt chastened. More to get rid of that feeling than anything I sat down next to her and said (what a conversationalist I am, come to that) "Do you live round here?"

She nodded. Encouraged beyond words ha ha, I said "Alone?"

Another nod. "Don't you find that a bit disturbing?" I said. Nothing, so I tried again. "I mean, the whole area feels hopeless, at least to me it does. You know, half of it's decaying and they're pulling down the other half and putting up concrete shelters. No wonder it's so violent, that's the only vitality that's left." And more of that sort of thing, which proves what a stupid turd I am, because of course she knew it already and that's why she was silent. She just kept gazing at me and I felt as if I were on some sort of truth drug, babbling away. I ended up saying how terrified I am by it sometimes. "Aren't you terrified sometimes?" I said, and she got up smiling sadly and left. Who could blame her.

Message from Jim via Lis and Pat. He's found out more about the Voodoo case. Doesn't think he'll use it, because it's too recent and too grim. Apparently the woman concerned lived round here until it drove her mad. He says he'll keep the material he unearthed for me to see. Just what I need. Still, I'd like to see Jim.

23/5/73: I'm going to have to put myself to sleep with a joint if I don't get my head together. Rolling around in bed last night again. Once I put my hand out and grabbed the wall, which was such a shock that it cost me another hour's sleep. Christ knows what I was reaching for.

I came home tonight and who was here to greet me? Unwashed plates and an unmade bed. Welcome home. I'm falling into the habit of the local despair.

But this is an anonymous dump. It even smells anonymous. I've been feeling something odd tonight: looking around the flat and finding that parts of it look empty. I mean, as if there should be something standing on the chest of drawers. And there's a crack on the wall I couldn't remember having seen before. I started trying to recall what used to hang over it. Nothing, of course. My head's in a weird state.

Found myself becoming obsessed with the whole area, and then I started thinking about the dark-haired girl living alone, and I went over to ask Lis and Pat about her. I had to wait until they and some friends had finished watching Chaplin. Then they didn't know who I was talking about. "But you were arguing about her when I left," I said. "Oh, that," Lis said. "Pat had been smoking too much again, that's all. He said he'd seen a girl we didn't know at the party. Nobody else saw her." "She was a ghost," Pat said. "She's waiting for you in the hall." "I wish you wouldn't do that," Lis said. "He just likes to upset me. She wasn't there." "She fucking was," Pat said. I left. Christ, I wish they wouldn't argue so much.

Tried to read the Camus again. Found myself slowing down to a dead stop—it was like a film getting caught in the projector, each phrase I read seemed to hinder me more until I came to one I simply didn't understand. The letters just hung there, looking meaningless. I've got to do something about my head.

Then someone tried to throw a brick through the window. Great fun. It hit the sill and missed the pane. There was a young brunette walking away. At least, she looked young, though I didn't see her face. I ran out but couldn't see anyone, and I tried to catch up with her in case she'd seen who it was. She heard me coming and ran. Can't blame her, round here at night.

No wonder my mind's running down. I was just about to go to bed when I started wondering when I'd bought the single bed. Don't ask me why, because surely I bought it when I moved here. That's what I remembered, but it felt wrong, as if it didn't really happen that way at all. I'm going to have to be puritanical about dope if this continues. I'll see if I can find the arrival of the bed in my diary tomorrow. Right now I'm exhausted.

MISSING

24/5/73: I'm just pissed off with this whole area. When I came home someone had broken into the flat. What makes it especially stupid is that they didn't take anything, not even the records. Couldn't have been classical freaks. They must have been annoyed that I hadn't left anything worth taking, because they threw all the dirty plates on the bed. Looks as if I'll be sleeping with baked beans tonight. Salvador Dali would be pleased. Their most inspired ploy was to tear up my diary. Or at least most of it, into tiny pieces. They must have gone at it page by page and got bored when they came to Lis and Pat's party. I didn't call the police, not with that excellent bush still in the flat. Of course, my visitors may have read about my vices and may enjoy tipping off the fuzz. That'd make my week.

And then I had to spend an hour unscrewing the broken lock and fitting a new one. Ran the screwdriver into my finger. Left hand, luckily, so it won't stop me writing. Just keep me awake all night.

They're screaming at each other upstairs again. Someone slashed their tires, by the sound of it. It's like living sandwiched in between two reproductions of my parents. I used to hear them when I was in bed. Makes me clench inside all over again. I've got to start looking for another flat.

25/5/73: I've got to laugh. Got to. Otherwise I'll be walking around all night.

Fran came round to make dinner. She was wearing a very short white dress—whenever she bent down it drew up from the curve of her bottom, which was nice. It was also quite an unequivocal signal for Fran.

It went wrong from the start. I bought some wine while she was making dinner, and when I came back and saw her I thought for a moment she was someone else. That must have been it, because I started when I saw it was Fran and stood there gaping, trying to think who she was (and who she wasn't). Then I had to explain by saying she looked beautiful, which was certainly true. It must have surprised her that I'd said it, though, because it's not my style.

Another thing: the place didn't smell anonymous tonight, but on the other hand it didn't smell right. Perhaps Fran's changed her perfume. No, I'm sure it's her usual. But I know I was searching for another scent. I'm becoming incomprehensible to myself and I don't like it.

We had dinner (which was very fine) and took our time over the wine, and Fran began telling me how her parents had invited some twat from a public school to go on holiday with her and them. "I'm sick and tired of being organized," she said. "They're not happy unless they think they can predict my every move. I told them I was going to a concert tonight. That's what they'd expect me to do, so no questions. It's horrible when you think about it, you know, like schizophrenia—*she'd* go to a concert, so *I'm* free to come here with you. I have to be careful which set of memories I'm remembering with them."

"I know how you feel," I said. "My memory's all to cock."

"Please don't say that," she said. "No, I shouldn't be telling you not to swear. It's envy, you know. Part of me's terrified of this place, and the other part envies you because you can do and say what you want. You can do exactly what you want, you don't know what that means."

"But can I?" I said, and I was kissing her and unbuttoning her dress.

"Did you know? When did you know?" she was saying breathlessly, and her head was twisting back and forth. "Are you predicting me too?" and her thighs were trembling round my wrist and relaxing again.

"I'm just happy," I said, and we fell in a heap on the bed. I was wriggling my trousers off because she wouldn't let me let go of her, and she began to cry as I took the plunge, and I was brushing her tears away and making her sneeze with the dangling bandage on my finger. Her hands were nailed to my buttocks and dragging me forward, and she was sneezing in my ear and pumping me violently each time she sneezed, and then a brick smashed through the window and landed on the pillow in a shower of glass. Fran leapt upright and screamed, leaving me behind, and all I could do was throw myself back on the bed and explode.

I still had enough energy to drag myself up to the window and see a woman in an old-fashioned dress vanishing into a side street over the road. Nobody else was in sight. I turned back to Fran, but she was already pulling on her dress, sobbing. "Don't," she said when I tried to hold her. "I shouldn't have come. I was trying to be fair to myself and not caring about being unfair to you. Please, get me a taxi." She didn't look at me at any time after the brick. I flagged her a taxi and stuck some cardboard over the pane, and sat around for an hour, and wrote this.

Christ!

26/5/73: Maybe the destruction of memory is the new malaise—further on from Camus: first Lis and Pat, now Jim and of course me.

Spent most of this morning thinking about Fran. Nothing I can do. I can't burst in on her at home, that would only wreck her more. Doesn't stop my head splitting with guilt.

Rang Jim eventually and had lunch with him. Had to force myself to ring him, and to keep the appointment. Perhaps my mind knows what it's doing but it's not telling me. Jim has one fault (two if you count telling horror stories to someone in my state)—the fault of people who tell you the punch line of a joke and then tell you the joke. Told me the whole story over lunch and then took me back to read exactly the same thing. I might as well fill the page with it. Anything to occupy my mind. Let's see how dispassionately I can tell it. The Camus syndrome.

A young woman—he told me and I read it but I can't remember her name—got married during the second World War. Her husband was crippled and so not fighting. They lived in Wavertree Garden Suburb a few miles from here; she was born there. In 1944 their house was destroyed by a stray bomb. With skillful manipulation of influential friends they managed to buy a cheap house in one of the side streets near here (now pulled down).

Some years later she freaked out completely. Jim tells me that interviews with her suburban friends, who eventually ceased to visit, suggest why. Their house was surrounded by bomb damage, which must have preyed on her mind. So did the whole sense of an area in decay. What obsessed her, apparently, was the sight of the old people round here, shut up in collapsing houses, unable to care for each other. All that and being thrown out of suburbia into the real world shattered her. I can understand that.

When she'd lived in Wavertree she'd been interested in the occult. She'd held séances and was a considerable hypnotist (probably a telepath as well). "Her eyes didn't need words," as someone reportedly said. This was where her insanity focused. She became violently racist and was convinced that the Negroes who lived around her practiced Voodoo. "I could beat them at that game. I could make my own magic and see them all dead," she told one of her visitors, who didn't visit again.

In 1947 she murdered her husband, obviously in pursuit of her Voodoo. A meths drinker discovered her in the cellar of a bombed house. She had her back to him and was bending over a man lying on a slab made of bricks. A few candles surrounded her. She seemed to be drawing something from the man's trunk. At first the meths drinker thought she was masturbating him; then he saw that what she was pulling from the body had coiled around her feet, and as he watched she arranged it into a pattern, chanting. My diary really is a load of laughs these days.

Anyway, he fled, upsetting his meths on one of the candles. She must have had petrol to destroy the corpse, because the cellar exploded almost immediately. The meths drinker didn't tell the police, but eventually someone overheard him telling the story. The police found her husband's corpse with the small intestine removed. They didn't find her, but clearly she couldn't have escaped. According to the meths witness when they traced him, she was chanting (as they interpreted the little he could remember) "le pouvoir" and "la jeunesse." Presumably she learned a little French to emulate Voodoo.

"Of course it was an invented ceremony, though her mind may have erased that point," Jim said as we walked back to the *Echo* building. "Entrails may figure in Voodoo, but not in that way. It's interesting to speculate."

I didn't want to, but I said "On what?"

"Well, on the function of that sort of ritual. I've heard the argument that it's not the ritual that counts at all, but the seriousness of approach it demands. It awakens your own dormant magic. So that could apply even to an invented ritual—if you believed in it, as she obviously did."

Not that he believed in it, of course. "I'm saying that if some of it's based on attitude then the attitude should have carried her. If I believed in it I'd be a fool to concentrate so much on this case. What monstrous and loathsome horrors might I be disinterring? Little did I reck when first I opened that cobwebbed file. . . ."

The *Echo* building's like a warehouse full of labyrinths of shelves, like an Orson Welles set. I felt claustrophobic, actually unwilling to go with Jim, though the poor sod's not that bad. When we reached the files he'd researched I found myself desperate to come back here, to read Camus (or to begin again, with my memory the way it is now).

Must have been depressed. There was enough sunlight and petrol fumes coming in the window to stave off morbidity.

So I read through the story, and at one point I stopped short. Because there was a photograph of the woman, and for a moment she looked exactly like the sad girl at Lis and Pat's party (and how come our paths have stopped crossing?)

I pointed this out to Jim and he said "Who?"

"The girl you tried to get me off with at the party. The one who fancied you."

"Listen, mate, I wasn't that drunk," he said. "What did she look like?"

"Like this," I said, and then I had to back down, because she didn't. There was a resemblance to the photograph, but nothing very striking. In fact, I don't know how I made the mistake, because the photograph was rather dim and so was the light at the desk; I found I could hardly see it. It was as if my mind had produced another photograph for me to flash, but I couldn't remember what that was or where I might have seen it. Shows how this whole scene is affecting my mind. I can understand how the woman went mad, and I said so to Jim.

"Yes, but you haven't gone mad, have you?" he said.

Well, that's true. Just about.

27–31/5/73: I'm going to try to write it all down. Might help me to understand myself.

On Sunday I didn't do anything. I sat around and went for a walk and had a few drinks. My mind felt as if it had been scooped out. I didn't smoke, because I felt prone to depression. In fact, I was convinced that dope was damaging me, especially my memory. Obviously my mind was preparing to get itself together.

On Monday I felt worse. I felt depressed and desperate for something, and my finger was on fire. I didn't go to lectures, partly because I couldn't have taken seeing Fran (and seeing me couldn't have helped her). Poor Fran—I hope she makes out with the public-school guy. She's been something of a victim. I suppose in situations like these there has to be one.

I went for a walk in the park, and that was where my trip started. I mean it was like a trip, at least the insights and some of the images were. Maybe my mind structured it that way to make it more comprehensible to me (or more bearable). I was walking by the lake in Sefton Park, and suddenly I began to hear bells. There was a kind of movement in my head as if something were about to flood in. I ran up a slope to be able to see the bells.

There was a church on the edge of the park. A wedding had just taken place, and I could see the bride standing in the churchyard. Her white veil was streaming out, the grass in the park was streaming on the wind, light was scattered in patterns on the lake like the sound of the bells. I knew all this was saying something to me, but I couldn't grasp it.

Then I became obsessed with the idea that the answer was here in the flat. I hurried home, even taking a bus instead of walking. My mind felt like a box that I was struggling to open. I dashed into the flat and gazed around. There was nothing.

It was as if I'd written something crucial on a trip and then come down and found I didn't understand it. I sat down on the bed, and I was nearly in tears. But deep in my mind there was a plea to keep trying. So I got up and started going over the flat, making myself trust my mind to stop me when I found whatever it was.

And of course I already knew, I'd even written it here in my diary. I came face to face with that crack on the wall that had troubled me before, and stood looking at it. I can reconstruct how my mind tried to ease me into remembering. There had been a photograph hanging over the crack. A wedding photograph. A photograph of me and my wife. I'd been married.

I felt as if I'd been groping about in the dark of the flat and suddenly discovered there was no floor. I fell back on the bed and just let my mind go where it would. I was more terrified than if I'd taken too much acid by mistake and suddenly felt it coming on. I didn't know where my mind was taking me.

Well, it didn't take me anywhere. It had given me the insight and now it was leaving me on my own. I had to do the remembering, and I couldn't.

For two days it was like that. I didn't go out. I searched the flat over and over for a clue. I ate what I had and then didn't eat. I figured out a few things: why the place had looked so untidy and anonymous, why I'd felt cramped in the single bed. But that only started me wondering again when I'd bought it, and where the double bed had gone. I didn't know (and Christ, I still don't) why I had destroyed every trace of my wife. She couldn't have taken everything with her. I even began to have a horrible suspicion that I'd murdered her.

But my mind was preparing me beneath all the horrors. It was as if someone were doing a jigsaw in my head, and it just needed one piece for the whole thing to fit together.

And yesterday it did. I was lying on the bed again. I'd realized that I'd be ill if I didn't eat, and I didn't care. I'd loved someone and they'd vanished—what was worse, vanished from my mind. I knew this was a kind of insanity. But I couldn't help myself, and I was terrified to ask anyone who might be able to tell me what had happened.

Then there was a knock at the door. I didn't start, even my muscles no longer cared. I said "Who is it?"

"It's Edna," she said.

And I didn't even have to open the door, because that was the piece of the jigsaw that fitted. Before I reached the door I realized that was the name of the woman in the files Jim had shown me, and that my mind had flashed my wedding photograph over the photograph in the file. I opened the door and there she was: my sad girl from the party.

Her eyes said everything. We didn't have to speak. We just held each other, and I drowned in memories. No incidents, just a sense of Edna: her stillness, her efficiency whose absence had troubled me so much, her voice that sang as it spoke, her perfume which had returned to the flat at last. When we released each other she said "You've hurt your finger. Let me see," and I knew she was home again.

So much makes sense now: why Jim tried to get me off with her at the party, why Lis and Pat were arguing about the fact that she'd been invited and then wouldn't admit that she'd been there. Because they didn't know how I would take it, of course. But they accepted that I didn't recognize her. They must all know what happened to separate us.

It can't have been anything too bad, surely. Edna wouldn't have come back. We aren't at ease with each other yet, and I sleep in a chair because the bed's too small, but she came back. I suspect that the tensions of the area got inside me and I freaked out, like the woman in Jim's case. He must have been trying to encourage me when he said I hadn't gone mad, though he didn't have the courage to admit that Edna was at the party. Well, I can't blame him. He isn't a psychiatrist.

Don't think I'll need a psychiatrist with Edna here. She'll help me back. But I still feel obsessively guilty about what I may have done, and I can't discuss it with her yet. I know she's waiting for me to talk about it—I see her watching when she thinks I don't. I shall, when we're on holiday. The Lakes for the rest of the week. No exams this year, not with my head as it is. Edna understands. She's paying for the holiday. Can't ask her yet where she got the money.

Went over to Lis and Pat's earlier. I was determined to make them tell me what I'd done, and how long ago. Their car was outside, but they didn't answer—probably tripping. Jim's never there when I ring.

When I came back Edna was staring from the window at an old woman in a wheelchair. She turned to look at me, touching her face as if searching for wrinkles. Hardly, but I know what she was wondering: whether I could look after her for the rest of her life. Well, I'll be useful to her. I scattered my bush out of the window this morning. See if that clears my mind.

Must finish. Edna's packed our luggage. She reminded me to bring my diary, in case someone wrecks it again. I can't remember telling her about that. My memory still isn't working properly.

"It'll be like a second honeymoon," I said, to be able to say it. "Like being married again."

And she nodded and smiled, watching me.

Reply Guaranteed

"I peeled off one of my nails once," Viv said, "to see what was underneath."

A bee buzzed in the warm evening. "And?" asked Jack finally.

"Hurt like hell."

A screen of sunlight cast through the open window behind her bed caught a metal trolley wheeled by a nurse and kindled it; Viv squeaked and squeezed her eyes shut. Photographed upon her eyes, Jack leaned forward from the chair against the ward; she pressed darkness down upon the image to blot it out and to bring Jack's departure nearer. Mary, her flat-mate, had not visited her tonight, and Tony had gone off in a huff on meeting Jack at her bedside. She opened her eyes; Jack was still there. A bee rose from the graveyard further down Mercy Hill and searched among the flowers on the table between the beds; a nurse, apologizing to the patient whose temperature she was taking among the visitors, pursued and slapped down the insect. Several of the parties round the beds applauded; laughter passed along the aisles and was absorbed into continued conversations. "Good shot," Jack said limply. The remark hung in their ears.

"Oh, yes," he said some moments later, "most bizarre ad in this morning." He rummaged in his raincoat pocket and brought out the evening's copy of the *Brichester Herald*, the paper for which he worked, together with a notebook page which he unfolded. "Listen: *Unconventional man-about-town would like to meet girl who values intellect more than good looks and adventure more than conservatism. Anyone who thinks she may be in a position to satisfy, write—*

and there's the address, on Mercy Hill somewhere, with a postscript: *Reply guaranteed.*"

Viv had yawned through the text, giggled at "position to satisfy." "Let's see," she said, then protested: "Why, you wrote this!"

"I copied it from the ad in Cooper's office. You'd have complained if I'd brought the real thing; it was typed, but the letters jumped so much you'd think his fingers had been falling off. I suppose it'll be in the *Herald* on Friday; Cooper won't know what he's let himself in for."

"Wonder who'll answer it."

A bell shrilled for the end of visiting. "Why don't you?" Jack said and bent to kiss her forehead; she submitted. She watched him make his way down the ward, bumping into the ward sister and apologizing with a blush, and as he shoved between the double doors the screen around the last bed in the aisle rattled and an old man eased himself out, his face pale. Birds sang and somewhere children scampered, shouting. Then Viv made a grab at her *Woman's Own* as it was slid from the bed-table by her neighbor, Mavis.

"Don't worry, I only want to read it," explained Mavis, snatching the magazine out of reach. Viv strained to retrieve it and the sister rebuked: "Your appendix won't heal that way, you know." She included them both in a reproving look and moved on to ask after the health of Mavis' neighbor, who answered "I feel a little better" with a weak smile and at once was dramatically sick.

Viv stuck out her tongue at the crisp rustling figure. Mavis tittered, then hissed: "Who was that gorgeous boy who came to see you? Not Jack, he's like you said: the other one."

"Who, Tony? He's not gorgeous, he's horrible. He has one side of his face higher than the other."

"No, honestly?" They both giggled. "He must have had his best side turned to me," Mavis spluttered. When they had recovered she opened *Woman's Own;* Viv recalled with a wry grin Tony's confrontation with Jack at her bedside and his "I haven't come all this way to face a selection committee!" As he had turned to leave he'd thrown at Jack "I wouldn't stay either if I were you," to which Jack had replied "Oh, I don't know," thus proving that his stock of repartee had fast declined since Viv had hurled a bowl into his lane at the bowling alley six weeks ago and he had returned it saying with reference to her name "For Vivacious, I suppose." Tony hadn't been bad, really; pity it hadn't been Jack who had taken offense. Still, there were always other boys.

"I'm going to listen to the radio," Mavis declared, distracted from her reading by the nurses leading the old ladies, blinking in the evening sunlight on the whitewashed walls and snorting at the smell of ether, to the Ladies'. The two girls fitted on their headphones through which filtered tinnily the tail end of the News; the announcer read: "The body of a six-year-old girl was found today in the Manchester area, where she disappeared from home three days ago." "God, isn't that terrible?" Viv said. "I can't bear to think of that poor kid, how she must have suffered. They should shoot men like that." They stared at each other, depressed, then Viv brightened: "Listen, this record's great!"

Some records later the sister switched off the radio. "I think you can walk to the toilet by yourself," she told Viv, meeting her furious glare. On the way back Viv felt as if she were being sawn in half; she bit her lip preparatory to screaming. Then, as the lights progressed through the hospital, darkening the dusk outside, she saw in the beds opposite eyes watching her with senile calm. She gritted her teeth and clutched the bed-rail. As she climbed into bed she had a brief glimpse of the warm dusk through the pane in the cold white wall. Over the sill she saw in the cemetery below a few white crosses like half-erased chalk signs, and a pale figure in a wheelchair drifting from the graveyard to a house beyond. She thought of being old and ill, and shivered; she would rather be dead.

"I'm going to live with Roy," said Mary.

Viv glanced across the bed at Jack; she felt the remark had been aimed at him to test his reaction. Ignored by the two girls, he had been patting his forehead with a handkerchief in the heat which settled into the ward as the sunlight dulled, looking up as a trolley's wheels squealed distantly, casting a hungry gaze at the pack of cigarettes on Viv's bed-table awaiting the visitors' departure. Now he was staring down the Hill to cover his embarrassment. Viv studied him, amused; but as the subdued hubbub from the other beds grew in her ears, she realized that Mary had not continued. "You're not serious?" she asked.

"I'm moving in with him this week."

"But you've only known him a month!" Viv's voice rose. Jack's head bowed lower; others turned to look. "What do you want to do that for?"

"You can be sure in less than that. Anyway, I can't say no. There mightn't be another chance."

"But what about me?" Viv demanded shrilly. "I can't pay all the rent by myself! Don't be mean, Mary. *I'd* stay if *you* wanted me to."

"I'll bet. Sorry, Viv, I didn't mean that. But I love Roy. You don't know what it's like."

"Oh, go to hell!" It might have been hysteria which edged Viv's voice. A nurse frowned at her before vanishing behind the screen around the last bed.

Mary went. Jack looked up eventually: "Er—" he said. Behind him a nurse bent over Mavis with, to judge by Mavis' expression, good news. Viv's eyes searched the groups around the other beds soothing the patients with murmurs of hope.

"Cooper didn't print that ad," Jack muttered. "More with-it than I thought."

"Well, I'm going to answer it," decided Viv, grappling with her depression, and took Jack's copy from the bedside drawer. The exertion made her feel a little sick, but she was determind not to weaken before Jack. " 'Dear—' How do I start? I don't know his name."

" 'Dear Friend.' "

" 'Dear Friend, I was pleased to read your advert—' "

"How about 'Your ad rekindled my hopes, for I too am seeking unconventional companionship'?"

"All right. . . . What comes after that?"

" 'My many bedfellows have educated me in their various requirements—no, desires, desires—but until now I have sought in vain.' " Viv giggled and wrote. " 'For despite my wide experience I have yet to find love.' " He bowed an invisible violin.

"That's a bit much, isn't it?"

"No, no, must sound sincere. How to end? 'I feel in my heart that we can build a relationship that will satisfy us both.' "

Viv signed with a flourish, which wobbled as the bell shrilled. Some of the bedside groups speeded up their conversations as they waited for the nurses to usher them out. "Wait a minute," Viv said, "I'll do the envelope and you can post it."

"Not likely."

"Hang on, it won't take a minute."

"You don't think I'm going to post that? Suppose he took you at your word!"

"Well, it might be interesting. Anyway, he won't. It's got the hospital address on it. It's only for a laugh."

"In that case you should think of the effect a letter like that would have on him. He's obviously lonely."

"Oh, forget it," Viv said and slipped the letter beneath the magazines littering her bed-table.

"Can't I have it?"

"No, I want it." She shut her eyes while he kissed her, so that she would not see his face looming up.

When the visitors had been cleared out and newspapers were

unfolding and pillows being patted, Viv said to Mavis: "Mary left me, you know."

"I thought that was what was going on. I'm going out tomorrow."

"Are you?" Viv made a decision. "Do you still want to leave your parents?"

"Well, I don't know . . ."

"Come on, Mavis, *please*. I've got half a flat going begging and I can't afford it. The rent's not much—your money from the store must cover it. They can't make you stay at home if you can keep yourself."

"No, I know that."

"And I don't want to be all by myself."

"I don't know, Viv, I'd like to."

A suspicion came to Viv. "You don't *like* your parents, do you?"

"No, of course not."

"Well, then?"

"I told my parents last night," Mavis said. "We had a terrible row."

An approaching storm weighted the sheets on Viv's damp limbs, stifling her; in the false dusk gravestones glimmered. "Never mind," she advised, "you'll feel a lot freer when you move in with me."

"I wonder what they feel?" Jack broke in.

"Who cares?" responded Mavis fiercely. "My father's busy with his accounts and my mother's got her social club, so they only come to see me twice while I'm here. They think I can look after myself. Well, now I'm going to show them how far I can go."

"There, you see!" Viv said triumphantly. "When are you moving in?"

"Tomorrow, if you're coming out tomorrow. I'd better go now, I've got to finish packing. Oh—I forgot about your letter, but I remembered to post it yesterday. And here's a letter to the flat that wasn't forwarded."

"It's from Tony," Viv announced. "Says he wants to be the only man in my life. Well, he's had that."

"Yes, the flat's only big enough for two," Mavis agreed. "I'll meet you here tomorrow, Viv."

"See you, Mavis." Viv stared down the Hill, waiting for Jack's question; in the deceiving twilight, one gravestone seemed to shift, teeter, thrust upward. She turned away from Jack to watch Mavis leave the ward; as the girl neared the screen by the door it was wrenched apart and the old man fell out, gasping wordlessly; as if at a cue nurses converged and swirled about each other with balletic timing, instruments in hand. Viv watched in unwilling fascination; behind her Jack mumbled something. A stern doctor strode to the screen and drew it gently to behind him, like a sheet across a face. The old man sat on an empty bed and gazed at nothing, and Mavis returned with the news: "The woman in the end bed's died."

"God, isn't that terrible," Viv said. "God, I hope we don't see her."

"I suppose they'll keep the screen in the way while they take her out. I feel all creepy. Just think, that'll be us one day. My father always used to say you've got to make the most of life, and for once I couldn't agree with him more. But that can't be all there is—you can't just *end* like that..."

"Oh, Mavis, shut up and stop being bloody morbid!" Viv cried. "I'll see you tomorrow morning!"

As Mavis strode past the screen and wheels screeched toward the ward Jack asked sombrely: "What letter?"

"What are you on about?"

"You know. The letter Mavis posted for you."

"Nosy, aren't you?" But why shouldn't she tell him? Let *him* try to order her about! "The letter I wrote to that ad in the paper."

"You haven't! Don't you realize he could find you here? I can't watch over you till you leave!"

"And I don't bloody well expect you to!" exploded Viv.

Jack was stunned into silence; the screeching wheels halted at the screen. At last he said: "I'm going to try to track him down."

"I'm not stopping you."

Jack hurried out, and Viv grinned wryly as she watched him go. Everyone seemed to be walking out on her today; well, what the hell. The cry of the wheels faded into distance, and the storm seemed to have passed.

But early next morning Viv awoke, sure that she had heard some sound inappropriate to this hour. She could visualize the ward, the empty bed by the door, the shapes turning beneath sheets in the subdued light like the clients of some uneasy morgue; she kept her eyes closed, wooing sleep, and listened. Down the corridor someone coughed painfully; a lavatory flushed. Then she heard wheels squealing slowly, softly, toward her. She could not judge their distance; perhaps she was dreaming. She fumbled a blanket over her ear, but the sound pierced the material, and a sickening smell of ointment and disinfectant reached into her retreat. The wheels approached her stealthily, then stopped. She was certain that a shape bent over her, peering down; nothing on earth would have persuaded her to throw back the blanket and open her eyes. She imagined she heard labored breathing, as from an open mouth; a stronger wave of the stench turned her stomach. One more second and she'd scream to wake up the hospital. At that moment the figure withdrew; another wave of the suffocating odor found her, and she thought she heard a creaking as of a figure settling into a chair. What was it doing now? Was it at her bedside locker? Before she could summon up the courage to confront it, the wheels whined off down the ward, carefully, with sinister stealth. As soon as she could no longer hear them beneath the blanket, she pushed back the covering and sat up. The ward was as she had imagined it; silent, huddled shapes, someone moving in a nightmare, a snore or two; but for an instant she thought the doors were swinging to a standstill, and through their glass a pale head moved out of sight as if propelled in a wheelchair; a trick of the light, perhaps. She glanced at her locker; the drawers had not been touched, and on top was nothing important; a glass, a bottle of Lucozade propping up the envelope from Tony. Awake alone among the beds, Viv shivered and snuggled down to sleep.

"I love this flat," Mavis said. "You're right, I do feel free."

"Do you want to unpack before we go out? You can have this wardrobe. Mary used to have it."

"That'll be great. Some of these need washing—I've never been to a laundrette before. Hope it'll be all right. Which is my bed? Oh, that's fine. Aren't they a bit close together? Maybe we can shift them when we have time. I don't know how to use these gas cookers, you'll have to show me. This was the bathroom, wasn't it? God, Viv, you dirty pig! Don't you ever clean it out?"

"You can clean it out when you need it."

"You know, I'm sure this wallpaper gets depressing. Look where it's coming off. Couldn't we get some new? I'm sure we could find someone to put it up. Jack any good at that sort of thing? Well, you never know. Say, aren't these curtains weird. Did you make them out of blankets?"

"I made them," Viv told her. "I bought the material. I like them."

Mavis giggled. "What're you sniggering about?" Viv demanded, but Mavis only sucked her breath in harshly and giggled afresh. She could get on your nerves after a while, Viv thought. "Look, Mavis—" Someone rang the bell, which clattered and swung further askew. Mavis howled with laughter. Viv glared at her and opened the door.

"Thank God you're in," Jack said.

"Oh, it's you. Mavis is just unpacking."

"Well, I'll help if you like. I've got something to tell you."

"What about?" Viv said with obvious boredom, closing the door and glancing at her watch; half-seven, and she and Mavis had agreed to reach the bowl by eight.

"One of you ill?" Jack asked. "Smells like someone spilled a jar of ointment in the hall."

"Nothing wrong with either of us," said Viv. "What were you going to say? We're going out in a minute." She began to brush her hair.

"It's about that letter."

"Oh, go home, Jack, will you." Viv groaned. "I want to enjoy myself tonight."

"No, listen, it's damned odd. The house from which the letter to the *Herald* was addressed—it's an empty house on Mercy Hill just below the graveyard: you must have been able to see it from the window at the hospital."

"If it was an empty house he must have been playing a joke too, so he deserved all he got," Viv said. "Are you taking a coat, Mavis? We said we'd leave at half-seven, and it's past that now."

"Will you *listen!* I told Cooper—I said I'd just been passing the house and remembered the ad—and he told me he thought there was something fishy when he saw the ad, because he remembered the address from years ago. Seems the owner of the house used it as a sort of one-man brothel, and when the police clamped down on that he started to lure in the neighborhood girls. When that got around the girls of the district wouldn't go out alone after dark—you know the Mercy Hill people would rather keep that sort of thing among themselves than call the police—and so he started cutting keys to people's back doors and getting in that way, even though by that time he couldn't get about on foot—you can guess why. The way Cooper heard it the people finally broke into the house, but they found him dead—you can guess of what."

"Are you coming, Mavis?" Viv called, grabbing her handbag. "You can finish unpacking when we get back."

"I don't know if Jack's finished. It's interesting."

"Well, *I'm* not interested!" Viv cried. "I think it's morbid! You've got a twisted mind, Jack, if you want to know about things like that. Come on, Mavis, let's go and have some fun!"

"But what about that letter?" Jack expostulated as Viv wrenched open the door and thrust him out. "Suppose some maniac is using that house for the same reasons?"

"I think you're a maniac, wallowing in that muck," Viv told him. She slammed the door and, head held high, marched downstairs.

"Who's got my comb?" a girl yelled. "Some bitch's nicked it."

"Maybe you've lost it," suggested one of her companions.

"Lost it balls," and she shoved open the cubicles to peer inside, kicking the doors of the *Engaged*. Viv and Mavis exchanged looks and ignored her, ostentatiously chatting louder as they retouched their faces, then emerged into the Bowl. Before them stretched the high clean walls and the alleys echoing to the reiterated hollow fall of pins, but first they had to pass through the gangs of girls waiting beyond the playing area to be picked up by their opposite numbers, and between the tables, treading on crushed paper cups, where groups dawdled over cold coffee and were moved on by an unsmiling waitress as she sponged the stained plastic. Viv and Mavis pushed through to an empty alley; two boys were standing near it, talking. "Are you playing?" Viv called.

"You go right ahead, kid. Age before beauty," the heftier boy laughed in reply, and continued to his thin swarthy friend: "Don't think you could bowl from a wheelchair."

"He must have been waiting outside for someone," the other commented, and watched Viv bowl. Conscious of being observed, she managed to twist the bowl into the trough beside the alley.

"You'll never make the title that way, kid." He swung his jacket from his shoulder and dropped it by the seat where Mavis sat watching. "Come on, Les, come and talk to dream-girl here," he called back, indicating Mavis to his friend, and crossed to stand by Viv while the bowl returned. "All mod cons," he said, slipping his arm round Viv's waist as the bowl came to rest beside them. "Go ahead, pick it up and I'll show you. What do they call you, kid? I'm Brian and that's Les chatting up your friend." As she fitted her fingers into the bowl he laid his hand under hers and drew her arm back; she felt his muscle swell. "Back here a bit." He positioned her legs with his other hand and patted her thigh.

"Watch it," warned Viv.

"Now don't you worry about me, kid. Viv, is it? Well, you bowl hard and get thirsty and I'll buy you a drink."

"This must be that girl's comb," said Mavis. "God, don't like to touch it." With her foot she pushed it under the pipe beneath the washbowls. "What do you think of them? You don't mind I got Les, do you? He's gorgeous. Anyway, Brian is too if it comes to that. God, isn't he big."

"I know. Listen, Mavis, where are we going?"

"For a drink, we said."

"No, I mean after. I mean—Brian said something about going back to their place . . ."

"Well, I hope so. What's wrong, Viv, don't you want to?"

"Oh, I suppose I don't mind if there's four of us. But—you know— Brian seems . . . I mean, I hope they won't expect us to . . . you know . . ."

"No, I don't. What're you on about?"

"Go all the way with them!" Viv forced out.

"I should think they will. That's the idea we've been giving them all night. God, Viv, you had plenty of chances to say if you didn't want to."

"You mean you've done it before? Well, I haven't and I won't!"

"Viv, you can't go now!" Mavis blocked the closing door with her elbow and hurried after her. "You bloody traitor! Don't you come to me for anything again! I'll ring someone and get her to make up a fourth and I bet Brian likes her better!" But Viv did not look back until she reached the exit escalator; she glimpsed Brian pointing angrily in her direction and Mavis gesticulating in explanation before she clattered down the moving staircase, fearful of pursuit, and out into the night.

Her bus was waiting patiently for an unsteady passenger. Viv ran wildly; her handbag clicked open and Tony's letter fell on the pavement. So what, she thought distractedly—but she stooped to retrieve it, and straightened up in time to watch the dwindling of the disinterested bus. Twenty minutes' wait for its successor. She'd walk; Brian might come out and find her at the stop.

As she set out beneath the suffused purple sky she found herself glancing back; she could not imagine what she sought. Though the night was humid she shivered once, then hurried onward. This was the area of transition between Brichester and Lower Brichester; the bowl represented an attempt to rake in the money from the Lower Brichester people on their own doorsteps, along with the odd Chinese fish-and-chip shops, the boutique in St. Anne's Gardens, the record shops, all angling for the enthusiasms of the students and other tenants of the flats which composed the dilapidated three-story streets between the city proper and the "desirable residences" at the edge of country. From an upper window roared concerted laughter, drowning the clink of glasses; on the ground floor of the next house figures sat intently round a tv screen, dead blue light playing stroboscopically on their faces. Viv wished she were home; she wondered whether she would have the energy to brew herself a coffee, or simply fall into bed.

Something hung from a telephone wire above the street and flapped in a stray breeze across the rooftops; Viv peered upward, then abruptly hurried past. A group of youths idling on the other pavement heard her and whistled; Viv smiled secretly—one up to me, Mavis. Then they were gone and once more she was alone beneath the buzzing streetlamps, dwarfed by the streets from which echoed her heels.

She passed the wrought-iron gates of Ellis Park; her feet were caught in the intricate shadow. Beside her railings multiplied to the corner of St. Anne's Gardens; above them a few packed fans of leaves, glazed by the electric light, swayed stealthily. Close to Viv a squealing sound began. She turned nervously; the street was deserted. Though the air seemed still, Viv told herself that some quiet breeze must be troubling the rusty hinges of the gates. But as she hurried to the corner, some part of her listened to determine whether the sound kept pace with her. As it would if it were coming from the gates, it faded. She turned right into St. Anne's Gardens, and saw that the gleam of railings was interrupted just before they ended at the slope down to the shops which rounded off the Gardens; a gap had been forced through the railings by nocturnal users of the park—in fact, several bars had been removed. She had passed it many times, even used it once or twice with Mary; now it yawned, sinister. She recalled that a path led inside the park from the gates round the corner, curved away from the street until an unofficial shortcut joined this gap. Was the squealing louder? Had it moved away around the curve and now was closing in on her? She peered in panic through the railings into the trees and beyond them the enigmatic silver shadows; for one moment she was sure that something moved rapidly ahead of her between the trees, gaining on the gap. She moaned and ran, past the end of the railings, down the hill between the first shops. Pain lanced her side; not from her appendix, which hadn't bothered her for days, not even at the bowl—but the nagging pain which weighs down flight. She had to stop, panting, beside the boutique.

In the distance a car screamed round the corners; someone played a tune upon its horn. Otherwise the night was soft and silent, soothing. Viv's sweater stuck beneath her armpits. Breathing normally once more, she took in the boutique display before strolling onward. Bloody Mavis, leaving her alone like this, letting her get frightened! Not that she was as bad as Jack with all that morbid drivel; if he hadn't come round she wouldn't have got herself scared just now. And by what? Grow up, girl, you'd think this was the first time you'd been out by yourself after dark.

She reached the junction at the bottom of the hill, and looked both ways; nobody in sight. Opposite her an alley led behind the buildings and came out just beyond 16 Desmond Street, where she lived; but inside the alley an angle of shadow cut off vision, and she turned left to take the long way round. Beside the alley was a record shop; she surveyed the covers as she passed. Then, in the depths of the display, something caught her eye; a picture, somehow illuminated, of a figure seated atop a hill. What record was this? Then it moved; the chair plunged down the hill; the figure raised its arms and from them tattered bandages flew; at her back the wheels shrieked closer.

Viv cried out and fled round the corner into Desmond Street, struggling with her bag to find her key. A few upper rooms were lit; light streamed from a garage beyond her door. But she had not reached the comforting light when she heard the sound ahead of her.

She backed into a doorway, grinding her knuckles into her teeth. If only she had the courage to ring the doorbell! But what could she say if someone came down? She wasn't even sure if there had been a lighted room in this house. She trembled, frantically seeking sanctuary. Beyond her house the squealing continued; it seemed to move no nearer. Then a car drew into the garage and an attendant emerged from the office. Viv tried to call out but could utter no sound; instead she ran blindly toward the light—and toward the squealing, which came from the garage's OPEN/CLOSED sign, pivoting back and forth.

A breath touched Viv's neck. She wheeled in horror. There was nothing but the deserted street and a night breeze. Terror filled her of some menace from some new direction, and she shouldered open the front door of 16 and fell into the hall. It was dark; the house was silent; the open door awaited the returning tenants. She fumbled for the light-switch. The car pulled out of the garage and poured its beams through the front-door pane to show an empty hall. Before the beams had withdrawn Viv was upstairs.

Her flat was on the right; at the end of the passage a tree waved in a window. Viv extracted her key with shaking fingers, and her eyes were drawn to the window; were the lines across it only those between the panes—or was there an extra bar, like the arm of a wheelchair? Was the vague darkness which moved against the night merely that of the tree? And where was that smell of ointment coming from? She thrust her key in upside down, tore it out and dropped it. Almost in tears, she stooped and clutched the glimmering key; a shadow brushed across it, perhaps her own. She froze, unable to look round, then with a last surge of panic leapt up, found the keyhole, wrenched open the door and slammed it behind her.

It took courage to switch on the light; but when she did her first sight was of Mavis' dresses in disorder on the bed. That bitch! Leaving her alone after she'd promised to stay with her! Well, this was *her* flat and she decided who was coming in—and that went for wheelchairs too. She began to giggle a little hysterically. She'd show Mavis. She locked the door and jammed a chair beneath the handle. Not that Mavis would be coming home tonight—but when she did, she could plead to be let in. Now Viv was going to bed, and to hell with everything; this was *her* flat and she was in control. She pulled off her sweater, skirt and stockings and threw them on the chair at the door; she was too hot and exhausted to do more. It was too hot even to be weighed down by sheets. She dragged the window down, sucked in the night air to clean her nostrils of the thick stench of ointment which seemed to fill the room, and climbed on her bed in her slip, catching her toenails on one of Mavis' dresses. Untidy bitch—did she expect her unpacking done for her? Tomorrow she could move her bed over, too. Viv lay down, yawning; she stretched one arm above her head to pull the cord for her own familiar domestic darkness, and throwing her legs wide kicked Mavis' offending dress. The cord clicked the light off and swung out of reach; the dark descended; Mavis' dress slid to the floor, and as the other dresses moved as they should not have, in the last split-second of light Viv saw that on the space where the dress had lain had been exposed a slowly moving strip of discolored bandage.

Jack's Little Friend

It's afternoon when you find the box. You're in the marshes on the verge of the Thames below London. Perhaps you live in the area, perhaps you're visiting, on business or on holiday. You've been walking. You've passed a power station and its expressionless metallic chord, you've skirted a flat placid field of cows above which black smoke pumps from factory chimneys. Now reeds smear your legs with mud, and you might be proposing to turn back when you see a corner of metal protruding from the bearded mud.

You make your way toward it, squelching. It looks chewed by time, and you wonder how long it's been there. Perhaps it was dumped here recently; perhaps it was thrown out by the river; possibly the Thames, belaboring and dragging the mud, uncovered the box. As the water has built the box a niche of mud so it has washed the lid, and you can make out dates scratched on the metal. They are almost a century old. It's the dates that provoke your curiosity, and perhaps also a gesture against the dull landscape. You stoop and pick up the box, which frees itself with a gasp of mud.

Although the box is only a foot square it's heavier than you anticipated. You skid and regain your balance. You wouldn't be surprised if the box were made of lead. If anyone had thrown it in the river they would certainly have expected it to stay sunk. You wonder why they would have bothered to carry it to the river or to the marshes for disposal. It isn't distinguished, except for the dates carved on the lid by an illiterate or clumsy hand—just a plain box of heavy grey metal.

JACK'S LITTLE FRIEND

You read the dates:

               31/8/1888
                8/9/1888
               30/9/1888
               9/11/1888

There seems to be no pattern. It's as if someone had been trying to work one out. But what kind of calculation would be resolved by throwing away a metal box? Bewildered though you are, that's how you read the clues. What was happening in 1888? You think you read somewhere that expeditions were returning from Egypt around that date. Have you discovered a lost archaeological find? There's one way to know. But your fingers slip off the box, which in any case is no doubt locked beneath its coat of mud, and the marsh is seeping into your shoes; so you leave off your attempts to open the lid and stumble away, carrying the box.

By the time you reach the road your excitement has drained somewhat. After all, someone could have scratched the dates on the lid last week; it could even be an understated practical joke. You don't want to take a heavy box all the way home only to prise from its depths a piece of paper saying APRIL FOOL. So you leave the box in the grass at the side of the road and search until you find a metal bar. Sorry if I'm aborting the future of archaeology, you think, and begin to lever at the box.

But even now it's not as easy as you thought. You've wedged the box and can devote all your energy to shifting the lid, but it's fighting you. Once it yields an inch or two and then snaps shut again. It's as if it were being held shut, like the shell of a clam. A car passes on the other side of the road and you begin to give in to a sense of absurdity, to the sight of yourself struggling to jemmy open an old box. You begin to feel like a tourist's glimpse. Another car, on your side this time, and dust sweeps into your face. You blink and weep and cough violently, for the dust seems to have been scooped into your mouth.

Then the sensation of dry crawling in your mouth recedes, and only the skin beneath your tongue feels rough. You wipe your eyes and return to the box. And then you drop the bar, for the box is wide open.

And it's empty. The interior is as dull as the exterior. There's nothing, except on the bottom a thin glistening coat of what looks like saliva but must be marsh water. You slam the lid. You memorize the dates and walk away, rolling your tongue around the floor of your mouth, which still feels thick, and grinning wryly. Perhaps the hitchhiker or whoever finds the box will conceive a use for it.

That night you're walking along a long dim street toward a woman. She seems to be backing away, and you can't see her face. Suddenly, as you rush toward her, her body opens like an anemone. You plunge deep into the wet red fronds.

The dream hoods your brain for days. Perhaps it's the pressure of work or of worry, but you find yourself becoming obsessive. In crowds you halt, thinking of the dates on the box. You've consulted such books as you have immediate access to, but they didn't help. You stare at the asymmetrical faces of the crowd. Smoke rises from their mouths or their jaws work as they drive forward, pulled along by their set eyes. Imagine asking them to help. They wouldn't have touched the box, they would have shuffled on by, scattering their waste paper and condoms. You shake your head to dislodge the crawling thoughts. You aren't usually so misanthropic. You'll have to find out what those dates mean. Obviously your brain won't give you much peace until you do.

So you ask your friend, the one who knows something about history. And your friend says "That's easy. They're the dates of Jack the Ripper," and tells you that the five murders everyone accepts as the Ripper's work were committed on those dates. You can't help smiling, because you've just had a flash of clarity: of course you must have recognized the dates subconsciously from having read them somewhere, and the recognition was the source of your dream. Then your friend says "Why are you interested?"

You're about to answer, but your tongue sticks to the floor of your mouth for a moment, like the lid of the box. In that moment you think: why should your friend want to know anyway? They've no right to know, they aren't entitled to a fee for the consultation. You found the box, you'll conduct the enquiry. "I must have read the dates somewhere," you say. "They've been going round in my head and I couldn't remember why."

On the way home you play a game with yourself. No, that bus shelter's no good, too open. Yes, he could hide in that alley, there would be hardly any light where it bends in the middle. You stop, because the skin beneath your tongue is rough and sore, and hinders your thoughts. You explore the softness beneath your tongue with one finger, and as you do so the inflammation seems to draw into itself and spare you.

Later you ponder Jack the Ripper. You've read about him, but when you leaf through your knowledge you realize you're not so well informed. How did he become the Ripper? Why did he stop? But you know that these questions are only your speculations about the box, disguised.

It's inconvenient to go back to find the box, but you manage to clear yourself the time. When you do you think at first you've missed the place where you left the box. Eventually you find the bar, but the box has gone. Perhaps someone kicked it into the hedges. You search among the cramped roots and trapped crisp-bags until your mouth feels scraped dry. You could tell the local police, but then you would have to explain your interest, and they would take the credit for themselves. You don't need the box. Tomorrow you'll begin to research.

And so you do, though it's not as easy as you expected. Everyone's fascinated by the Ripper these days, and the library books are popular. You even have to buy a paperback of one of them, glancing sideways as you do so at the people browsing through the book. The sunlight glares in the cracks and pores and fleshy bags of their faces, giving them a sheen like wet wax: wax animated by simple morbid fascination. You shudder and hurry away. At least you have a reason for reading the book, but these others haven't risen above the level of the mob that gloated squirming over reports of the Ripper's latest killing. You know how the police of the time must have felt.

You read the books. You spread them across the table, comparing accounts. You're not to be trapped into taking the first one you read as definitive. Your friends, and perhaps your spouse or lover as well, joke and gently rebuke you about your singlemindedness. No doubt they talk about it when you're not there. Let them. Most people seem content to relive, or elaborate, the second-hand. Not you.

You read. 31/8/1888: throat cut twice, head nearly severed, disembowelled twice. 8/9/1888: handkerchief wrapped around almost-severed neck, womb missing, intestines cast over shoulder, relatively little blood in the yard where the corpse was found. 30/9/1888: two women, one with windpipe severed; the other, less than an hour later, with right eye damaged, earlobe cut off, intestines over shoulder, kidney and entrails missing. 9/11/1888: throat cut, ears and nose missing, also liver, and a mass of flesh and organs on the bedside table. There's a photograph of her in one book. You stare at it for a moment, then you slam the book and stare at your hands.

But your hands are less real than your thoughts. You think of the Ripper, cutting and feeling his way through the corpses, taking more time and going into more detail with each murder. The last one took two hours, the books tell you. A question is beginning to insist on an answer. What was he looking for?

You aren't sleeping well. You stare at the lights that prick your eyeballs behind your lids and theorize until you topple wakefully into sleep. Sometimes you seem almost to have found a pattern, and you gasp in crowds or with friends. They glance at you and you meet their gaze coldly. They wouldn't be capable of your thoughts, and you certainly don't intend to let them hinder you. But even as their dull gaze falls away you realize that you've lost the inspiration, if indeed it were one.

So you confine yourself to your home. You're glad to have an excuse to do so, for recently you've been growing hypersensitive. When you're outside and the sunlight intensifies it's as though someone were pumping up an already white-hot furnace, and the night settles around you like water about a gasping fish. So you draw the curtains and read the books again.

The more you read the stranger it seems. You feel you could understand the man if a missing crucial detail were supplied. What can you make of his macabre tenderness in wrapping a handkerchief around the sliced throat of Annie Chapman, his second victim? A numbed denial of his authorship of the crime, perhaps? If there were relatively little blood in the yard then surely the blood must have soaked into the Ripper's clothes, but in that case how could he have walked home in broad daylight? Did he cut the windpipe of Elizabeth Stride because he was interrupted before he was able to do more, or because she had seen too much for him simply to leave her and seek a victim elsewhere? An hour later, was it his frustration that led him to mutilate Catherine Eddowes more extensively and inventively than her predecessors? And why did he wait almost twice as long as hitherto before committing his final murder, that of Mary Kelly, and the most detailed? Was this the exercise of a powerful will, and did the frustration build up to an unprecedented climax? But what frustration? What was he looking for?

You turn to the photograph of Mary Kelly again, and this time you're able to examine it dispassionately. Not that the Victorian camera was able to be particularly explicit. In fact, the picture looks

like a piece of early adolescent pornography on a wall, an amateur blob
for a face and a gaping darkness between the legs. You suck your
tongue, whose underside feels rough and dry.

You read the Ripper's letters. The adolescent wit of the rhymes
often gives way to the childish illiteracy of some of the letters. You
can understand his feelings of superiority to the victims and to the
police; they were undoubtedly at least as contemptible as the people
you know. But that doesn't explain the regression of the letters, as if
his mind were flinching back as far as possible from his actions. That's
probably a common trait of psychopaths, you think: an attempt to
reject the part of them that commits the crimes.

Your mind is still frowning. You read through the murders again.
First murder, nothing removed. Second, the womb stolen. Third, kidney and entrails stolen. A portion of kidney which had been preserved
in spirits was sent to the police, with a note saying that the writer had
eaten the rest. Fourth, the liver removed and the ears and nose, but
the womb and a three-month-old fetus untouched. Why? To sate the
hunger which motivated the killings, presumably, but what hunger
was that? If cannibalism, surely he would never have controlled himself sufficiently to preserve a portion of his food with which to taunt
the police? If not, what worse reality was he disguising from the
police, and perhaps from himself, as cannibalism?

You swallow the saliva that's pooling under your tongue and try to
grasp your theories. It's as if the hunger spat out the kidney. Not
literally, of course. But it certainly seems as if the Ripper had been
trying to sate his hunger by varying the delicacies, as if it were a
temperamental pet. Surely the death of Mary Kelly couldn't have
satisfied it for good, though.

Then you remember the box. If he had externalized the hunger as
something other than himself, could his mind have persuaded him
that the hunger was alive independent of him and might be trapped?
Could he have used one of the portions of Mary Kelly as a lure?

Would that have seemed a solution in the grotesque algebra of his mind? Might he have convinced himself that he had locked his hunger away in time, and having scratched the dates on the box to confirm his calculations have thrown it in the river? Perhaps the kidney had been the first attempted lure, insufficiently tempting. And then—well, he could hardly have returned to a normal life, if indeed he had left one, but he might have turned to the socially acceptable destruction of alcoholism and died unknown.

The more you consider your theory the more persuasive it becomes. Perhaps you can write it up as an article and sell it somewhere. Of course you'll need to pursue your research first. You feel happy in a detached unreal way, and you even go to your companion willingly for the first time in, now you think about it, a long while. But you feel apart from the moist dilation of flesh and the hard dagger thrust, and are glad when it's over. There's something at the back of your mind you need to coax forward. When you've dealt with that you'll be able to concentrate on other things.

You walk toward her. The light is flickering and the walls wobble like a fairground corridor. As you approach her, her dress peels apart and her body splits open. From within the gap trails a web toward which you're drawn. At the center of the web hangs a piece of raw meat.

Your cry wakes you but not your companion. Their body feels like burning rubber against you, and you flinch away. After a minute you get out of bed. You can't stand the sensation, and you want to shake off the dream. You stare from the window; the darkness is paling, and a bird sings tentatively. Suddenly you gasp. You'll write that article now, because you've realized what you need. You can't hope to describe the Ripper or even to meet a psychopath for background. But there's one piece of first-hand research you can do that will help you to understand the Ripper. You don't know why you didn't read your dream that way at once.

Next day you begin searching. You read all the cards you can find in shop windows. They aren't as numerous or as obvious as you expected. You don't want to find yourself actually applying for a course of French lessons. You suppose there are magazines that would help you, but you're not sure where to find them. At last, as the streets become grimmer, you notice a group of young men reading cards in a shop window. They nudge each other and point to several of the cards, then they confer and hurry toward a phone box. You're sure this time.

You choose one called Marie, because that was what Mary Kelly used to call herself. No particular reason, but the parallel seems promising. When you telephone her she sounds dubious. She asks what you want and you say "Nothing special. Just the usual." Your voice may be disturbing her, because your tongue is sticking somehow to the floor of your mouth, which feels swollen and obstructive. She's silent for a moment, then she says "All right. Come up in twenty minutes," and tells you where she is.

You hadn't realized it would be as swift as that. Probably it's a good thing, because if you had to wait much longer your unease might find you excuses for staying away. You emerge from the phone box and the sunlight thuds against your head. Your mouth is dry, and the flesh beneath your tongue is twitching as if an insect has lodged there. It must be the heat and the tension. You walk slowly toward your rendezvous, which is only a few streets away. You walk through a maze of alleys to keep in the shade. On either side of you empty clothes flap, children shout and barks run along a chain of dogs.

You reach your destination on time. It's in a street of drab shops: a boarded betting shop, a window full of cardigans and wool, a Chinese take-away. The room you want is above the latter. You skid on trodden chips and shielding your face from the eyes of the queue next door, ring the bell.

As you stare at the new orange paint on the door you wonder what you're going to say. You have some idea and surely enough money, but will she respond to that? You understand some prostitutes refuse to talk rather than act. You can hardly explain your interest in the Ripper. You're still wondering when she opens the door.

She must be in her thirties, but her face has aged like an orange and she's tried to fill in the wrinkles, probably while waiting for you. Her eyelashes are like unwashed black paint-brushes. But she smiles slightly, as if unsure whether you want her to, and then sticks out her tongue at a head craning from next door. "You rang before," she says, and you nod.

The door slams behind you. Your hand reaches blindly for the latch; you can still leave, she'll never be able to pursue you. Beneath your tongue a pulse is going wild. If you don't go through with this now it will be more difficult next time, and you'll never be rid of the Ripper or of your dreams. You follow her upstairs.

Seeing her from below you find it easy to forget her smile. Her red dress pulls up and her knickers, covered with whorls of color like the eye of a peacock's tail, alternately bulge and crease. The hint of guilt you were beginning to feel retreats: her job is to be on show, an object, you need have no compunction. Then you're at the top of the stairs and in her room.

There are thick red curtains, mauve walls, a crimson bed and telephone, a color tv, a card from Ibiza and one from Rhyl. Behind a partition you can see pans and knives hanging on hooks in the kitchen area. Then your gaze is wrenched back to her as she says "Go on then, tell me your name, you know mine."

Of course you don't. You're not so stupid as to suppose she would display her real name in the window. You shake your head and try to smile. But the garish thick colors of the room are beginning to weigh on you, and the trapped heat makes your mouth feel dry, so that the smile comes out soured.

"Never mind, you don't have to," she says. "What do you want? Want me to wear anything?"

Now you have to speak or the encounter will turn into a grotesque misunderstanding. But your tongue feels as if it's glued down, while beneath it the flesh is throbbing painfully. You can feel your face prickling and reddening, and rooted in the discomfort behind your teeth a frustrated disgust with the whole situation is growing.

"Are you shy? There's no need to be," she says. "If you were really shy you wouldn't have come at all, would you?" She stares into the mute struggle within your eyes and smiling tentatively again, says "Can't you talk?"

Yes, you can talk, it's only a temporary obstruction. And when you shift it you'll tell her that you've come to use her, because that's what she's for. An object, that's what she's made herself. Inside that crust of makeup there's nothing. No wonder the Ripper sought them out. You don't need compassion in a slaughterhouse. You try to control your raw tongue, but only the throbbing beneath it moves.

"I'm sorry, I'm only upsetting you. Never mind, love," she says. "Nerves are terrible, I know. You sit down and I'll get you a drink."

And that's when you have to act, because your mouth is filling with saliva as if a dam has burst, and your tongue's still straining to raise itself, and the turgid colors have insinuated themselves into your head like migraine, and tendrils of uneasiness are streaming up from your clogged mouth and matting your brain, and at the core of all this there's a writhing disgust and fury that this woman should presume to patronize you. You don't care if you never understand the Ripper, so long as you can smash your way out of this trap. You move toward the door, but at the same time your hand is beckoning her, it seems quite independent of you. You haven't reached the door when she's in front of you, her mouth open and saying "What?" And you do the only thing that seems, in your blind violent frustration, available to you.

You spit into her open mouth.

For a moment you feel free. Your mouth is clean and your tongue can move as you want it to. The colors have retreated, and she's just a well-meaning rather sad woman using her talents as best she can.

Then you realize what you've done. Now your tongue's free you don't know what to say. You think perhaps you could explain that you sneezed. Perhaps she'll accept that, if you apologize. But by this time she's already begun to scream.

You were so nearly right most of the time. You realized that the stolen portions of Mary Kelly might have been placed in the box as a lure. If only you'd appreciated the implications of this: that the other mutilations were by no means the act of a maniac, but the attempts of a gradually less sane man to conceal the atrocities of what possessed him. Who knows, perhaps it had come from Egypt. He couldn't have been sure of its existence even when he lured it into the box. Perhaps you'll be luckier, if that's luck, although now you can only stand paralyzed as the woman screams and screams and falls inertly to the floor; and blood begins to seep from her abdomen. Perhaps you'll be able to catch it as it emerges, or at least to see your little friend.

Beside the Seaside

Milne left the garage and began to descend the hill to the town at the edge of the sea. Above the water the sun sank like an orange windblown seed, furred by a faint mist. He'd stopped to read *Playboy* in a layby, but when he'd closed the magazine the car had coughed weakly and had barely staggered to the lip of the hill down to the sea. It would be repaired in the morning, they'd told him, and he could stay in the town. He strode past white Victorian houses wedged into the hill, balancing his case full of samples of the new perfume; below, along the beach which was a leg stretched in a *Playboy* posture, a few figures hurried through April, and a lone green car vanished up the coast road.

The town's few streets were drawn to the promenade, and in the first hotel—one of a line whose intricate verandas had been chafed into sameness by sand—he found a room. "Oh, are you a salesman, Mr. Milne?" But it wasn't an echo of the inevitable joke, for she ushered him into his room with a smile, not a grin.

Well, the room would be gone in the morning, and he might find a club for the night. But his mind shouted: good God, what a holiday! Who could leap up eager for the day between these walls like slabs of yellow sand? Who could meet his face reflected between those patterns of wood tangled as brown seaweed? Who could live beneath the pencilled misspelt sign "No drinking in bedrooms" strung between two corners of the room like "Thou God Seest Me"? Beyond the balcony the thin line of the sea was russet, but the sun was sinking fast. Yet as Milne hurried from the room he glanced speculatively at the double bed.

At the end of the hall a net curtain unfurled across the window like a wing drifting forth from a cocoon. Milne locked his door and glanced up. A woman crouched on the ray of light along the floor, where the curtain's shadow bunched and spread. No, he hadn't seen her; he'd remembered seeing her, or remembered an insomniac notion, for the shadow whipped away and the floor was bare. A strange idea, given even his previous sleepless night in a disembowelled bed: it wasn't as if she had been crouching, more as if she had been a sketch glimpsed as she folded in half. He passed through the ray of light, his shoes crunching on sand.

In the dining-room, among the marine prints and the teapots in their knitted coats, sat groups Milne might have predicted: a family holidaying and laughing out of season, two pensioners and a stained wheelchair, a typist who couldn't afford Majorca. The last, a timid eager teenager who smiled with the family, sat alone. "I'll put you two together," the landlady said, taking Milne across to her. "You look right as rain now," she told the girl.

"Have you been ill?" Milne asked as he waited for his chop.

"A bit. I'm all right now, though. My friend went on a coach trip and she won't be back till late. I didn't want to spoil her week."

"How do you intend to pass the time?" Milne felt that was unequivocally conversational. Her nose was shiny, and fifteen years ago—at her age, in fact—he'd rejected women with shiny noses.

"There's not much to do down here," she said. "You can always walk along the prom, I suppose."

"No doubt you could."

"There always seem to be a lot of people on the beach at night. And other people watching."

"You've more or less sold me on an early night," Milne said, intending no ambiguity.

"Did you have to have a double bed? We got one even though we didn't want it."

"Oh, I'm surprised," Milne said.

But the room couldn't sustain an early night. Perhaps clubs were beyond her experience, Milne thought as he emerged to search, strolling along a quarter-mile of promenade to the first turn, past flurries of sand and shifting embryonic humps of the beach. In the inky light half the freaks of breeze and sand might have been embracing.

He made his way up the first hill. Already crumpled newspapers and trodden chips gathered outside the fish-and-chip shops; further on, buckets and spades clanked against a tube of fitful pink light in a shop doorway, and in an amusement arcade glowing plastic men leapt up and howled as they were shot. An alcoholic twitched away from a cracked Woolworth's window as Milne approached, snarling "Now gerraway, boy! Gerraway, won't you?" and poking forth fingers coated with wet sand which Milne saw had smeared lines on the window.

Milne cut through an alley, past a lone string of garish cardboard fat women, and found himself in what might have been the same street. No, there was a cinema; the posters peeled like wallpaper in an abandoned house to advertise *Bullitt* or perhaps a tattered *Sound of Music*. Bored by the colorless night, Milne quickened his pace. Beyond the grey shop windows, the glowing gibbet of a neon sign, "The Submarine Club"! But when he came closer he saw the groups of shaved heads jostling down the steps, boys whose hair was minute tips like grains of sand, and the pursued groups of factory girls, vanguards of a new and equally disturbing race of close-cropped blondes. As he turned away, however, a Jaguar drew up and its driver coaxed forth a girl. Milne watched engrossed, as he might have pored over a *Playboy* centerfold. Even beneath the goosenecked sodium lamps she glittered, turning a cold facet to dazzle the defensive skinheads, whose laughter shattered. She was intricately perfect as a brooch, and Milne wavered in the shadows. Then she moulded back into the car and was gone.

Milne walked down toward the sea. Above a shop in whose doorway lay a broken plastic windmill, a room flickered around a television. He thought about the girl: during the night he knew her surfaces would melt from her, dangerous as ice over quicksand. He didn't envy the driver of the Jaguar. Neither, he realized with an insight he could usually avoid, did he envy himself.

He reached the promenade. A half-mile to his left it merged with the coast road which he would take tomorrow for the next large town, Liverpool. He turned in the opposite direction, toward the hotel. A chill breeze crept across the beach, which glimmered beneath a moon that bulged out briefly like white flesh from between strips of cloud. The sea was seeping darkly over the horizon. Yes, of course the old jokes were accurate; he had his transient women as he drove around the country, but hurriedly before he sped on to outdistance ennui or worse, reflection. It frightened him how fluid housewives were beneath their sleepy "Good morning," how their lives could slacken with their muscles. Sometimes he envied them their chameleon natures, although he suspected what that revealed of him. Sometimes he saw himself as a lone traveller—but he was no cowboy, for what did he leave except often a sample of perfume, and what did he take with him except some shreds of memory sticking to him like burrs, all anonymously smelling like his suitcase of the latest perfume?

"What do you want?" he demanded as he leaned on the railing and peered out at the sea. On the drowned sand, patches of mud glistened like dead bruised jellyfish. Perhaps ideally he needed a woman whose aspects he could fit together at leisure, like a jigsaw, fascinated then triumphant—not the eager typist, not the determinedly brittle girl in the Jaguar, for they would draw him down into themselves. "Go on then, where is she?" he demanded and pressed his lips together, for he was talking to the sea, whose refusal to be defined and violent ecstasy he detested. Not that this was violent; rather was it an oily sea which slumped sluggishly across the beach. That must be why so many couples lay down there, darkly huddled along the mile of beach. My God, they must be damp and daft, he thought. The grains of sand which settled on his own feet were clammy enough. Or perhaps they weren't couples. In the feeble bursts of moonlight it was difficult to see. Certainly one embrace on a glistening stain of mud was of coils of rope and limbs of sand.

He moved back from the railing and halted, disturbed. Along the railing, as far as he could see up the promenade, figures were leaning, peering out across the beach. He couldn't count them. The nearest man must have felt Milne's gaze, for he jerked out of his inertia and hurried away, almost running. The others still gazed down. What could they see? Milne wondered. Momentarily, before he erased it in fury, he had an autoerotic image of sand: once, gazing at a handful of sand slipping between his cupped palms, he'd thought how like a vagina it looked. Balls, he told himself, that's not the explanation. From what he'd seen of the town he could imagine that watchers had nothing else to do; why, even the sand which surged up the slope of stone below the promenade and trickled about his feet was more alive than they. He shook his toes free of the amoeba of sand, but already it glittered on his legs. His trousers were covered with the drifting grains; he might as well take the chance to slip beneath the railings and stride toward the sea. But he turned instead and strode toward the hotel, past the sign of a deserted taxi-rank through waves of sand which washed across the pavement.

It was close to midnight. The hotel was silent and paler than the moon. Over the table full of women's magazines and *Reader's Digests*. Milne stared blankly back at himself through the lounge door; his hair had yellowed. He hurried past the scatter of redirected letters on the hall table, past the vase of plastic ferns, and upstairs.

Before the entangled mirror in his room he combed sand from his hair; grains sprinkled whispering on the glass top of the dressing-table.

The hotel was still quiet; the jovial family had taken a tour, the old couple and the typist were doubtless asleep. He lifted the window a little. A roll of moon squeezed out between two tight clouds, and Milne glimpsed the line of figures propped intent at the railing, above the beach where sand lifted palely whirling in the breeze. Slashed by a blade of the wind which pierced between window and frame, Milne undressed hurriedly and burrowed into bed.

A shout awoke him. Perhaps it echoed down a dream; perhaps it was the last laugh of the jovial family. Disorientated by sleep, Milne felt without believing that he was walled into a sand-pit. The sheets weighed on him heavily as sand and rustled like grains. He shifted restlessly, his eyes closing. Then he blinked. Half-awake or not, he was sure he'd caught sight of something which had reared up on the balcony like a semi-opaque wave and vanished.

But the white sky streamed past and nothing else moved. He hung alert for a few minutes, then sank into sleep again.

Ants massed on his face, crawling. They pressed into his mouth, gritting between his teeth. He threw off the sheets and awoke—at least, he was sure that was the order of his actions. His face prickled and chafed against the pillow; his tongue grated against his teeth. He jerked upright and clutched the light-cord. As he pulled it and light blazed his fingers recoiled. They were excruciatingly gritty with sand.

He swung to sit on the edge of the bed, and grains rained on the carpet. The sand must have crept through the window on the breeze. He heaved the window shut, half-noticing that the air no longer moved but was an invisible block of ice. As he peered out at the faint dilution of night on the horizon, a shadow swept across the room behind him.

He stared at the light-bulb. Had the shadow been cast by an insect on the bulb? Somehow he associated the shadow with insects, a whole swarm of them crawling across the wall. He didn't intend to return to bed until he'd found the intruder.

THE HEIGHT OF THE SCREAM

Dressed, he began to search. In one corner of the room he killed a torpid earwig; in another he found a tiny blackened cog from a child's toy. Beneath the bed he found what seemed to be a plastic mouse's tail, and either a cat or the child had scraped the bed's legs to the bone. He peered beneath the dressing-table. The bottom drawer had sprinkled splinters on the carpet, but otherwise there was nothing. His face lifted in the mirror, and behind him the "No drinking" sign moved.

It couldn't have been an insect. One side of the string had risen and fallen back. It couldn't have been a swarm—yet unless his eyes were failing, one corner of the room had slipped out of focus because its entire surface was alive with minute specks. He caught up a shoe and rushed at the wall.

Nothing. But the corner of his eye caught movement, a swirl of shadow across the window. He stood in front of the bed, instinctively protective. A diagonal of movement streamed back to the first wall. In a second the wall scintillated like an anthill. Milne snarled incoherently and threw the shoe, then struggled to remove its twin. As he did so he saw in the mirror the reflected shoe strike the reflected wall, beneath a swarming yellow oval which might have been the unstable impression of a girl's face.

The wall screamed.

It might have been only the image of a scream that tore his mind. It was an echo, or a memory, before he could tell. Already it had disintegrated into a hiss like rain and pattered on the carpet. He was on his feet before he could think and clutching for the door. But his feet skidded on shifting sand and his nerves tore, for the doorknob was acrawl with grains unbearable as powdered glass.

He stared at his fingers, shocked not to see blood, and lunged for the window. The floor rolled apart beneath his feet. He fell. The floor and the walls were whispering voicelessly. He scrabbled to his feet, his fingers scraping together like rusty iron, and thrust at the window.

BESIDE THE SEASIDE

On the pane, against the dawn, stood the bed; and the sheets moved.

Milne turned as though in treacle and saw the girl's face on the pillow. No, it was too shapeless for a tanned girl's face; it must be a stain. But it moved, although it had fallen in half. The lower half of the face, from the upper lip downwards, swarmed into shape and crept up the pillow to meet the cheekbones. And the sheets rose convulsively, furiously, as if limbs were drawing themselves up only to disintegrate and collapse again. As Milne watched mutely, the crawling particles of the face massed into a new pattern, and the mouth smiled.

He was across the room in one leap. The doorknob was clean. He fumbled and wrenched the door open. Behind him, a weight struck the floor with a spread flat thud which at once became a pursuing hiss. He stumbled limping down the stairs, his shoeless foot flayed by sand, and fell out into the dawn.

He peered about weakly. A quarter of a mile away one taxi slept at the taxi-rank. If Milne could reach the garage he could drive back later to collect his suitcase. He began to hobble along the promenade, shivering in a breeze which scooped up the sand from the pavement into his face. A few minutes and the dawn would splay forth. But now he could see little in the flecked crawling light; only the indistinct vista of the promenade dropping one edge to the beach, and at some distance still the taxi, guarded by a dim figure. Milne limped forward, brushing at his face, somehow unable to bring himself to call out or wave. There was so much sand in his eyes, like desiccated tears. Heedless of his chafed foot, he began to run.

The Cellars

Julie felt no precise emotion at the sight of Vic, approaching up the office. The lunch hour had dawdled by; she had nothing to read, nothing to chat about to her colleagues, and was bored—but Vic would hardly have been her choice of a visitor to relieve her boredom. She turned from the window and the dandruff of snow slipping from the ruined church's shoulders as he rounded her desk.

"I say!" he began. "I'll bet you didn't know there were catacombs in Liverpool? Down near the river, off a cul-de-sac, steps leading underneath the street—I'd never have known they were there if one of my friends didn't work nearby. Most extraordinary, though. Heaven knows what they're used for."

She found herself becoming interested, and regarded him expectantly.

"Do you want to explore them sometime?" he asked after a pause. "Tomorrow lunchtime?"

She considered. Agreement committed her to nothing: no more than she had committed herself by giving Vic a photograph of her at his request. "Yes," she said eagerly. "See you here one o'clock tomorrow."

Several minutes later he left reluctantly, detaching himself from her presence as though from a fly-paper, and she imagined him making his way down the office, round the corner at the end, across the bridge linking the two halves of the building which were divided by a well up to the fourth floor where they worked, down his leg of the floor and sitting at his desk. Across the well, through the coinciding windows opening onto it, she could have viewed him seated opposite her, had she wished. But the division across which they had used to wave had widened into a gulf which she had no inclination to bridge. Some months ago he had become her regular escort to the cinema; this had been well enough, but she'd wondered why he never put his arm round her, never even spoke during the film unless she spoke to him. He was too engrossed, she decided; but she could not invoke this theory when he was as frozen as ever in a movie she knew he was attending under protest. She assumed outright that he felt nothing for her, and ceased to go out with him. She supposed he might be shy, but shyness for her was evidence of effeminacy. Why he continued to visit her she did not attempt to deduce; his visits, in any case, were often a nuisance and sometimes a bore. But this time he had aroused her.

Nevertheless, on the following day her anticipation of their trip to the vaults had palled before one o'clock. Once there the vaults would no doubt excite her enthusiasm, but how to alleviate her tedium while she waited? She had ten minutes to kill. She reached for the phone and dialled Alan, her call was batted back and forth between extensions at the factory, and it was three minutes to one before she heard him speak and, her hand deafening the telephone, called to Alice at the next desk: "Ring Vic and tell him to come round at five past, will you?"

Vic had her coat over one arm when he arrived. On the other hand, he lacked a torch with which to guide their exploration; but Julie solved this problem by commissioning a candle from the stock kept in the office against a power cut. "There'll never be another cut so soon after the last one," she affirmed, leaving one candle asleep by itself in the storage box. He held the door for her and they emerged before the lift.

Her nose against the crack between the doors, she watched the elevator's steady ascent of the shaft. Behind her Vic offered: "Cigarette?" His hand curved into view around her face, a hopeful box of his usual Turkish brand on his open palm. When she had begun going out with him she had expressed a taste for these Turkish cigarettes. "No thanks," she replied. He shrugged; smoke creamed from his mouth.

The lift's lips closed behind them. She leaned against the back wall and watched the floor numbers wink at her: 4, 3, 2. . . . "Of course different people may react to the vaults in different ways—said warningly," Vic was saying from his post at the controls. "I went out of curiosity, morbid of course, seeing it's me, but as for your reaction —romanticist that you are . . ."

This image of her he had derived from her fondness for slushy Hollywood movies. She asked: "What's that mean?"

"A romanticist—well, someone whose outlook is—you view the world through rose-colored glasses, one might say. This place isn't romantic. It may do something for you, all the same."

Having flaked all color from the sky, the snow had stopped, but an insistent rain troubled the pigeons picking their way among the debris of St. Luke's Church. Vic jerked Julie's umbrella and it bloomed above them, the same sunny orange as her coat. They started out; she walked on his left while he balanced the umbrella in his left hand. Above them the rain tapped for admission. They crossed into Bold Street and passed the sonorous entrance of the Odd Spot Club—"Have you ever been there?" Vic asked. "I don't know anyone who'd take me," she replied. Vic was about to speak when a furtive-looking man with an armful of bottles pushed between them and was lost in the vestibule of 69A.

"Where is this place anyway?" Julie demanded, returning under the taut shade of the umbrella.

"Ah, no—*that* you must wait and see in due course."

The flowing arrow-headed ripples in the gutter accompanied them into Church Street, where commuters ventured from the cold grey bulk of Central Station and ducked back. An icy wind slanted the rain toward them down the narrow two-way street; Julie plunged her hands into her damp pockets. The drenching gusts raised goose-pimples on the cars and herded the pedestrians into shop doorways to choke on the stench of raincoats. A soaking dog, with wetly lolling eyes and tongue, flinched among the darting feet. Julie ostentatiously averted her gaze as they approached. "I don't like to look at things like that," she explained.

"There's a hell of a lot worse than that in the world, and you can't look away from it all."

"But if you think about that all the time, how are you going to have any fun?" she retorted, and without warning darted across the road. Car wheels screeched in fury. Vic grimaced and waited with the army at the curb for the traffic-lights to permit him to join battle with the mob across the street, each seeking gaps in the press through which he could slip. The drivers sat and cleaned their windscreens with their hands. When he reached her Julie was enjoying the brief plush warmth of the Tatler Cinema entrance, before the padded splendor of the House of Bewlay and the Kardomah Coffee House. He urged her on. The rain still streamed down the toadstool-buff or sooty buildings to the kaleidoscopic shops which served as their foundations, their windows full of lifeless shoes and dresses; over all, detached, the streetlamps pored, and above the roofs the Liver Building clock stood with hands on hips.

Fewer feet splashed through the dirty puddles at the end of Church Street. They skirted the cloaked black figure among the Victoria Monument's pillars and hurried down the line of parking meters like hooded cobras. On either side the discrete life insurance buildings with their golden nameplates mounted to wild turrets. Vic led the way below the regimented windows and cream rain-striped walls of Exchange Flags; scattered men and women, dwarfed by the ebon figures chained below a wartime motto, ran from the scything rain. Here Julie lost her way; they wandered through a maze of streets whose sides descended to unlabelled blackened doors, past makeshift bookstalls cloaked in drooling oilskin, between opaque windows and boarded doors. Very far away, it seemed, a steamer blew its nose. Then, when she was least expecting it, she was led through a gaping arch between two silent storage houses into an inner court, across the slimy cobbles to a railing which boxed in a heavy long trapdoor, hooked back to show treacherous stone steps burrowing into rectangular darkness. Vic sheltered some steps down to light the candle, then looked up at her. "Right, Julie-ette," he said, using her full name by which few people called her however much she pleaded. "Down we go—said ominously," and he reached up for her hand. Briefly hesitating, she clasped his hand and let him draw her down into the blackness.

The rain's persistent patter faded. Down some twenty feet the stairs came on a corridor; it stretched both ways to unlit depths. Vic steered her to the left. The candle's aura pulsed on pock-marked walls, the floor carpeted with moss like ancient flesh, the beaded ceiling. The silence had already closed around them, bespeaking secret lightless halls. *"Une fois de plus—le long de ces mêmes couloirs,"* intoned Vic, and urged her through an archway beyond which the light expanded dimly to suggest low vaulted rooms on every side. They stooped beneath an entrance on the left and flat black walls again enclosed the flame.

A table slumped against the wall on dislocated legs, and in the corners cartons massed, almost shapeless in the shadows. Vic rummaged in his pockets for a pen and notebook and copied down the number of the telephone abandoned on the table, while Julie tried to open an enigmatic spongy crate in the half-dark, and failing kicked it viciously. She wandered over to the phone as Vic, becoming interested in the crate, drew away the candle's circle and left her groping through the murk. Julie stretched out her hand to determine whether the phone still rang—and pulled back with a squeak of horror; for the receiver was enveloped in yielding moss and fungus—it was like blindly touching a drowned corpse. Vic's shadow loomed and billowed as he returned to protect her, but she refused to explain what had happened.

He took her hand again and together they came out into the widening subterranean night. Grey curves against the depths implied archways beyond archways, an emptiness expanded through long-forgotten dusty echoing rooms. Vic strode ahead. Hinted cracks between the bricks shifted and flickered as they explored. In the vague distances of alcoves off the passages they glimpsed grim rusted cogs and levers of some disused machinery, the strained-back lids of grimy tins, the minute reflection of the candle flame in a black sheet of broken glass as if across a spatial gulf. From one red-brown nail on a door a *Danger* sign still hung; but Julie, hoisted up by Vic, could not see what lay beyond the insecure grille. They meandered on, avoiding the black pools which formed beneath the ceiling's sweat; beneath a beam from which grime-weighted cobwebs hung like distended stomachs, and beyond it stretched their destination.

The limits of the place hung back from the light; they could sense oppressive walls on either side and saw the start of lines of iron pillars which supported the roof as they dimmed into the depths, but what lay at the extent of the hall Julie did not know. Somewhere a shrill drip of water stressed the silence. Chunks of moss-smoothed rubble caught their feet as they moved toward the right-hand wall; the candle's luminous wand conjured the stone out of the blackness and picked out an oval pallid shape at eye-level. Julie's grip tightened.

"It's a face," Vic whispered.

It was in fact a patch of mould; the walls were soft as those of some decaying padded cell. Vic stumbled onward and Julie almost tripped over piled shards of wet green stone; as she regained her balance Vic was already peering into what appeared to be a cupboard in the rock, half-revealed by a creaking stout wood door. The niche was shallow, slightly over six feet high and two feet wide. Vic held the candle close to the uneven rheumy brick; the space's floor was hidden by a tangle of what might have been hair and fungus, and up in the left-hand corner was a bulge of something white. Julie poked it with her umbrella and it peeled away, dragging pale strings which held it to the stone. She brought it near her face to squint at it then, shuddering in revulsion, scraped it off against the edge of the door. It oozed down to the floor.

"And what's this cupboard for?" mused Vic as Julie tried to drag him away. "You could be shut in here with the mould—how would you come out?"

"Don't be soft," she rebuked, prying him away at last. They continued forward and were blocked by the boundary wall. They inched along it hand in hand, uncertain of what lay ahead, the cloying smell of candle wax blanketing them in the dripping quiet. The featureless grey rock gave way to rust-scaled iron; the yellow glow gradually included the lower regions of a pair of metal doors, towering above them. A heap of rubble blocked the foot of the portal, and the way was further sealed by a massive iron bar, cemented to the wall across the doors. One end of the bar hung loose, however, and the other rested only in a powder of cement, but the bar was held by supports set in the rusted panels. Handing Julie the candle, Vic clambered over the jigsaw of stone and reached the iron beam. He had his shoulder under it before she realized his intention; and instantly she saw herself, at the wrong end of a maze of lightless underground tunnels, before a pair of giant doors deliberately sealed up, cut off from the city far above and unaware of her. "Vic, don't!" she said.

"But this is why we've come down here," he protested. One end of the bar grated from its socket and clanged reverberantly on the pile of rubble.

"No, Vic, it's time we got back," she reasoned desperately. "We've got half of town to cross even once we're out of here."

He slipped along the shifting fragments to the other door. "Perhaps you're right," he said at last, "but we'll have to come again to see beyond those doors. Or I will anyway." He slithered down to join her. "After all, what can be the connection between them and that cupboard? It's as though something came from that place beyond, whatever's through those doors, and shut people in with the mould . . . Made pets of them, perhaps, or collected them. . . . Imagine what they'd look like if they ever escaped—it ought to be easy enough to get that cupboard door off its hinges once they'd finished screaming for help . . . You could scream all you liked down here, nobody would hear you . . ."

"Shall I scream?" she suggested.

"Go ahead."

"Do you dare me?"

"Sure."

"No," she decided after surveying the dark bulks swelling the shadows which must be passed before they escaped. Vic held up the candle and his other hand in warning—"Scream *now,*" he told her —and blew out the flame. The echoes of his voice raced down the pitch-black corridors and into alcoves, awakening them. Julie stood awkwardly, her hands clutching empty air, and somewhere in the silence pressing round her she heard a muted grind of metal, as of a rusty surface rumbling over rock. It came, she thought, from behind her. "Vic," she called and realized that she could not feel him at her side. Something near her rattled sharply. Something scraped and light exploded silently, revealing Vic who watched her quizzically from behind the candle.

She did not speak, but grabbed his hand and made for the yawning arch beyond the glistening pillars. Sinking in mould and toppling balanced debris, they ducked out of the hall, and Julie glanced back at last to the double doors: they appeared to stand further ajar, but by the sickly light she could not be sure. She turned quickly and they hastened through the maze of passages past half-glimpsed rooms.

With every step she sensed the unknown depths behind and ahead of her.

The stairs stretched up into a washed-out sunlight. Vic and Julie rested for a minute on the swimming cobbles at the top; Julie tentatively stretched her fingers and Vic immediately released her hand. She started for the exit of the court and heard his call behind her; looking back, she was met by his other hand which clawed toward her face, white tentacles protruding from its leprous peeling fingers. It was only icicled and embalmed in candle wax, but her scream was genuine enough.

The next day she was short of money, and Vic seemed the obvious person to approach. Leaving her desk she stared through the building's windows and found him seated in the distance. Clear and minute as an image in a reversed telescope, he was dialling the telephone. She determined to contact him later, but when she went out for a time-passing walk she chanced upon Frank in a crowd. His feeling for her was not dead, and she speedily forgot about borrowing from Vic—and, as the days dragged onward, about Vic as well.

"Got two bob?" asked Julie. Alice rummaged in her handbag. They stood like mannequins just inside the entrance to the store; the doors swung back and forth as customers pressed past each other, ruffling the receipts dropped by the clientele before they reached the street. Julie gazed across the counters. Above the hubbub rose the howls of babies in distress. Purchasers waved merchandise in vain attempts to catch the shop-assistant's eye; register drawers slammed and rang; samples of stock were hoisted like severed heads on steel poles above the crowd, which forced its sluggish way through gaps, met and engulfed itself in avenues, leaving its moraine of customers before displays. Detached from the commotion, an amplified voice proclaimed from above: "Reported missing in the store—a small boy aged four, royal blue overcoat, blue eyes, fair hair—"

THE CELLARS

"Look for a kid with fair hair," ordered Alice, extracting her purse.

"You mean *fur hur*," said Julie, catching and exposing the suggestion in Alice's speech of the thick Liverpool accent. "Found the money yet?" She strode to the automatic photograph booth guarding the basement escalator and ripped aside its half-length curtain. Faces of previous subjects, smiling, romantic or preoccupied, were exhibited on the outside of the booth. "It's something to do," she explained, climbing into the cramped cell and seating herself. "From now on anybody who takes me out can bring me to one of these."

"I'd rather have one boy than look at a lot of pictures. What'd you want them for?"

"Souvenirs. Besides, you can do what you like with them. Anyway, so long as he's paying, he could have one too."

"Do they have to pay to get pictures of you or something?"

"They should be interested in me, not a bit of cardboard. It's been ages since I gave one to anyone—the last one must have been—um—Vic."

Snap-closing her bag, Alice handed over the coin and squeezed in beside Julie. "What's with him these days anyway?" she enquired.

"How should I know?"

"Well, didn't you hear what happened? I thought it went all round the building. Jackie told me all about it. She was really messed up over it—well, you know how she used to fancy Vic but he never knew about it. Anyway, she comes up to me—'Alice,' she says—"

The rejected coin clattered in the basin. Julie slipped it out. "Got another one?"

"I should coco, I just gave you one."

"Give me another and I'll give you this one back." Julie dropped the coin she held to waste a mite more time; they heard it totter and fall on its face. "Now, where'd that go?"

"Here it is, there." Alice retrieved her initial outlay in exchange for a thicker copy, which fell within the slot and was rewarded by a whirr and click of levers; Julie and Alice embraced, disclaimed, grimaced and were seeking inspiration when the camera's fourth flash faded. They piled out and waited for the photos to develop.

"Anyway, Jackie comes up to me the other day— Hey, Julie, do you want me to tell you about this or not?"

"If you get to the point, yes. What did Jackie say happened to Vic?"

"Well, she says he hasn't been in since weeks ago and he didn't ring up to say what was wrong. Last anyone saw of him he was at his desk phoning someone, they didn't hear who, and it looked like it was urgent or something, 'cos he got a funny look on his face and just walked out and didn't come back the rest of the afternoon. So that was weeks ago, and then they got round to sending somebody round to see what was up. Well, his mother answers the door and she looks nervous as anything. You met her once, didn't you?"

"Yes—she was all right, as mothers go. She wasn't the nervous type at all, though—wonder what changed her?"

"She didn't say. No, they asked her what was wrong with Vic, and she wouldn't let them in. She says he won't be coming back to work and it's none of their business why, and they'll be getting a letter of resignation if that's what they want, then she slams the door in their face and leaves them there."

The booth put out its tongue of photographs and Julie giggled over them. Alice interrupted: "Jackie told me one thing that was funny. Vic's mother was sort of, you know, blocking the doorway so they couldn't see into the house, but they thought Vic must be in there, 'cos they could hear someone sort of gargling in the bathroom."

"Someone *what?*"

"Well, Jackie says that's how she heard it, supposed to be upstairs somewhere, only it sounded like he was trying to talk while he was at it. And they looks up past her and thinks they see at the top of the stairs— Look, are you *interested?*"

"Not really." Julie consulted her watch. "Come on, we've got to get back."

St. Valentine's was a day like any other, only worse. So Julie thought as she was borne along by the press of passengers boarding the 5:30 ferry. A young man on the landing-stage was shouting to his mate on the boat as he cast off to him. "Seen any muddy hunchbacks tonight?" he shouted. "Or do you reckon that one the other night was some rain in your eye?"

Aboard the boat she climbed to the upper deck; it was her habit to avoid the crowded lounges, enveloped in tobacco-smoke obscuring people fighting down nausea—but though she usually enjoyed the view of the far white lights drawn up to define the Mersey banks off into space, this evening they looked as miserable as she behind a sheet of drizzle. As the ferry tamed the river's surge and began to ride across it, she gazed down into the thick wrinkled water from which the rain extracted bubbles like the last breaths of the drowned. Nobody had asked her out that night, and the hours before sleep promised unrelieved monotony. The sooner she was home the sooner she could read her Valentines; but by the same token, the longer she would have to sit and cast about for entertainment until she tired enough for bed. She blinked at the stark Birkenhead landing-stage as it rocked toward her, and received the stinging raindrops on her cheeks.

Once inside the bus at Woodside she was at least able to relax in its shelter. She craned to watch the commuters below; darting around or colliding with each other with an apology or glare, they sought their transport with downcast heads like fleeing spectres of the drowned through the black glistening night of the terminus. It was like watching the antics of fish, she thought, and acknowledged Vic's authorship of the image: "well, back to the aquarium" he had remarked to her once as he quitted the bus. Now Julie's vehicle took a deep breath and ground away at last, its headlamps catching drops of rain in flight. The drenched disorder of the terminus quickly fell behind and was forgotten.

Set down at the end of her road she struggled through the half-seen rain to her house, the last in the row. On her right the first residence, its brown and orange bricks, its stern rectangular frames imprisoning windows and doors, its suppressed flowered curtains behind greyish panes, was duplicated down to hers at the end; here and there a street-lamp's nimbus staged an example. On her left a green, which on fine days children trampled, curved easily to the river; occasional shrubs poked through it, and Julie was surprised to note that the bush nearest her house had under the downpour acquired a dim shape as if a figure were peering from behind it, watching her. She pulled open the black creaking gate and ran to the front door; behind her rainfall rattled on the adamant board fence through which the privet hedge clawed for release. She managed to unlock the door, which swept the morning's mail before her as she staggered inside, shutting the storm behind her at last. The colored lines and angles of the wallpaper seemed almost welcoming, but she did not expect them to stay so for long.

Towelling her hair, she returned to the hall, picked up the envelopes and carried them back to the kitchen, where her discarded coat drooped over a chair. On this entrance she noticed the note propped against a cup on the table, facing her. She read her mother's message, black against the sheet of paper and the larger white of the kitchen: *Sorry, must leave you to your own devices 'till 11 or after. Eat well. Books in the bookcase should you fancy a read. No men friends whilst I'm out, please.* Julie looked away to the percolator as if for companionship, but the jug was engrossed in its own attempts to boil. She rapped the envelopes into line but instead of examining their contents, let them slap loose on the table and left them for the hall. The open left-hand door of the sitting-room attracted her briefly, but

THE CELLARS

she did not enter; the pale-green armchairs and abstract pictures on the walls would not welcome her—there was nothing of her in that room. She knew all that the bookcase had to offer without approaching it: the blocks of authors—Iris Murdoch, Muriel Spark, Mary McCarthy, Penelope Mortimer—did not appeal to her. Instead she chose the right-hand room; the mushroom-colored furniture was faintly hostile, but at least she had made the record-player virtually her own. She caught up a pile of naked records, slipped them on the spindle and waited while a disc dropped from the bottom of the column and was taken by the turntable.

The room had two windows, equidistant from the far righthand corner, each titled on the outside with a different street name. As the music started with a trill of strings, Julie stared out upon the darkened green and the oily river beyond. The rain which lashed the privet leaves had slackened, but veins of water still rolled down the glass, so that the view through it rippled and was obscured; and Julie therefore was unsure whether she saw an unusually plump figure slowly making its way over the green in her direction. She rubbed her breath from the pane to sharpen her vision, and above the music the percolator cried for help. Julie switched out the light, setting the door ajar to give the tunes the run of the house, and having sipped at her cup of coffee, sat down at the kitchen table to give the Valentines her attention at last.

A long thin rectangle bore Alan's signature; two amorous skeletons declared undying love. She smiled at that and went on. Frank had mailed a crimson heart and on the back a lengthy scribble requested, in as many words as possible, that she get in touch with him. Lovesick teenagers Dave and Chuck had settled for drawings of lovesick teenagers. The largest she had saved until last. The unstamped envelope bore only her name, written in a hand so magnified and unsteady that she assumed it was the work of an illiterate or cripple, and she did not admit to knowing either. She turned it over. The back flap had been shoved clumsily inside; she inserted a finger to extricate it, but froze in that position—for looking closer she saw adhering to the sharp edge of the envelope's V a blob of white mould. She shuddered and in a flurry withdrew the card. It showed a couple arm in arm against a sunset idyll, and inside a romantic verse, but no signature. She hurriedly laid down the card, for it felt oddly slippery to her touch; and she was remembering that a nearby card shop had been broken into before the dawn of a recent day, though nothing had apparently been stolen.

Having stared into her cup until it cooled, she finished off the coffee and stood up. The white planes and surfaces of the kitchen were serving only to reflect her confusion back to her. Swinging her handbag, she climbed the stairs, below the china dogs enshrined up to the landing, and entered her room. Corners of pop singers peeled from the walls as she opened the door. Sitting on the bed and reaching under it, she came up with her scrapbook. She leafed through it, every so often glancing up to catch herself watching, mirrored in the panel of one of the wardrobes, listening to the last squeezed-out patter of the rain; finally she went through her bag and found the strip of photographs of herself and Alice as they had been taken two weeks before. She taped it to the page; her hand resting on the paper pressed through it on various versions of Vic.

The record-player, its repertoire exhausted, clicked silent. Julie groaned and went out onto the landing. Silence hung about the house, weighted with raindrops suspended at the tips of leaves; and in that silence she heard someone padding slowly round the building. Julie listened down the stairwell, and the footsteps stopped. Viewed from above, the china dogs seemed as intent as she. Her breathing tightened painfully, but she tiptoed down to arrive before the doorway of the record-player's lounge.

Inside, along the wall to the left of the door, electric flickers from a fake coal fire spread out to illuminate the shadowed room. The cold pulsating flame lit up the window which confronted her, and picked out the indistinct mass of a face peering in. Julie's heart contracted. She reached around the doorframe to switch on the light, and the watching figure withdrew. But she thought there was something wrong even as she rushed forward and came close enough to see that the face had left upon the pane an imprint, with gaping holes for eyes, like a mask of some dull white substance glued to the glass. She knew without approaching closer what that substance was. She started back with a moan of horror—and as she did so she felt a shape appear at the window nearest the river, look in at her, and pass on.

She stood there for a moment, trapped and helpless, thinking frantically—whatever happened, she could not léave the house, she could not even bear to stay downstairs so near what plodded about the garden, though there was a telephone in the hall—and without conscious volition she dashed for the stairs, fell into her bedroom and slammed the door. Her breathing slowly eased. Then she looked toward the curtains. A fear of what she might see should she pull them apart gradually took hold of her. She told herself that this was the upper floor, unreachable via the slick wall outside. Yet that window was directly above that at which she had last sensed a bulky form watching her. She forced herself forward and ripped back the curtains. Then she released and pushed open the halves of the casement, flinching back as her hand crossed the sill, and at last she leaned out into the wind and its hint of spray, and looked.

The filtered light of a still tearful moon and the restrained glow of the streetlamps laid vague pale patches on the green, and across the flattened grass Julie made out a humped figure progressing painfully away from her, toward the river. Its ill-defined shape seemed swollen, and she thought that parts of it protruded lumpily as if it were the victim of some deforming malady. Her terror had dissipated, leaving only nausea; secure in her warm room, she felt detached from the spectacle below. Revolted yet fascinated, she watched as with an agonizing slowness, as if crushed by knowledge as well as cumbered by its body, it approached the river's edge and swayed there as if uncertain; then it fell forward with a distant splash, disturbing the moon's path on the black water, and sank. The last trace of the ripples which it caused to spread was soon absorbed by the glassy surface; but by that time Julie was already downstairs, listening impatiently as Alan's number rang.

The Height of the Scream

"Hurry up with the joint or it won't seem worth going," Martin said.

But I was watching the skin of the joint roll back from the glowing glans as I inhaled; my head sailed back; I heard the glittering flutter of a bird outside the window. "I'd really like to go now," Martin said. "I'm an hour slow."

"If you look at the clock across the road you'll see you aren't." He shook his head and I had to look myself. It was an hour later than I'd thought. I'd been sure that my time wasn't so personal. Martin was standing at the window with the joint, exposing himself as it were. "Sorry. They must just have remembered summer time," I said. "I'll get my coat."

The soft whoosh of cars on Princes Avenue met us halfway down the stairs. We ran out to find a taxi, and a raucous argument rose from the basement through a hole in the lawn. "Listen, I'm starting to feel bad about this," Martin said. "That joint won't help this party. I mean, it's the sort of party you watch, not enjoy."

"You knew that when you had it."

"I knew I wouldn't enjoy the party. The joint will show me why."

"You'll forgive me if I reject your preconceptions."

The taxi swung into Granby Street. A shamefaced man hurried out of a shop doorway from which urine trickled. "We could have brought a joint if you'd thought," Martin said. "They're trendy enough where we're going." I stared from the window until we reached Childwall: placid ranks of cars and Siamese-twin houses, a synagogue, a few people walking, a few gnomes squatting, the occasional garden crowded with wooden arches and ivy. The taxi left us at the Slaters' house and an enormous quiet descended, interrupted by a distant hoarse dog.

Betty opened the door to us. A low-necked ankle-length black dress streamlined her thin body, and a silver-coated marihuana leaf dangled between her freckled breasts. "Hello, Martin. No doubt we invited you," she said. "And I think I know your friend as well. Yes, I've seen you behind the counter in the music library." She handed us glasses and wrote our names on them with a marker pen. "So that we don't have arguments about who pays for breakages," she said. "Well, wander in. Our protégé is going to make an announcement soon."

The party was located in the main room, which most resembled a long hall scattered with bean-bags and pieces from the gallery two streets away, which Betty ran. Around the walls were plaques which mixed colors slowly or hooted when you breathed on them; on the windowsill stood Jack-in-the-boxes from which members of the city council popped up grimacing. The room was roaring with conversation, for Betty's gallery was fashionable, particularly in Childwall. The adagio from Mahler's 10th, of all things, was trying to make itself heard. I knew some of the people from similar functions I'd visited with Martin: young morose painters and bemused academics; reporters from Radio Merseyside and the *Daily Post;* Betty's sister Mildred, an executive officer in the Civil Service who was given to saying "I want to talk to you, which means I'm going to be horribly truthful again" and who had a corner to herself at the far end of the party. Almost everyone seemed either to be surrounding Peter Hale, tonight's painter, or to be waiting for a chance to speak with him. "Don't let the crowd put you off," Martin said, pouring himself sherry. "He'll talk to us."

I hoped so; I was beginning to dislike the indeterminate blur of hermetic conversations. I'd attempted to join two, but they hadn't opened. Martin edged his way into the circle around Hale, and I followed.

"Hello, Peter, it's really nice to see you again. I must come to your exhibition, specially if your friends get in free. I saw one of your science-fiction things the other day. Very typical, I thought. Here's someone you ought to meet, I can't remember why just now. He works in the music library, I suppose that's a reason. Hey, aren't you playing the meeting game? Peter, you can't have dried up already. Look, I've known you as Peter for twelve years. Oh come on, Peter, Fatman, talk to us."

Hale insisted on being called Fatman in memory of Sydney Greenstreet and his father's hoarded wartime National Comics. "If I'm going to make myself what I want to be I might as well start with my name," I'd heard him say on Radio Merseyside, in a booming voice which he often covered with his fingertips as if it were too loud for what it had to say. Seen striding through town, he seemed to be carrying his girth to an exhibition. "You've come a long way, it's really nice," Martin said.

"But look where I have to go."

"Don't deprecate yourself because it's fashionable," I said. I'd seen some of his paintings and thought them fairly evocative—his series of Musical Thoughts, which had balked at Henze and halted at Gerhard: an attempt to show an infinity of crystalline figures descending transparent staircases under a stormy sky. He didn't strike me as the type you could ask what he had against Handel and Haydn.

"Who's fashionable, him? Listen, he started the fashion," Martin said. "Don't you remember that painting the headmaster liked, Peter? He said it was brilliant, if I remember. He wanted you to give it to him but you really felt it wasn't that good, and he never spoke to you after that."

"I don't need reminding," Hale said, touching his mouth. "I know I'm not much good at giving."

"Fatman, here's someone from the *Daily Post*," Betty said. "He's anxious to talk to you," and she ushered them away. I frowned. There was something grotesque about a roomful of people patronizing Hale for the fee of having to call him Fatman, all the more so when I felt that it was almost a nickname a child might adopt in order to reject his childhood. And the clock on the wall showed the time we'd assumed when we left the flat. Martin caught my eye. "Don't let it get through to you," he said quickly. "It'll get worse."

Mildred returned to the room, wearing sparkling trousers beneath which her large buttocks churned. "Dressed for battle, I see," Betty said. "I'm sure you'll win." Laughter was suppressed around the room, more out of politeness than compassion. Once, after a concert at the Philharmonic, I'd passed the Slaters standing near a crushed and bloodstained car. "You see what happens when you lean on things," I'd heard Betty say, and Mildred had been pursued by nervous slavish laughter all the way to the car park.

The Mahler reached its orchestral outburst. "Could we have that thing turned down, do you think?" someone said. The theme disintegrated and the orchestra shrieked in inarticulate despair, and Betty kissed a painter a passionate thirty seconds' adieu and turned off Mahler's reconciliation. Several drinks passed. People slid off beanbags, laughing or turning pale. An art master panted aggressively at a hooting plaque for five minutes. Betty and a young dishevelled sculptor returned to the room and Mildred frowned at her and shrugged. "What did you mean about not letting it get through to me?" I asked Martin.

"You're not watching," he said.

"And at the center of all these films, no matter how bad, there's a truth called Bette Davis," Betty said to a rush of silence. Hale was standing up and bellowing 'I'm sorry but I wonder if I could have everyone's attention for a moment," and massaging his lips wildly as he realized that he had it. "Go on, Peter, let's hear some honesty," Martin shouted.

"Well, all I wanted to say really was thank you to Betty and Mildred." He paused and there was a drizzle of applause. "I said say it, but I meant I wanted to give them something as a sign of gratitude."

"That's enormously good of you, Fatman," Betty said, falling into a bean-bag.

"It was the first sketch for my ABC of SF." I'd seen a few of this series: a towering flowerbed for Aldiss, a sinking New Brighton for Ballard. "I've framed it for you," Hale said to Mildred.

"She can't find words to thank you," Betty said.

"As a matter of fact I can," Mildred said. "It's one of my best presents ever, Peter."

"Well no, it's me thanking you," Hale said. "I mean, if it weren't for you the gallery would never have made it at all and a lot of us would still be having to listen to our friends telling us how talented we are."

"We are all very grateful for your money, Mildred," Betty said.

"I think Peter's a little embarrassed by your wit."

"Now watch," Martin said.

And as if a slide had clicked into place in my brain I found myself sharing part of his consciousness. It was the joint, of course; it had happened before, although not with him. I had a flash of Mildred in a short black pleated skirt and navy-blue knickers and white knee-socks, up at the far end where nobody would play with her. "Come on," I said. "It's not as simple as that."

"No? Watch."

"At least I'm not boring him," Betty said, lying back in the bean-bag with her knickers displayed and her immature breasts weighing down her grey sweater, Betty and her gang laughing at Mildred. "I'm not boring Fatman. He doesn't like you to call him Peter."

"It doesn't matter, really," Hale said.

"Nor anyone else in the room am I boring," Betty said, swaying to her feet. "Or if I am I'm sorry. This sort of squabble is usually kept private. In normal homes."

"And what isn't normal here?" Mildred said.

"This is hardly the time to discuss that. Look, you see, everyone agrees. They'll be leaving if we don't talk about something else."

"They're your friends. Tell your friends what isn't normal here."

"Well, it's normal for someone to be the breadwinner. But," Betty said in a whisper I could hear even as I edged toward the door, "it isn't normal for the breadwinner to sit around the house all weekend pawing at herself."

"At least that way I know who's touching me."

"Well, you know what I'm always looking for in bed. My father's balls."

"You exhibitionistic little Judas!" Mildred cried. "You wouldn't have dared say that to him, you fucking—oh now look what you've made me say, you bitch!" and she began to snatch books from a shelf and hurl them at Betty: L. P. Hartley, Elizabeth Bowen, dialogues with Stravinsky. "There's some bruises that won't turn you on!" she cried as Betty advanced on her, rubbing her thigh where the spine of a book had struck it. Mildred grabbed a Picasso collection and Betty swung in front of her the first defense that came to hand, Hale's sketch. The book tore through. For a moment they grappled, clawing and pulling hair, then Mildred pushed Betty away and ran upstairs sobbing.

People collected around Betty to apologize before leaving. "I'll be all right so long as you come to Fatman's exhibition," she said. Martin mopped his forehead, gulping air. "That's all," he said.

Hale joined us as we put on our coats. "And these are the people I'm reaching," he said.

"You've got to realize sometime," Martin said. "Everyone's like that when you break the shell."

"No," I said. "I'll see you," and before Hale could find his coat I was out of the house and taking deep breaths of a cold prickling rain.

And now he's gone off to sulk, I heard Martin say. Never mind. I wasn't staying to gloat.

And two days later Peter Hale was dead.

I wasn't working until one o'clock, but I intended to meet Martin at the public opening of Hale's exhibition. Smoke billowed from fires in the back yards as I brushed my teeth. The phone rang and I answered it, foaming and swallowing toothpaste harsh as bile. It was a police inspector at Hale's exhibition. Hale had shot himself. "Mr. Hodges says you knew him quite well," the inspector said.

"Martin Hodges? I don't know where he got that idea."

"You're saying he isn't telling the truth?"

"I don't mean that. I suppose I knew quite a lot about, er, Hale." Though I was angry I didn't want to revenge myself on Martin by placing him in an awkward position, and I was half-amused by the way he seemed to have undertaken to educate me. "I'll come down there if you want," I said.

My shock at Hale's death began to accumulate on the bus. Children with sketch-pads were sitting in Princes Park. There had been too much of him, most of it unexpressed, to have vanished in an instant. I restrained myself from trying to imagine what had happened.

At the gallery I could only stand uncomprehending. People stood talking and letting their heads edge round the shop doorways on either side, and the manageress of a bakery ordered her girls away from a reporter. Martin was leaning on his umbrella and frowning uneasily out of the gallery window. Inside, Hale's paintings lay smashed in a heap in the middle of the floor, among the derivative record-sleeve psychedelia: idealized men with flaming green hair, ornate birds the color of orange juice. "Here he is now," Martin said.

The inspector and a small moustached man, Hale's father, came to meet me. Mr. Hale's lips and the skin around his eyes were trembling, like a bubble about to burst. "It wasn't a girl, was it?" he appealed to me. "Was it someone who'd got a hold over him?"

"I'm just shocked. I don't know."

"Please, Mr. Hale," the inspector said. "They'll take you in the car."

"I told him he'd be a success one day. He was on his way already, wasn't he? This was his chance. But he used to say I didn't know anything about it." Mr. Hale was groping for the door. "It was my gun. I didn't know he had it, I hid it years ago. I killed in the war with it, you see, and I knew he wouldn't have wanted to know that. God knows I tried to understand."

When Mr. Hale had left the inspector said "Was he taking drugs? Was it as simple as that?"

"No, he never tried them."

"And how is it you're so sure of that?"

His tone had sharpened. "He was quite forthright about it. It was well known," I said, sharing Martin's memory of Hale's refusing a joint and lecturing him.

"So you've no idea of how it might have happened?"

"I still can't believe that it did. If you'd asked me where he'd be in ten years I'd have said he would have been at least a very able minor artist, and very possibly he'd have surprised us all by then. Of course he had doubts, but never to this extent. Destroying all his work as well, I find that almost harder to believe."

"Perhaps not quite all. There's something I'd like you to see. Please be warned it isn't pleasant." He opened the office door and pointed. "As far as we can tell he stood with his back to that canvas when he shot himself. It was blank then."

"Christ almighty. I just can't take that in," I said, and Martin sat down and stood again. "It's just the sort of romantic crap he wouldn't have gone near."

"I'll be outside if you want me," Martin said. "I'm feeling rather bad."

THE HEIGHT OF THE SCREAM

"I should say you're all right," the inspector said to me, "but him —I'd stay away from him. The things they do to themselves with these drugs. Sometimes I wonder how many of your generation will be with us in ten years' time. Was Hale like him, would you say? Is that why it happened?"

"I can only think it was a terrible fit of depression," I said. "And I'm sure Martin can't have been involved."

"Oh, we've no suspicions of him on that score. He was outside and the door was locked. He saw there was something wrong and called us, but you could tell it was an effort to do so. I sound resentful. I have a son, you see, and I hope he'll never prefer not to ask me for help. Still, I'm wasting your time. Tell me about Hale."

I ran across the road to a bus. "I feel like seeing people. I'll come with you," Martin said.

I sat facing the engine at the rear, watching the road stream away. "He warned you against me," Martin said.

"What makes you say that?"

"I could feel it coming. That was why I went out."

"He was talking about Hale. What do you think—"

"Don't make me think about anything like that," Martin said. "I've done enough."

A child sat opposite me, blocking my view. His face bore an unchanging reproachful grimace. Two stops later a middle-aged couple in frayed clothes sat a reproof apart at the other end of the back seat. "Don't touch me," said the woman. "Don't speak to me," said the man. All I could see now through the side window were cramped flashes of the bottoms of shop-fronts and the antics of litter in side streets. I wished I'd used my bicycle. I gazed at the emergency door and Martin followed my gaze. "I see what you mean but I don't think the driver would agree," he said.

A man with a grey wax face and waxwork's black hair and a nose like a trampled candle lowered himself onto the seat opposite our touching knees. The bus jolted on the patched road, and he steadied himself with a hand that lacked two fingers. I drew back into myself. I blinked my gaze away from the space like a toothless gum between his fingers. The roar and sweet stench of the engine and the prolonged deafening howl of the brakes seeped through to me; I felt as though I were trapped in a box three feet wide. Once when I was ten a purple boil had appeared at the base of my jaw like a plum trying to grow through my cheek. Whoever it had appeared on I shouldn't have been able to touch it, and my compassion still sometimes regresses to sensitivity. Which is true of everyone, I told myself, staring at a hill that swept up the back window between the frieze of shoulders.

"You've been kneeling," the mutilated man said.

My toes clutched at the soles of my shoes as he brushed at my knees. "You'll get years out of those trousers if you keep them clean," he said. "Kneeling like that. I hope it was to pray. I knew a boy once, about your age, who wouldn't pray before a battle. Said his god was in a flask. His flask got his head shot off and I only lost these." I smiled and nodded and clenched my toes.

"You've been kneeling too," he said to Martin. "You've both been at it."

"Right, okay, but not right now," Martin said, lifting the man's hand away by the cuff.

"It won't bite, you know," the man said. "It's only a hand. Don't you want it near you? There, look, it was shot for you. No? Where shall I put it? Out of the window? Do you want to put me out of the window? Eh, and kick me when I'm down?"

"Please piss off," Martin said.

"My stop," I said, grabbing the pole. As I half-tripped into the swaying aisle I realized that everyone on the bus was staring back at Martin. One man in blue overalls was gripping the back of the seat, and the woman next to him was pulling at his arm. "It's all right, no," she said, her eyes fixed on his face. As Martin passed the man stuck out his foot and drove his toe into Martin's shin. "That's right, leave him now," the woman said.

Martin's eyes and mouth widened and he hobbled to the doors, supporting himself on his umbrella. The tip of the umbrella slipped from the edge of the platform, and he almost fell. Gasping, he caught the pole. The umbrella rolled under the bus.

"Get it if you're going to," the driver said.

Martin stared at him, and the skin around his eyes puckered. "I don't want to go under there," he said.

"You don't have to go under," I said. "Just reach."

I could see the people on the bus craning to watch; some were laughing loudly enough to be heard. Martin knelt down, staring at the driver, and groped under the bus. He leaned further and his armpit scraped the curb. "You won't find it unless you look," I said, and the bus began to roll forward.

I almost spoke but didn't know what to say, I almost dragged Martin to safety, but he was already on his feet and leaning against the bus-stop. "Brakes. Brakes went," the driver said, but his eyes weren't so sure of themselves. "I'll move the bus and you can get your umbrella," and as the bus groaned away toward the Pier Head I snatched the umbrella.

"It's all right now. It was an accident," I said. "Do you want a quick pint before I go to work?"

"You're really fantastic. Incredible faith you've got," Martin said. "You'd really like to go in there?" and he pointed at a faded brick-and-plastic pub outside which several youths in leather were laughing. As he pointed they stopped and took a step toward us. "Wha sup, umbrella man? Didz we upset syer? Yerve ruinedz our fun now," one said. I felt as if someone had plunged a hand into my stomach and were trying to drag his fist free. "Come into work with me," I said.

"Christ, just go and I'll be fine!" Martin shouted, halting a taxi and slamming himself in. I stared after him, then I hurried toward the music library with laughter rising in my wake. A Beethoven quartet was playing, but all I registered was the name.

I didn't think about the morning, but it lay like a block of lead in my mind. I still hadn't thought about it three hours later, when Martin came in. "I'm sorry I went off like that. I've got my head together a bit more now," he said.

"All right. I know you must have been pretty disturbed."

"It was bad. Do you like these people you work with?"

I couldn't tell whether he meant to relieve my tensions or his. "Yes, I think so."

"That's really nice. I mean, I'm glad. You want to hold onto that. Specially if you can get them to buy some good sounds instead of all this decadent classical stuff. Listen, you told me once you had some friends with a cottage in Wales. Do you think they'd notice me if I slept in a corner?"

"I'm afraid so. They'll be practicing natural childbirth about now."

"That's a drag. There aren't many places I like to go any more. Are you going home when you finish work? I suppose you'll have just about enough to eat for yourself?"

"No, come round if you like."

A man entered the library. "You've a thief among your members," he said. "Someone's put some pop rubbish inside this *Sound of Music* cover."

I frowned in order to control my face. "I really want to visit you. On your own you're one of the nicest people I know, I really mean that," Martin said. "I'll buy you a meal sometime. If they don't take me back at the University I'll get a job soon. But I really want to talk to you tonight. There's things I have to tell you."

When I returned home Martin was turning round and round in the alcove of the doorway. "Christ, I'm glad you came," he said. "Some spades were doing something horrible across the road. They were making one of them run and catching her. You could hear her screaming."

"It's over now," I said, patting his arm.

"Not in my head it isn't. I don't know how—Christ, I was going to say I don't know how you can live round here. As if that mattered."

I opened the door of my flat. "Dinner won't be long once I open the packet," I said.

I heard Martin slump on the bed. "I've just come from the Slaters," he called. "They've made it up."

"I'm glad to hear it."

"You wouldn't be to see it. I was there for an hour and it feels like walking in melted sugar. It's sickening."

"At least the strength to forgive is something."

"I'm sorry to have to disillusion you. They need each other to tell them it wasn't their fault about Peter Hale, and they know they've still got to live together. That's all. You saw the real Slaters at the party."

"Come on, Martin. You know, after the party I honestly felt that you wanted these things to happen. It's almost as if you were making them happen."

There was a silence. I could hear a slight creak from the bed-springs as if Martin had sat up. I could hear a saxophone two rooms and a main street away. I became very still. Martin said: "That's what I wanted to talk to you about."

I could feel him waiting for me to go to him. I went into the main room, thinking. "I didn't mean it literally," I said. "It's just coincidence. Or at most, perhaps you're one of those people who attract the bizarre."

"Please let me try to tell you about it," he said. "Maybe I can get it together that way." Shouts and laughter rose from Princes Avenue, and he shut the window. "The less I suspect the less I can make happen," he said. He lay down and closed his eyes. "The first time I knew what I was doing was three weeks ago. I'd gone to see my parents. My mother was trying to make my father tell me to get a job. He's been impotent for years. When he wouldn't say what she wanted she started saying he wasn't a man and that was why I was like I was. Well, I'm not much good that way myself. I was quite stoned, and I got this idea that she was going to get it out to show me he wasn't a man. And by Christ, all of a sudden she tried."

"Well, perhaps after years of frustration—" but I didn't believe whatever I'd intended to say.

"She couldn't have done that by herself. It just wasn't her scene. Anyway, he pushed her off and slapped her, and I went into the kitchen to wash up. I couldn't have stayed with them. When I came back they weren't speaking. Have you ever been in a completely silent house? Nothing except one of them turning on the box and the other one immediately getting up to turn it off. I haven't dared go back since."

"You should go back," I said. "Not to make something happen in the way you mean. Just to try to talk them out of it."

"You don't see it yet," he said. "For the first time in my life I can see them as they are, and if I go back it'll only make sure that they stay that way. If I keep away perhaps they can pretend. I can't pretend, you see. That's what's so bad."

"But you could try to change your view."

"How? Don't you think it's enough to try not to think it? It's like having a floodlight up against your eyes and not being able to blink. For three weeks. You just try to imagine it. I don't know what opened me up this way. Acid or THC, I don't know. And it can happen at a distance. Like with Peter Hale. I told him he'd destroy himself if he didn't reach people he could respect, he was that sort of person. Then I started thinking how he'd do it. I didn't tell him, but I remembered his father had been in the war, and he was just the type who'd bring his gun home to brood over. I was outside the gallery when Peter shot himself, you know. I saw him do it. It was weird, because I'd already imagined it and so it wasn't any worse actually seeing it happen."

"And whose idea was that canvas?" I said, clenching my fists.

"Mine, of course. I'm not proud of it," he said, tightening his eyelids. "I've been seeing too much Ken Russell."

"All right," I said. "Suppose all this is true as you interpret it. Obviously you mustn't think too deeply about what's happened, that would only make it worse. But you have to try to change your outlook, for everyone's sake."

"Christ!" he shouted. "Change how? I've been fighting it for three weeks, you tell me when I've had the chance to take time off and change. Listen, have you ever had premonitions? You try to imagine what it would be like if you knew that having the premonition would make it happen!"

"But they aren't premonitions. They're preconceptions."

"Jesus, I like you a lot but you do piss me off sometimes. You think you know it all. Let me tell you something that'll bring you down a bit. Until today nothing's ever happened to me, until that thing on the bus. That wasn't just me. That took two."

I almost spoke, then thought. "I suppose you could be right," I said.

"And you're so smug about it."

"Me smug!" I shouted. "Me smug!"

"Look, let's stop there. You think about it and we'll talk again in a while. I don't want to screw you up, of all people."

"Sit down!" I shouted. "You're so perceptive about everyone except yourself, you tell me what's wrong with me!"

"You asked, remember. All right, I'll tell you. Like today in the library, you and the rest of them laughing at that poor guy just because he liked *The Sound of Music*. I managed to keep my head together until I got away, otherwise you might be out of a job, so you can thank me. Now please, I want to go."

"Not yet you aren't," I said. "Now we've got that crap out of the way we can talk about you," and I shoved him back on the bed. His head thumped the wall. "Let me go!" he screamed.

"Shut up!" Something like a short circuit occurred in my brain, bypassing all the restraints of compassion. My fist was back and looming over his face when, with a shock that drained me completely, I realized what had happened. I sank on the corner of the bed, trying to analyze swiftly. I'd felt an uncontrollable flash of self which, so it had seemed, I had to express or burn myself out. Martin pushed past me. "Martin, please don't go," I said. "I can tell you how it felt, what you're doing. It must have been the same for Betty and Mildred and the rest. If we talk it may be a step toward a solution."

"You of all people," he said. "I set you apart from the rest. It's just people, that's what I have to get away from." The shouts on Princes Avenue were closer. "There's a mob out there but it's only the same as staying here," he said.

I heard the door slam, and punched the bed in undirected rage. From the street came renewed shouts and the thud of wood on metal. I threw the window up and saw five youths bludgeoning a car with sticks. "Stop that!" I roared. They looked up and laughed, and I grabbed the phone and called the police. I had just replaced the receiver when I heard someone shouting "Jesus, that's a stupid way to behave." It was Martin.

I reached the window in time to see one of the youths shoving Martin's head back against the stone gatepost. I leapt downstairs, but by the time I reached the gate it was all over. A police van had arrived, and another was blocking the side street. Thumping with their clubs, the police herded the youths into the van.

"Listen, don't say no, please," Martin said. "Can I borrow your bike? I want to get away from people somewhere. Then I'll come back and talk to you, I promise."

"I'll get it," I said.

THE HEIGHT OF THE SCREAM

When I came back Martin was staring wide-eyed at one of the policemen. "Say that again," he said.

"I was just saying these have bought themselves a holiday," the policeman told me, grinning. "They duffed up two Negroes half an hour ago, just like that, for something to do. We'll be in touch with you, Mr. Hodges."

"It wasn't me," Martin said. "It doesn't need me to make it happen. It's there already."

"Yes, and that means you can stop worrying," I said, and then I heard all his barriers go down. It was like the shriek of the Mahler, beginning as a low almost inaudible rumble, then speeding up: a scream which rose and grew until it reached a pitch thin as wire, slicing through my mind, and still rose until it was only a point, tugging in agony at me. I think the policeman heard it too, for he frowned and rubbed his forehead before getting into the van. "Martin, don't go yet," I said, but he was already cycling away between the cars and the trees, and the thread of his scream was stretched to the moment where, indistinguishable from my aching memory of it, it vanished.

My name and address was scratched on the frame of the bicycle, and next morning the police called me almost as soon as they found Martin's body.

He was lying on Freshfield Beach, surrounded by the bricks with which he'd been battered to death. Tears and terror disfigured his face. "Bricks, of all things," the inspector said to me. "Why bricks?" I could understand his perplexity; the beach was scattered with bottles and tins, and pollution lay in the hollows of the sand like dirt beneath nails, but the bricks had come from a housing development a quarter of a mile up the road. "These bricks were piled up by the houses," the inspector said. "Some hooligans knocked them into the road and your friend may have ridden into them. Look, you can see where the wheel's bent. I'm sorry." I didn't know whether his sorrow was for Martin or the bicycle, which they'd tied onto their car as evidence; I nodded and shrugged sadly, and promised to help when called upon, and walked away from the beach, beginning to suspect I understood.

Perhaps I did, for as I walked along the gravel road between the green strata of the pines and the banks of trodden sand flashes of Martin met me: cycling wildly along the road in the dark, hearing thuds among the trees and the splintering of wood, and a pursuing rumble like the stumbling gallop of horses. A bird hovered overhead, flutter-tonguing, and as I reached the houses I felt the wheels wobble uncontrollably beneath me, obstacles thumping the ground around me as I fell, and an engulfing stillness as I realized that something in the darkness was hostile.

Perhaps I was inventing evidence of my suspicions. It would have taken considerable power to conjure attackers from the inanimate, and indeed to leave the traces that I thought I'd glimpsed. But equally power would be required—and this was what struggled to be resolved in my brain as the police car sped by—to perceive the last traces of Martin. When he'd shared my fears on the bus, had he propped my mind open too?

The train was about to leave Freshfield Station when three children of about ten, two boys and a girl, piled into my compartment. Clouds began to roll across the sky. "The sun's gone out," said the girl. One of the boys was showing her how a pointed piece of wood resembled a knife. "Give us a kiss," said the other. "No, gerroff," she said. I talked to them all the way to Seaforth. "Listen, the way the train's jolting us around you might stab yourself or me with that, and I wouldn't like that," I said. When the train moved out of Seaforth I sat staring at the piece of wood he'd left under the seat, thinking: But this is only the beginning.

Litter

I used to walk through the market at night.

I mean the new construction of plastic and tiles and glass, where the old street market used to be. I work at Radio Brichester—producing the folk-song program, among other shows—and it's handy, late at night when the last bus has gone, to cut through the market and take a taxi from Central Station. I used to do so often, even though I grew to dislike the route.

Why? There were several reasons, some of them banal. Perhaps I should describe the market. It's two storeys high, cloven by a cross of avenues. Avenues—they're corridors, to be less pretentious, but that's the name the city council has given them. Each corridor is walled by two levels of shop-fronts, largely plate-glass and plastic signs, and at the crossroads in the center escalators carry you up to the balcony level.

If my description sounds dull and featureless then I've succeeded. Even in the afternoon, during its crowded hours, the place is leaden with anonymity. Some people visit the shops, of course, but the mass use the market as a thoroughfare: hurrying through, their minds dulled by muzak, occasionally halting to gaze at televisions gagged by windows. Unlike the street market, a bewildering, deafening and dazzling maze which might infuriate you but could never leave you unmoved, this new development offers the mind no purchase. It most resembles a colossal supermarket, but that hardly explains why I began to find it disturbing.

The market was deadening: that was the first thing I noticed. Since

THE HEIGHT OF THE SCREAM

I'd always been working late when I used the shortcut, it seemed unremarkable that I could traverse the market without a single thought occurring in my brain. Obviously, I was exhausted. But one night I knew I wasn't exhausted: I'd compared in passing the melody of an English ballad with that of an Indian folk-song, and at once a whole program had begun to take shape in my mind. I came out of Radio Brichester juggling with ideas. Enjoying myself, I entered the market—and it was as if an old grey dishcloth had been pulled over my head: I couldn't think or perceive, only struggle. Not until I emerged could I function properly, and by then half my ideas had suffocated.

Well, I blamed the market. I wasn't sure what was wrong, but I was convinced it wasn't wrong with me. So, making an effort (and it was fairly strenuous) I set out to notice things. After a while I discovered that there was a feeling—or less a feeling than an aching lack of any personality at all—about the center of the place, near the escalators, which were surrounded by several hefty pillars, as much for decoration as for support. They were carved with cogs and levers and more abstract symbols, the work of one of our local artists. At night the metal and rubber of the escalators chafed, and the machinery trumpeted and groaned. With its jungle sounds and its deliberately primitive carvings, the center might have seemed reminiscent of an abandoned temple, no doubt; but between the off-white walls, among the echoes of traffic and footsteps, it felt simply empty, unnervingly so, and sounded rather like a ghost train someone had forgotten to switch off. I felt as if its planners had attempted to fake atmosphere with inappropriate juxtapositions.

The noises, though, puzzled me. While walking through I'd often heard swishing sounds, rustles up on balconies, a sort of limping patter and scuttle out of sight in the other corridors. Nothing remarkable, but they served to draw my attention to something stranger: that even when I crossed the market earlier than usual, I never met anyone. Window-shopping couples seemed to keep to the main streets, even the homeless never sheltered in the market. And yet it was a shortcut.

Which brings me, I suppose, to Jamie Macdonald.

Not that he has any bearing on what happened, only the aftermath. His real name was James, and he'd never been to Scotland in his life, but when the Radio Brichester staff was invited to a mayoral dinner Macdonald turned up in a kilt. His fat hairy legs improved nobody's appetite. I can't say I ever liked him. He was a disc-jockey, and his program consisted of two hours of anonymous vintage rock and intermittently Scottish logorrhea, although it was professional of its kind. Off the air, with his ten-year-old Beatle cut and his three thirty-year-old chins, he was less impressive. However, around the time I began to feel there was something wrong with the market he issued a warning against fashionable witchcraft to his listeners, and this made me feel we might have attitudes in common. That's how he enters the story, or this is:

One night in mid-November I finished a folk program of which I was quite proud. I made my way across town feeling peaceful and acutely perceptive. The market looked pale and squat beneath the concrete hooks and gleaming eggs of streetlamps. I strolled along the flagged path to the market, and my mood soured. The city council had planted a few scrawny trees in wire tubes among the paths to add color, but I could see that long before they grew into trees one could be proud for they would be swamped by old newspapers. As it approached its first anniversary the market seemed more and more determined to fertilize the surrounding streets with trash. I thought of the cleaners I'd glimpsed early one morning, silently scrubbing a waste of tiles. Our cleaners at Radio Brichester were anything but silent. I pondered this, and then I saw a man hurrying along one of the paths toward the market. It was Macdonald.

"This isn't your usual route," I called.

He halted and frowned. He was wearing mauve trousers and

carrying a transparent umbrella. "I don't always come this way," he said.

"I'll accompany you, if I may." We entered the market; an alarm was ringing somewhere, and televisions flickered. "I hope you don't mind my asking," I said, "but if this is your shortest route home, how is it you avoid it?" We'd often met in the lift and parted at the street.

"It's a bloody peculiar question, if you don't mind my saying," he said.

"It's not mere curiosity."

"You surprise me." Among the pillars the escalators creaked like tethered boats. "You tell me why you want to know," he said, "and perhaps I'll tell you."

I should have been furious, but I felt he might have something to reveal; besides, the conversation and the market were beginning to stifle my emotions. "There's an atmosphere to this place I've come to dislike," I said. "No, it's more a lack of atmosphere, that's precisely the trouble. You know how most places have a personality. This place is about the least haunted I've ever encountered, and it makes me uneasy. I mean, if you dig into most cultures you'll find the notion of the genius loci. What sort of spirit could this place have?"

Macdonald was gazing at me. "That's all, is it?" he said.

"Well, nothing's actually happened."

"You know, you're all right," he said. "I thought you were having me on, but I can see you're not. You ought to come outside your folk music sometime and take a look at what's going on. Sorry to spoil your story, but I don't come this way because I don't live this way. Only my wife's away for the weekend and one of my fans wants to know what I look like without ma keelt."

I should have known, I thought sourly: as banal as that. Somehow it was the sort of thing I should have expected to learn in the market. Hostile clichés jostled in my brain, how pleasant for you, I wish you luck, but instead I pointed and said "What's that?"

LITTER

Along the corridor ahead a small white shape was scurrying. Occasionally it gave an ungainly leap and fell awkwardly; once it somersaulted, once it came to a halt and seemed to dwindle before puffing up and hopping closer. "It's a plastic bag," Macdonald said.

And of course it was. I was still expecting too much of the market. The bag bumbled along, skipping and falling playfully like a puppy. It exhaled, then wrapped itself around my ankles. "It's after you," Macdonald said.

It seemed to be. As soon as I freed myself it filled again and pressed against me. I turned and let it drift away, but it rolled back and moulded itself to my leg. Suddenly I felt disgusted, as if I were trying to shake off a limbless mindless embryo. "You can have it," I said to Macdonald, and kicked it toward him. He tried to knock it away with his umbrella, and I hurried off down the corridor. I heard him trampling the bag and tearing it with his umbrella. Looking back, I saw tatters of plastic grasping at his legs.

In the morning I awoke still thinking of the incident. It seemed indefinably squalid, and my mind was smeared with it. At Radio Brichester I encountered Macdonald. He winked and grinned secretively, and my mind produced an image of his struggle with a pale shapeless night-creature. I hurried on to see the station manager, who told me that he'd like a Christmas folk show, lots of carols and the better known the better, and no more talk than absolutely necessary if I wouldn't mind. Of course I minded, but there was little I could do except sulk and eventually begin to construct the program.

But at least it kept me away from the market. For a couple of weeks after the scene with Macdonald I consciously avoided the place, for less conscious reasons; and by the time the memory began to lose form I was sorting out the Christmas show and leaving the station early. In fact, if I hadn't stayed for the station's Christmas party nothing more might have happened.

It was an enjoyable, if incoherent, party. Someone wandered in from one of the pantomimes, wearing a stuffed parrot on his shoulder; the type of a news bulletin was unfocused, and its reading slurred, by Guinness; a theatre pianist made progressively vainer attempts at the Hammerklavier. Macdonald left early, having been harangued by his wife over the telephone. I left late, taking half an hour to bid goodnights.

The ice of the night didn't reach me, warm as I was. I bumbled along, slapping bus-stops amicably on their waste-bins, patting traffic meters on their heads. A few cars skated on the dull mirrors of the roads. Down on the Severn a tiny line of lighted windows slid by. I'd thought it might be the season for taxis, but none was about, and so I headed for the market.

Before I reached it I determined not to let it affect me, to preserve the mood of the party. Let the place be as stiflingly anonymous as it wished: my personality could pass through intact. I rounded a corner and there it was, squatting glumly, wreathed by my breath like a tomb amid studio mist in a film. I laughed. I balanced along the line between the flags of the path, and the thin caged trees hissed and rattled softly, snake-like, in the wind.

The ceiling of the corridor drifted above my head like a white shadow. My footsteps hammered on the tiles. I passed the fish-shops, their slabs sluiced clean, a boutique from whose windows bald nude androgynes stared expressionlessly. In a shop near the escalators identical silver heads danced, grew and shrank, but before I could make out the face the television screens went blank for the night. Somewhere ahead came a fluttering, as of birds' wings.

My footsteps continued to knock, measured, regular, like the sounds of workmen. The featureless muzak of the escalators hummed, faltered, hummed again. They must have been overhauled, I thought. I passed the last shop before the pillars, and the white of the tiles closed on my eyes like fog. Or more like the beginnings of snow-blindness. Among the pillars something fluttered again. My mind groped

LITTER

for a song. At the top of my voice I began to roar *Matty Groves*.

As I did so the fluttering intensified. I could locate it now; it came from behind the pillar nearest which I had to pass. It sounded as if the bird, which might be nesting there, had trapped itself among the carvings of the pillar and were struggling to pull free. But somehow I didn't want to go round the pillar and free it. Surely the carvings were too widely spaced to trap a bird. Instead, I made to hurry past.

Then the escalator caught my eye. The escalators rise straight from the center of the floor to the balcony level, and they're enclosed by glass. Where the sides of the treads back the glass as they climb, they form mirrors. These mirrors are dim and unstable, of course, but nonetheless I could glimpse fragments of the pillar in them. And the reflected pillar seemed to be covered with a multicolored mass that shifted and crawled.

I hesitated, then I began somewhat unsteadily to run. I came level with the pillar and with the transverse corridors. A gust of wind struck me, and the mass that had been pressed to the pillar detached itself and hurled itself in my direction.

It consisted largely of paper: old grey newspapers, paper bags puffed up like lungs, tendrils of receipts, scraps like leaden moths. As the wind tore it from the pillar and threw it at me, the mass resembled a hulking attacker swooping from concealment; it was almost my height, and for a moment gave the impression of a similar build, and of a sort of faceless impersonal aggression. Then it flew apart, scattering on the floor, pasting itself to the walls and to me.

I brushed it off furiously, my heart pounding, and hurried away. Or began to, for I hadn't taken three paces when I heard a fluttering behind me. I turned and saw the litter falling from the walls into a heap and reforming.

I was still drunk, and so I stood and watched. The heap was dwarfish now the support of the wind was weakening; two feet high at most, it shuffled about a little as if questing before it collapsed into a quarter of the size. Eventually I wandered away, glancing back frequently. The heap tried to rise, failed and began to drift away in fragments.

Next morning I had a headache which jabbed out of shape any notions I tried to ponder. At lunchtime I went out on the roof above Radio Brichester to clear my head. A wind plucked at me, and six floors below the city muttered monotonously. I gazed toward the Severn, where light fluttered silently on the water about a few boats. I glanced toward the market, left like a plastic lunchbox among the peaked Victorian facades, and all at once I remembered last night's incident and realized how unlikely it was. How drunk had I been? As I mused, the door onto the roof opened. I turned and saw Macdonald, chewing a thick-lipped ham sandwich.

"Trying to catch a cold?" he called.

"No, just trying to clear my mind a little."

"Been chased in the market lately?" he shouted.

"Well, as a matter of fact," I said, and stopped. I could hardly expect a sympathetic hearing. But I was damned if I were going to let his opinion matter. So I told him.

Telling him seemed to free me of the obligation to investigate the market. He smiled and shook his head when I'd finished, and walked away munching. He left me convinced that if there were something odd about the market I had no wish to encounter it again, and if there weren't then I didn't propose to depress myself with the place after a day's work. In either case, I shrugged it off.

Until a stormy night a fortnight later.

All evening layers of black cloud had been racing each other past the studio windows. When I left they had slowed, and were unfurling overhead. The hail began just as I was passing the market on the way to the station. I didn't intend to walk through, but I saw no reason not to take advantage of the shelter of its overhanging roof.

I stood and watched. Hail slashed across the mercury-vapor lamps like the teeth of luminous combs. Above, a blurred moon was threshed by tattered clouds. A man rushed stumbling across the mud between the paths, past a large battered plastic Santa Claus left over from the street's Christmas display, trampling the adolescent wisps and stubble of grass. He was a vandal in an unthinking way, but I couldn't altogether blame him; the place commanded no respect. The surface of the paths crawled beneath the onslaught of the hail, and paper bags winced in the mud like dying fish. A young couple arrived panting beneath the shelter, bearing a radio full of tinny pop music. I gazed at the moon, enjoying it, thinking how few people in cities ever look up. When I glanced down, I saw Macdonald running toward the market.

He didn't see me, and I looked away. Almost at once I heard his voice.

"—chart-topper if ever I heard one, really great sound, and confidentially I'll tell you what their lead guitarist told me, they got the tune from Johann Sebastian Bach and he wrote some really good ones, so they tell me, but he's finished with them. Anyway, we've got some awfy braw wee records on the turntable for you now but listen, here's a warning for you next time you're in Brichester Market, don't go dropping litter or it might drop you, that's what someone was telling me who got jumped on the other night by a crate of beer-bottles, and who said he emptied them all first?"

The music recommenced and the couple with the radio stared at me, alarmed, because involuntarily I'd punched the wall of the market. But I whirled and ran toward the entrance beyond which Macdonald had vanished. He wasn't getting away with that. I was going to catch him and keep him in the market until something happened. The episode after the party overwhelmed my memory, and I knew I hadn't just been drunk. Tonight I felt it would happen again. I would make it happen.

I couldn't see Macdonald ahead, but I could hear his footsteps.

"Macdonald!" I shouted. "There's something in here I want you to see!" The echoes of his footsteps multiplied, as if hurrying. I slipped and almost fell; the tiles were wet as the edge of a swimming-pool.

Balls of newspaper and cartons huddled against the shops, unmoving. I ran faster, one hand ready to catch the wall. Pink cardboard girls in a travel agent's flashed by, but there was still no sign of Macdonald. His footsteps were hemmed in by echoes, and sounded unreal. In a moment I would have passed the pillars and he would be in sight.

I reached the center of the market and halted, surrounded by the echoes. The sound of footsteps clattered from all four sides. The market's acoustic was odd, I knew, but not so spectacular. At once I realized that I had not been following Macdonald at all, but the sound of restless cardboard.

I was still looking both for Macdonald and for the source of the sound when that source emerged from behind the pillars and advanced on me.

It sounds absurd, and it looked so as well. A few empty milk cartons clattered into sight, pale water dripping from their torn mouths. Some sodden newspapers flapped dismally at the corners of the pillars, detaching themselves at last and falling to the tiles to flutter feebly like dying birds. A couple of magazines lay face down in dirty pools, trying to raise themselves. A ragged sheet of polythene rippled along the floor like a grey flattened caterpillar. Then cardboard boxes began to lumber into view, tumbling and rolling on their distorted edges, and a wind buffeted me from all four sides; an odd wind. All of a sudden I found myself cut off on three fronts, and the litter waiting, flapping and clattering nervously.

It was absurd, I repeated to myself: grotesque and unpleasant, but absurd. I turned back the way I'd come, slowly as if the litter mightn't notice. I took a step, and ahead the cartons I had passed shifted slightly away from the wall. I moved again. One of the cartons shook itself, tipped forward with a wet slap and skidded toward me.

LITTER

I watched it come, ready to side-step. But I maneuvered too soon, and I hadn't realized the weight of the thing. It teetered and brought one corner smashing into my shin.

I cried out, as much in surprise as in pain. As I did so I remembered the couple with the radio. They'd seen my reaction to Macdonald, and I could hardly look other than foolish. Nevertheless I shouted for help. I shouted twice before a beer-bottle rolled beneath my feet and sent me forward, almost burying my face in a pile of squelching newspapers, its corners shivering with what could have been anticipation.

I thrust myself to my feet and controlled my fury. If I kicked the paper I should never be rid of it. I forced myself to think calmly, or began to—until several bottles rolled against the wall and smashed.

It was then that I realized that I might be in danger, when the paper and cartons began to grope toward me, shards of glass glinting in their midst and on their surfaces. I backed away, searching for a means of escape, and saw what might be one: the escalator. The toothed paper rose up quivering, and I ran. I wasn't sure, but I thought I remembered an exit from the balcony level.

I gained the escalator and began to stumble upward as it moved. I gripped the moving banister, feeling the rubber bump and swell beneath my hand like the muscles of an arm. At the foot of the escalator the litter was massing and toppling forward to be carried upwards. Then above me I heard a crash of metal.

I glanced upwards and stood on the step I'd reached, overcome by despair. On both sides of the point where balcony and escalators met were dustbins. Two had fallen over, spilling their contents onto the balcony. Some of the rubbish, including trampled flowers from a florist's, had already trailed as far as the down escalator and was being carried to meet a waiting huddle of cartons below.

I felt myself being lifted inexorably, and tried not to cry out again. I knew nobody was within earshot, and crying out wouldn't help. On the contrary, if anything.

I gasped, not immediately knowing why. "On the contrary"—but why? I knew—I knew I knew. "Been chased through the market lately?" Below me on the escalator I heard the tinkle and scrape of glass. I remembered the night of the party, when I hadn't let myself be chased. A mindless threat has no motives of its own. And at last I realized how I'd escaped.

I reached the balcony and stood for a moment, taking deep breaths with my hands protecting my nose. Then I walked calmly, only, my face twitching, to the down escalator and stood on it. I tried closing my eyes, but this proved worse than watching the impatiently trembling cartons rise toward me.

At the bottom of the escalator I stood for some minutes. Behind me I could hear small objects scuttling down the stairs. When the cartons made no move I edged past them. I had just inched myself free when the cartons, and such contents of the bins as had made their way down, hobbled toward me.

I had hoped that they would subside before reaching me, as in the previous episode, but clearly this time they had gained more energy from the chase. They kept coming for some considerable time, and were hideous, particularly the trodden flowers smelling of fish that managed to reach my face. I sustained only a couple of scratches, but I had to walk slowly out of the market before brushing off all that had clung to me. Afterwards I felt ashamed to approach another human being, but I managed after some argument to hire a taxi. I spent hours in the bath, knowing I would never sleep.

I haven't spoken to Macdonald since, for he made it impossible for me to broadcast a warning. I haven't even attempted to guess the city council's reaction. But I continue to fear, no, to know that the market isn't unique; and perhaps other victims of its species may be more capable than I.

Cyril

A tentative flame felt its way along the edges of the pages, seeking to open the book. It leapt up the corners; a brown crisp of cellophane lifted from the cover; Flora bent closer, and the doorbell rang. She swore and stood up. She'd told Lance to let himself into the flat, hoping that he might—it would have augured well. She threw the window high and looked down; at her back the flames buzzed and muttered over the book. Beneath the streetlamp borrowing fire from the chaotic sky, Lance stood before the basement railings, adjusting and readjusting the parcels beneath his arm. She'd sworn at him; she felt ashamed, and swore. "Here, Lance!" she cried. "Something for you," and cast the keys down. He gaped and smiled; he wavered between her voice and her keys. One of the parcels slid free, only to be caught by his thigh. She hoped to God it wasn't the bottle. Off balance, he juggled the parcels, somehow swept up the key and scurried out of sight beneath her balcony.

Minutes later she heard him hurrying upstairs. On the landing there was a pause while perhaps he regained his hold on the parcels. She should have gone down to help. She glanced about the flat. She hadn't time to hide the *Lysistrata* prints; they were bound to terrify him, too soon. He was hastening down the long linoleum hall. She ran to the door and found him contorted round the parcels, which refused to be set gently down.

"Let me," she said, catching what must, beneath its crumpled wrapping, be the bottle. "Could you find the wine I wanted?"

"I think it must be," he said. "I don't know much about wines."

Not that it mattered; any alcohol would do—indeed, anything she could ask him to buy for her without arousing his suspicions and so lure him to her flat. But when she'd watched him yesterday sipping shyly at his half of beer in the office lunch-hour, she'd realized that wine might prove useful indeed.

"Well, come in," she cried. "Oh, you must for a few minutes," she pleaded. "You're cold." She took his elbow to usher him inside, but at last she had to let go. "Here's the fire," she said, thrusting a cup aside with her heel. "Try not to notice all this crap. I'm bloody lazy, I should warn you now." He clutched the other parcel to himself and edged forward, almost into the flames; she could smell his trousers warming. As the ash split into flakes and flew up the chimney, the title stood out black: *Bringing Up Baby*. "Oho," Lance mumbled. Or it might have been simply "Oh"; she could never be sure.

"Know a man by the books he leaves," she said. "A friend of mine, a late friend, let that book slip last night. Christ, men are so unsubtle!"

As Lance huddled closer to the fire she could smell his coat, faintly smoked by November fog. "I didn't mean you," she apologized. You're about the only sensitive man I know—but she knew that would drive him further inward. "Oh for a sensitive relationship, you know? Perhaps I should try a Lesbian or two. There are few things I wouldn't try once." He laughed and tried to hide behind his shoulders. Christ, she thought, it's almost love. If I could fall in love with anyone I'm sure it would be Lance.

"You'll catch fire in a minute," she said. "Do take your coat off. I know you'd like a coffee." She would have loved to unbutton him, but waited for a chance to draw the sleeves free. "And what have you been buying?" she asked as he fumbled with the parcel over the fire.

"Oh, this." Her fingernails on his coat collar ran down his palm as it withdrew. "It's a, I mean it's just a doll. I saw it, you know, shopping. I thought you might like it. You said you collected things."

"You are a darling," she said, thinking: I shouldn't have said that yet. She unwound the woollen scarf from his neck and, as he wasn't looking, brushed it across her cheek. It was tangled with lumps of fluff. Then she laid his clothes on the camp bed and tore the wrappings from the parcel. As she lifted it to look closely the doll's eyes turned down in a chubby face, perhaps proud of its neat Tyrolean shorts and T-shirt. I wonder why he felt this was appropriate—or maybe he was desperate, she thought. "It's very sweet. You're very sweet," she said. If he had been anyone else she could have pulled the clothes from the doll and slid her tongue into each crevice, although it terrified her to know that the doll was sexless. "I should explain," she told his shoulders, "that I wasn't burning that book for symbolic reasons. There are things you must burn to enjoy them, and things you must eat." Almost she offered him her piece of basalt, cold as catatonia on the tongue. "Speaking of which," she said, "you must eat before you return to the cold."

"Oh, I mean," he said, half-turning. "Thanks," he said.

She'd succeeded. "And what can I tempt you with?"

"Well, it's all right," he said. "I'll eat anything," still turning tentatively like an injured man afraid to test a limb.

"We'll have omelettes," she decided. "But first let's put Cyril to bed. I shall call him Cyril," she explained, "because that's the name I'd call a child I wanted to dominate. You know, Lance, if I had a child—which thank God science has helped me to prevent—I think it would only be so I could beat him. One must channel one's aggression." I don't mean this, she thought, do I? All I'm trying to do is to force Lance to talk, if only to shut me up. I'd like to feel present for five minutes. She kicked a coffee-bean toward the fire. "God, what a craphouse," she said.

Cyril wouldn't stand gazing from the window; she sat him on the sill, facing toward her bed, and tucked the curtains behind him. Lance watched from the bedroom doorway, hands behind his back. "How do you like my room? Come on, let's eat," she said, and captured one of his hands.

As she scraped the omelette from the pan she reached vainly for conversation. They would have to talk first, she thought, if only to soothe him. The news? She never read newspapers. His silence was crushing her skull. She peered round the curtain which veiled the kitchen from him like the entrance to a dressing-room. Lance was glancing up again at the *Lysistrata* prints and quickly recoiling. If I can't release him from himself then nobody can, because nobody cares.

She poured wine into the glasses and carried the tray to him. "I'm sure it's not what you're used to at home," she said, "but I trust it's less than emetic."

He waited for her to sit, then took a mouthful. "It's good," he said. "Honestly, I mean. I like it."

If he weren't so anxious she might have believed him. "If you drink your wine it might be better," she suggested.

"I haven't drunk much wine."

"I don't like to drink alone."

Success again, she thought, but how slowly! "You'll sleep tight tonight," she said. "Do you ever dream?"

"Well, I suppose so."

"About people you know? I'm sure you must dream things you couldn't tell most people." But he'd looked down to realign his knife and fork. "The things you can do when you dream. I enjoy delirium for the dreams, you know, because then I'm at the mercy of myself. If there's a real me then Christ, that's where she is."

A flame throbbed like a muffled drum. Flora was silent. From somewhere Lance asked: "Don't you ever get frightened, living alone?"

"Good Lord, my flat is open house. It's like a station sometimes." She took his glass. "You live at home?" she asked.

"Oh, yes." Of course, he said.

"And what will you do eventually?" She picked up the bottle, burning from the hearth.

"No more for me, really," he said, glancing at the clock and leaping up; crumbs of omelette tumbled down his trousers. "No, honestly, I mustn't."

"Lance, I should have warned you," she said, tensing herself for the lie. "I thought you'd have realized the clock's an hour slow. The last bus has gone."

His eyes turned up and retreated above his round mouth. Christ, she thought, I love him. I'll protect him. "You can't walk, it's too cold," she told him. "You must sleep here. Give me your number and I'll phone your parents."

The telephone stood grey upon the wedge of silver light along the wall; above it numbers were entangled, some in handwriting she couldn't place. She glanced up the wooden staircase to the dark mouth of her floor. Even if Lance were still sitting with his hands tight in his lap, he wouldn't be able to hear. When the receiver squeaked urgently, panic-stricken, she pressed in the coin like a knife.

"Is that Lance's mother?" she quavered hoarsely. She hadn't realized the voice would be so difficult to sustain.

"Who is that?" a woman demanded. Flora knew her face was sour and wrinkled as an orange. "If that's Eunice, I'm surprised you haven't rung before."

"I'm nobody you'd know," Flora said, crabbing her hand on the wall to help her voice. "Just an old lady your son helped to get into her house when she was locked out."

"Well, I'm glad to hear it," the voice conceded.

"I'm sure you've been worried about Lance. I know I would be if I had a son. I'm sorry I didn't ring sooner, but it's difficult for me to get up and down stairs. I just wanted you to know that he'll be staying here with me tonight. He'll be quite safe, but I'm a bit upset," she said. But the phone was noncommittal. Suddenly Flora continued: "And he bought me a little doll. I thought that was a nice thing to do for an old lonely lady like me."

"That's the way I brought him up," the voice said through an electric hiss like the rush of a wave. "Always take a present when you're visiting."

Flora prolonged a cough into the mouthpiece, wishing germs travelled, and replaced the receiver. God, she thought, how could anyone release him. God!

Beside Lance's leg the wine had spilled from the bottle and mixed with the ashes. She could see he hoped that she wouldn't notice; she looked away. "I usually go to bed about now," he told his hanging hands.

"I've been known to go to bed early." But even weaving his conversation into hers wasn't enough. She must fail while he was so conscious of what and what not to do. She couldn't break through his fidelity. "You'd better sleep in here," she said. "Just leave everything. I'll clean up in the morning."

As she undressed each movement was so heavy she wondered, why bother? Her body was lithe beneath the nightdress which twice had been torn from her, and yet she was incapable of holding what she really wanted. She peered into her somnolent bedroom fire as it shifted, then returned to the other room.

Lance was covered by the blankets; somewhere beneath was his body. Behind his head his clothes hung on the chair as on a line. He gave a smile, generally appreciative rather than for Flora. "I won't be asleep for a while. We insomniacs, you know," she said. "If the fire goes out come in and see me. Or if you need anything." She would ask point-blank, but she knew how dreadful that would be—and besides, that was one thing she would never do. Instead, she tucked the blankets about him. But she couldn't find his body. For a moment she was poised to spring; but she held back, seeing him helpless, on the edge of dream. She had almost kissed him when she turned and quietly closed the door behind her.

A distant train rushed muffled through a tunnel; a dog yelped.

CYRIL

Flora thrust her arm beneath her head, the better to hear the night. It was a decade since she'd lain and listened to the sounds of midnight; she'd lived at home then. These days she would be buried somewhere with shrieking guitars or tramping the night with friends, peering upward for a lighted window and a party. And Lance would be lying quiet, his hands stilled, his mind released— She turned toward the wall. Through the thin plane she could hear him breathing. As she accepted the night she extended. She embraced the streets she'd walked wet and echoing at four in the morning. Peaceful, she sensed that she could merge with whatever she wished. Instantly she merged with her love; she was sharing Lance's peace, and somehow this erased the agonies of the evening; at rest, he was himself. A red coal crinkled and fell. His breathing was so clear that she could imagine him next to her in bed. This at least was hers alone, she thought.

Her eyes heaved against their weight to open. His breath was suffocating her. Good God, she thought, is he ill? The harsh exhalations seemed on top of her, preying on her lungs; he might be in the room. Then inadvertently she shuddered; perhaps he was. For a moment she imagined him inching the door open, crawling in on hands and knees so as not to disturb her, raising his head and peering at her, shy as before her prints. She trembled upright. The room was black; the introverted fire smouldered; through a chink between the curtains she glimpsed a bright fragment of streetlamp. The blackness breathed. She sank back, drawn down by sleep, and heard something strike the floor at the foot of the bed.

It was small. A baby. But surely a baby's fall would never be so hard and menacing. She wrenched herself awake; half her mind was in darkness. It must be Cyril. Only her eyes were free above the sheet, waiting, anxiously alert; her body was hemmed in, she couldn't lift the sheet from herself. Around her the breathing quickened, panting. The transparent curtain drew back from the ostrich neck of the streetlamp, revealing the room beyond her vision. Then, close to nightmare, she saw that the neck of the lamp was swaying, questing back and forth outside the window. No, it was not the lamp. The curtain was appearing and withdrawing as what had fallen fought its way free.

The breathing had slowed; its pace was deliberate, like an approaching tread. Flora knew her first wild notion had been right. Lance was in the room. What she had declared impossible had happened. She closed her eyes. She must not move; Lance must approach in his own way. But the cold silver light flooded her, penetrated her, exposed her helpless. If only she could see him! She'd never known fear—well, perhaps once, but even then less than most women. Now she tingled at the edges. She knew she was safe with Lance, of course. This was every kind of experience at once; it was delicious. She felt the bed shake. Lance, on all fours, afraid to awaken her, had bumped against the foot. His breathing choked, then recommenced more softly, faster. In a moment she would know what he meant to do. She embraced fear.

At her feet the bedclothes tugged. She pressed her eyes shut and lay still. A weight crawled over the coverlet and crept toward her toes. When it touched her a charge coursed through her body; the light within her eyelids blazed. Lance's hand moved over the arch of her foot, gradual as his breathing. The blanket rested on her face, soft wool yet a prison. The hand traced her leg. Flora's fingers splayed out like antennae to determine what was wrong. Then she knew why she was troubled; the hand was approaching up her leg in rapid breathless stages, as if climbing. Suddenly her mouth opened, but the wool caved in upon her cry. The hand scaled her body; the room held its breath. Incapable of waiting longer, she opened her eyes. The icy light poured down; from the corner of her eye she saw the fire collapse and show forth a red heart. Otherwise, nothing. Still the hand crept upward. It reached her shoulder and lay inert. In a moment she must see his face. She would know. The hand moved from her shoulder to the coverlet over her neck. Then, hard and black against the precise light, a head rose into view.

Love or fear thrilled through Flora; she surged upright to embrace him and saw that Lance's head was shrunken, pale as a dead baby's. She recoiled, gasping. The head fell back and the plastic eyes rolled up to gleam in the steely light.

Oh God, Flora thought, revolted. Is this a game? What's wrong with him? She twisted free of the bedclothes, vaulted over the pillow and stumbled to the light-switch. In control again, she turned, already prepared to pity. But on the floor next to the tossed bedclothes was only the doll. One leg was bent beneath it; it rocked as if struggling to rise and walk.

And Flora, furious, strode forward. As she gripped it, digging her fingers into its side, its eyes turned blindly upward. She raised her hand to strike it, and then threw it into the heart of the fire. As it began to buzz like an agonized insect in the silence, she knelt down to watch.

Its clothes burst into flame. Naked, its arms warped upward as if pleading. A pink liquid bubbled from the elbows, and the arms fell broken into crevices of flame. Exuding, its legs drooped and lay bent outward on the orange coals. At last its head sank back. One eye-socket writhed, and the eye hurtled out to roll by Flora's knees.

She had to be rid of the eye; otherwise her release would be incomplete. She bent forward to pick it up between thumb and forefinger, and froze.

For an eternity she was petrified. Then she pressed her hands to her ears. The fire boiled close to her cheek; the eye had rolled beneath her knee. But Flora only dragged her head down and wished, cursed, prayed that the screams from the next room would stop.

Smoke Kiss

King was hurrying along London Road, self-consciously carrying the bottle of ink before him, when he saw the old woman. She was sitting in the doorway of a large store. She wore a stained black coat and slippers. "Go on, you sods," she was shouting. "I'm dying. You don't care. I don't either," and she threw back her head and sucked at a bottle of spirits. Her mouth was blackened and her yellow teeth were askew; blood had splashed the whole of her face from within. Shaken, King lit a cigarette as he hurried on.

By the time he reached home he had focused his mind on his work. He sat down at the drawing-board and wrenching the top from the ink-bottle, drew the last panels of *Mucky Matt*. That would see him through the next month's issues of *Nut Cutlet*. He lit a cigarette and addressed an envelope to his agent. He stubbed the cigarette out half-smoked and sat staring at the ashtray. Suddenly it looked to him like a stained mouth full of broken teeth.

None of that, he thought, you can't afford that sort of contemplation, not now you're a professional. Three strips for different comics had enabled him to go freelance fulltime. To daydream on your boss's time may be immoral, he thought, but when you're your own boss it's suicide. But his mind was full of the face mottled with blood and the staring eyes in which a spark was dimming. All right, all right, he hushed himself. Let's paint for a couple of hours. Good practice. Never know when someone might commission a cover.

The page of *Mucky Matt* was dry. He lifted it from the drawing-board. One corner of it jabbed the ink-bottle. It's all right, he shouted

SMOKE KISS

as his lungs gulped and his heart twinged, it's only paper, it won't knock it over—but the bottle rolled and ink leapt over the sheet. Jesus. Oh Christ. Control yourself. Let it dry and copy it.

While the page lay by the window, glistening in the July sun and curling up, he calmed himself harshly with a cigarette and began to paint. He gouged at the color, seeking the emotions he wanted to convey. Scrolls of smoke rushed up from the ashtray and curled toward his eyes. He squeezed his lids together and drawing on the cigarette, aimed the smoke at the canvas. Interesting effect of texture. Pockmarked. The *Nut Cutlet* editors would really go for that. Might as well try action painting on them while I'm at it. And sign on at the dole.

When he'd finished he stood back from the canvas and gazed. Really splendid. Quite remarkable. The mouth hung open, broken and slack; in the eyes there was the suggestion of a last faint gleam. I can just see that in someone's entrance hall, he thought. Jesus, how much time I do waste. I know, I'll call it *Death Embodied*. That'll really get the old ladies bidding.

He stood the canvas by the window. Above the roofs smoke poured from factory chimneys like huge black cigarettes. Mucky Matt would love them. He pinned the stained page to the wall and began to copy it. Mucky Matt was having a fine time this week, kicking dustbins over and emptying them over the head of our hero Tom, until Tom lured him into a bin and rolled him downhill into the town dump. "I think your idea is well-timed," the editors of *Nut Cutlet* had commented. "Like everyone else these days, children are becoming pollution-conscious." I'd take your word for it, King thought, if I didn't think we were trying to kid ourselves. Seems to me that when I was a kid I read comics just for enjoyment. Who knows if the kids read me at all. Who knows what they think. Not me. Maybe if I could talk to them, if I knew how to approach them.

He finished a panel and threw down the pen with enough control not to splash the page. No good, he thought. I've lost it for today. No point in trying to force it. He looked at the painted woman's face, staring upward as if in search of the light that was fading. No wonder, he thought. I know I've wasted an afternoon, no wonder I'm not in the mood. Well, she's not staying here. He grabbed the canvas and carried it out into the unkempt grass of the back garden. Then he tied newspaper in knots and thrust them beneath the canvas. I really must have had a moment when I thought someone would buy that, he pondered. Well, I don't want to be reminded of death either. We all know it's on the way.

Smoke began to squeeze out from beneath the canvas. Washing flapped like sleepy inverted birds on a line in the next garden. They can complain if they like, thought King. It'll be the first time they've spoken to me. But the smoke swung toward him and slipped up the wall of his house and over the roof. I could have used that canvas. Christ, I am in a self-destructive mood today. Coughing, he turned away and lit a cigarette. The woman's mouth charred and smoke sprang from the hole. As flames sputtered from her lips he threw the cigarette into the fire and waving away the thick smoke, retreated into the house.

Later he walked along Everton Brow. The pale boxes of high-rise flats were scattered down the rubbly hill to the Mersey, like minutely checked cartons left in a junkyard; on the other side of the river cranes nodded and picked among the sludge. Ah, inspiration. More happy fun with Mucky Matt next week, kids. Suddenly he threw his cigarette away like a grub and stamped on it. Moist brown leaves spurted from its end, but so did smoke. He scraped his heel across it and walked on. Looking back, he saw a thin grey stream still rising from the pavement. Go on, go back, don't let it pollute the air. He walked past waste ground rough with bricks and litter. Just like the inside of my lungs, koff koff.

He couldn't even bear to walk back across Everton; he caught a bus.

SMOKE KISS

All the windows upstairs were shut. Smoke hung in layers in the aisle, and its originators coughed. Maybe there's a new race, the pollution-breathers. The sharp tang of nicotine reached his nostrils; he inhaled, held it for a moment, then blew it out loudly and angrily. Christ knows where it's been.

Once home he stared along the terrace. Only a dog and a piece of newspaper moved, and beneath the yellow streetlamp the houses looked flat and synthetic, like a row of clones. He felt trapped inside his head. Someone had washed the pavement in front of his house. Well, that's a start. Could do with some order inside. Inside me, come to that. I should start cleaning there. That night he dreamed that the old woman was lying on her back in the doorway. Fumes billowed from her mouth. He knew that the spirit was charring her from within. He awoke panting and had to smoke a cigarette before risking sleep again.

In the morning he returned to the pages of *Mucky Matt*. The ashtray was full of torn stubs and pieces of ash like grey turds; fragments and a stale pungency surrounded it. He emptied it and reached for the packet. No, let's see how long I can hold off. He drew a few outlines, which looked empty. He felt half-awake and dull. No use. He pulled the tab of the packet and a cigarette arose. As he absorbed the smoke his mind began to buzz, then grew heavy.

Behind the stain on the pinned page his drawing had become indistinguishable. Never mind. Let's start again. As he redrew the last panels the impulse grew stronger. He was smiling. Christ, this is what it's all about. He drew faster, more surely, lighting a cigarette at the end of each panel, at the end of each dialogue balloon, at the end of each figure, coughing. A squashed stub rolled out of the ashtray and hopped over the floor.

When he'd finished the page he looked up and saw the smoke hovering over him. It had been built up into still grey strata. He waved his hand through it, and it dilated and reformed. He shouldered his way through it and opened the door. But the smoke had settled inertly over the drawing-board. Bugger off, he thought. I don't need you hanging around to remind me. He shoved the window up. Gradually, very gradually it seemed to him, the smoke dissipated. He remembered the fumes from the mouth in his dream, which had settled on his face and lips, growing heavier like mud. He strode around the room waving his arms to drive out the clinging smell. Perhaps the smoke hadn't taken so much longer than usual to disperse. His head was swimming so much he couldn't be sure.

Ravenous, he made himself dinner. When he'd eaten his dizziness had vanished, and he enjoyed the taste of tobacco as dessert. Then he worked out two stories for *Clara Caterpillar*. Let's see how they look. No, must discipline myself. If I feel this way tomorrow I can start early and draw them both.

Instead, he cleaned up. He swept the mites of ash from the table and carried a dustpan full of stubs and empty packets to the dustbin. Then he emptied the remnants of spaghetti into the kitchen bin and dumped the contents. As he washed up an idea was worrying the back of his mind: I had a full packet of cigarettes somewhere. I'd taken the cellophane off and put the packet somewhere. On the table. No, I couldn't have. Oh no. He held his breath and searched among the slime of spaghetti and ash in the bin. All the packets were empty.

He went to the corner shop to buy cigarettes. Among the sweets and tights on the counter he saw a few dog-eared copies of last week's *Nut Cutlet*: none of the current issue. "No, it's not doing very well," the proprietor said. "The children buy the ones they know. The new ones don't go. They're not very good, that's why." Thanks for the encouragement, King thought. Must tell my bank manager. No doubt he'll be sending me a begging letter soon. He pulled off the cellophane and lit a cigarette. As he passed a refuse wagon he crushed the cellophane and threw it in, and then the packet. Christ, I'm losing my grip entirely. Sorry to trouble you but could I have my cigarettes back. No, my mind knows best even if it doesn't tell me what it's doing. The money was wasted anyway, so let's be blatant about it. If I go to bed I can't want a cigarette. Then I can make an early start.

In the early morning he found himself in the doorway, stooping over the old woman. A light was fanned up in her eyes, and her arms clung to his neck. Vertigo pulled him down toward her mouth, which fastened on his. His eyes sprang open. He was half out of bed, his arms clutching the bedside table. His mouth was moving on the ashtray; stubs adhered to his lips, and one was in his mouth. He reached the bathroom barely ahead of a rush of vomit. Each cough ripped his chest like a saw.

When he awoke later he felt purged. He was weak, but once he'd eaten breakfast some of his strength returned. His head floated. As soon as he'd washed up he sat down at the drawing-board. The first panels of *Clara Caterpillar* appeared quickly and easily. In the fourth he had an old caterpillar coiled on a toadstool. Bit for the Lewis Carroll fans. Pipe in his mouth. No, absolutely no pipe! He halted the pen so violently that his elbow jarred the ink-bottle. Christ, not again! But it didn't spill, although it was some time before his harsh breathing ceased to fill his ears.

If he hasn't got a pipe then the next panel doesn't make sense, nor the last. He sat staring at his thoughts. Come on, the pipe isn't essential. He looks too decrepit for a kids' comic, anyway. Maybe I should start again. He grabbed his sketch-pad. Christ, why have I made him look so senile? All he needs to complete him is a beard of drool. It's that old woman.

King couldn't think. There seemed to be a grey patch hovering behind his head. He twisted round. Nothing, but his movement drew a stale aroma of smoke from the walls and the furniture, on which his nostrils fastened avidly. This is pointless, he thought. If I'm going to be like this while it seeps out of me I won't be able to work. He hurried out and bought a packet of cigarettes.

For the rest of the day he drew in halting stages. He worked out a new story and sketched it in, stopping to suck on a cigarette and stare at the glowing tip, on which a flaking coat of ash accumulated like thick dust. Then he thrust it into the smouldering tangle in the ashtray and scratched the grey paste from his fingers.

By the time he'd finished the room was heavy with smoke, and the smell from the ashtray stung his nostrils. His head seemed filled with grey mist. Before he reached the window he was coughing uncontrollably; a fire sputtered in his throat and collected in his chest, which clutched at itself in agony. He had to slump into a chair and hug himself, for the grey in his brain had turned red.

All right, he thought. That's it. No more. His limbs were shaking and his lungs felt waterlogged. After an hour he ate some cheese and tottered into the bedroom. He emptied the bedside ashtray into the toilet and left it on the side of the bath. The stubs uncoiled like charred anemones. Then, still trembling, he slipped into bed.

His mouth felt dry and metallic. He lay watching the light sink into darkness. Somewhere behind his eyes the old woman waited. No, I'm not having her tonight. She can stay outside. He let her face swell up toward his consciousness and then with an effort of will thrust her into the darkness of the room. Now stay there. You're no ghost, just death. Let me sleep.

As sleep accumulated he felt his mouth working against the sheets. A drink. A cigarette. Well, you're not having any. He blacked out for a moment, and as he waited for the next more prolonged intimation of sleep he searched his mind for the old woman. Not there.

He awoke coughing, unaware that he'd been asleep. He sat up more shocked than at any time since he'd once fallen into the void of anaesthetic. He fought off the blankets that hung about him. His limbs were free but his face was caught in the sheet. No, it wasn't a sheet. It was smoke.

He wrenched his feet free of the bed and plunged forward through the smoke. He was unsteady, and grabbed the dressing-table to support him as he made for the window. As he did so he glimpsed his head dimly in the mirror. The smoke clustered about his face, and as he strained his eyes it seemed to be pouring from his mouth and nostrils.

He staggered across the room and switched on the light. The smoke was whirling over the bed, but when he forced himself to look in the mirror it was nowhere near his face. He supported himself to the window. Within the pane he could see the smoke drifting closer behind him. He moved his shoulders uneasily and threw the window open.

As he turned back to the room the smoke seemed to gather itself. Then it rushed toward his face. Perhaps it was merely being drawn into the night behind him. He put up a hand to ward it away from his eyes. Before he could cover them he thought he saw the mass extend twin plumes of smoke toward him. He sucked in his breath, and they plunged into his mouth and nostrils.

He stared at the mirror and breathed out until his lungs gulped with pain. No smoke emerged. He panted, tearing at his lungs with air. Nothing. He could feel the smoke growing heavier in his lungs, and his head was spinning. He punched his chest, weeping. He forced himself to cough. He coughed harder, hacking at himself. Nothing; only the taste of stale smoke that emerged as far as his tongue. Then, as his lungs clutched at air, he began to cough in earnest; his body burned as the coughs flayed his throat; the hot agony focused on his chest and magnified, and he fell.

Five minutes later his body felt hot and inert, as if his flesh were rubber. As he crawled and then wavered to his feet, he saw falling away beneath him a butt that had charred the carpet. It was surrounded by saliva where his mouth had rested. When he returned to bed a mouth with smouldering teeth gaped above his sleep.

In the morning he forced himself out of bed and bought a week's supply of cigarettes. As he worked he lit the cigarettes and left them smouldering in the ashtray. The sawtoothed fumes trickled toward his nostrils. Got to wait for my mind. Wait until it's suffered enough to grab the whole lot and burn them. Then it'll always be ready to tell me what a bloody fool I am.

Last night's stale taste had vanished, except where it coated belches. As his nostrils flinched from the interminable smoke he thought: how could I ever have enjoyed inhaling that? I didn't. Because it didn't taste as it smells. That's where I've gone wrong, rationalizing. The justification is nothing to do with the smell. He gazed at the empty outlines on the drawing-board. He felt his first and second fingers open tingling toward the ashtray.

The Words that Count

Amen to that, because it did seem to be the words that counted. That's a bit short storyish as a beginning. But after all, I know this morning would make a good short story, and this is going to be it. So I'll buck my ideas up, as my father would say.

Evil is something you read about, but what you read is only very approximate, if that. (That's better!) Even the Bible can read like a story sometimes, if you permit your mind to slacken. I'm lucky to have had my father to read the Bible to me, rather than one of those teachers who try to indoctrinate their charges in the lie that it isn't meant to be taken literally. But evil is clever today. It takes forms that aren't in the Bible. It comes through the letterbox in a plain brown envelope with a threepenny stamp.

From Mike, I thought as I heard the letterbox click. I was in the kitchen, making my father's breakfast. Mike's my boy friend, my first and only real one. He's only a bus ride away but we often exchange letters, because it makes me feel secure to read them during the day. And my father doesn't insist any more on opening them, which makes Mike all the more my boy friend (I won't call him Mike if I send this off, of course; in fact, he doesn't really come into the story at all unless I make him.) Anyway, I turned the stove down and went to get the letters.

"Us, is it?" I heard my father call. "Yes, but it's nothing," I called back, because it didn't seem to be. It was just a flat brown envelope addressed to me, without a return address. "Just a circular," I said.

"Deliver us from circulars," my father said, which is the one thing in surprisingly bad taste he sometimes says. I suppose all men suffer from the temptation to shock, even Mike, although he has great self-control. I threw the envelope on the kitchen table and took my father's scrambled eggs up to him. That's his weekend treat; on days when I'm working I only have to slice him a grapefruit.

But I didn't take the envelope to him. I don't know why, because of course I felt guilty, and kept telling myself that I didn't want to bother him. "I'm sorry," I said. "Shall I throw it away?" "Yes, unless it's anything worthwhile," he said. He wasn't wearing his dressing-gown, so I left the tray outside his room, but he put his head around the door and smiled at me. He often does that, and his hair is usually standing up like a silver halo; it's as though someone were leaning out of a stained-glass portrait to smile. I don't think that's blasphemous. I went downstairs and had my own breakfast, and there was the envelope waiting in front of me.

Temptation is a dreadful thing, because it insinuates itself among your thoughts and mixes them up. I kept reaching for the envelope and drawing back. You see, I was beginning to be convinced that someone had sent me one of those things they're trying to stop, a catalog of aids to love. As if the sacrament of marriage weren't enough of an aid! I know it will be for Mike and me. But what scared me was that I didn't know how much I'd have to see before tearing it up—or taking it to my father, who would know what to do. I almost threw it away unopened, except that I felt I'd have to grow up sometime; but my head was throbbing as I thought about it.

"Into the jaws of hell, then," I said to myself, and snatched the envelope and ripped it open, holding my breath. I shook out the contents, then I breathed so hard that I had to hold it again in case my father had heard.

Not that I was completely reassured by what I'd found. It was a pamphlet bound in a soft black material on which light rippled slowly. It felt like fur. I shivered, because it seemed too enticing for its pages to be innocent. But I closed my eyes and let the pamphlet fall open, and looked.

"Us." That was all: just one word on the page, in delicate mauve letters on a darker purple. It was strange—I mean it was even stranger, because that was a word I'd been thinking about a good deal. I don't think I have space in my diary to explain, if I'm to finish my story. I remember wondering whether all the pages were like that, and whether any of the words were ones I shouldn't read. But I steeled myself and turned over.

"Lead" was the next, in a pearly pink against mauve. I stared at this, because the colors seemed beautiful in a quiet way, like the Oriental paintings on our tea service. Then I let the pages run through my fingers. I had to stop, not because any of the words I'd glimpsed were foul, but because the colors were throbbing against my eyes like a kaleidoscope gone out of control.

And I'd almost forgotten to run my father's bath. Perhaps that should have shown me how the pamphlet was, if I may permit myself the word, seducing me. But I couldn't have known then what it was. I ran upstairs and turned on the taps. "I'm sorry, father. I've been reading," I called. "I'm sure you needn't blame yourself," he said. "The day was meant to be used." I heard him put the tray on the landing as I turned off the taps. I took it downstairs and washed up, thinking.

"Us," I was thinking. That was how the pamphlet worked: by putting claws into your brain, and that was the first. And to stop myself being confused I thought about the pamphlet. What I'd seen reminded me of a book of poetry Mike had shown me once. Some of the poems weren't the sort of thing I should have read, and he'd apologized. But some seemed to be just words arranged attractively on the page, and I thought the pamphlet might be similar. It depends on the kind of attraction, of course. I was even beginning to think Mike might have had the pamphlet sent to me as a present!

Against yourself there's sometimes no defense. It comes of not making yourself be straightforward. I should have waited for my father to come down and shown the pamphlet to him, but I saw no harm in reading it. A bird was sitting on my childhood swing and puffing up its feathers, and the garden sparkled like the night with dew. It seemed pleasant to listen to the bird's trills and read. So I sat at the table and began to read the pamphlet slowly from the beginning.

"Trespass" was the word that made me frown. "Thou shalt not trespass," I found myself thinking, and yet the pamphlet seemed to be urging the opposite. But the word wasn't important, I told myself; the artist had simply wanted a pattern of dark blue stretched across lilac.

Who could have produced such a thing? That's the thought that shocks me most, although perhaps the idea fed them lies to justify itself, as it was doing to me. I can only shrink from myself as I was then, my head bent close to the table, my eyes and my brain separated. My eyes were drinking in the colors while thoughts scrambled in my brain, my own thoughts being silently suppressed while others moved into their places. My head was twinging, and I sought peace in the slow turning of the colors. I had forgotten where to seek true peace. "Who" was the next word, then "those."

"Those as can, does; those as can't, teaches." I'd once heard my mother shouting that at my father. Of course she didn't really talk like that, she was only affecting vulgarity. She died of cancer when I was ten, and my father and I prayed for her soul before every meal. I missed her, although my father told me that was presumption: everything belonged to God. Something of her was still in our house, even after my father gave away her clothes to Father Murphy. Her letters were in a drawer in my father's room, and he'd honored her photograph by putting it next to the Sacred Heart in the lounge. This was what I thought as I looked at the word. All that from one word! And I remembered their argument.

"Forgive her," I'd cried. I'd felt guilty because in a way it was all my fault; my mother had been proud because a teacher had liked a story I'd written, but my father had said nobody needed fiction when there was the Bible. Looking back, I think he wanted me to write something he could sell in his Catholic bookshop, not a fairy tale. But then I didn't know; I'd squeezed myself into the couch, crying and screaming, feeling that it was wrong for my mother to take my part against my father. "Those as can—" I heard her shout, and I ran to my father to intercede for her. I felt he would listen to me, and after a while, holding up his hand for silence, he did. I felt guilty again when my mother died—in fact it was worse, and I've never understood why.

We were closer after that, though; there wasn't so much tension in the house and in me, I suppose because I knew my mother was with God. There was a different sort of tension when I brought Mike home, after having met him in the library where we work; an odd sort of tension, because although I knew I shouldn't I half-enjoyed it. Not that this is helping my story, but I like to be able to write it down for myself.

As I turned the pages I was thinking all this (so perhaps it does fit into my story). My mind felt strange then, though, like a slippery surface across which my thoughts were scurrying, sliding out of reach as I tried to catch hold of them. The room felt oppressive, and so did the sound of my father getting out of his bath. I must have been overpowered by then, because I began to turn the pages faster in case I shouldn't have finished by the time my father came down.

"Trespasses" stopped me again. I knew it should remind me of something but God help me, I didn't know what. All I could think was that when I'd brought Mike home the first time my father had treated him like a trespasser. My father had wanted me to work in his shop but there wasn't enough money, so he managed to persuade the city librarian to let me work in the Religion Library, making me promise solemnly to choose my friends. I found that there were books on spiritualism and black magic on the shelves but I didn't tell him, although I should have; I simply told people when they asked that all the books were out. I believe you can lie in the service of God.

Our house felt brighter when Mike continued to visit. My father rebuked me after his first visit, but I told him that Mike had been to the best Catholic school in town. I didn't tell him that he'd lapsed, because I know I can bring him back to the Church. After all, I'm twenty-three and I want to help people. That was why I left the convent, that and the way all the silence and rustling terrified me; they were kind but I couldn't make sense of the gap between life in the convent and the people we tried to save from alcohol and drugs. I wanted to see ordinary people so much that I couldn't sleep for weeks. Perhaps I wasn't ready. I think I did the right thing, because once I met Mike I knew I was ready for him. I felt God was watching over us.

"Us"—there it is again, but let me get on. That word was troubling me then too, and I began to walk around the house, still reading. It was as if the kaleidoscope had got into my head, and my thoughts were about to fall together. I found myself staring at the television set. My father is a member of the National Viewers' and Listeners' Association, and recently he watched part of a wrestling match before writing his weekly letters (one to Mrs. Whitehouse, one to each of the broadcasting companies). I'd been both repelled and fascinated by the wrestlers. They were pink as the inside of a shell, and their muscles kept wobbling and then growing taut. I'd once seen Mike fight, to take a broken bottle away from a man who was threatening his wife, and I'd been terrified and proud. Terrified most in case my father heard we'd been in a pub, for he would have forbidden me to see Mike again. I stared at the television, thinking all this, and then my thoughts fell together.

Forgive me, father, for writing this down, but I think it's better out of me. I began to think of all the subjects Mike had to avoid discussing, his lapse, drinking and the rest. Suppose he betrayed himself one day? I imagined them fighting over me, like knights over a lady, or wrestlers. I would belong to whoever won. Of course my father would win, I thought, because if I were honest I had to admit that right was on his side. And having won, what would he do with me then?

And I can't remember what I thought after that, because I backed into the sideboard and knocked over a cup. It wasn't broken, and I began to giggle nervously, listening to the china chattering against the saucer like a tiny monkey running into the distance. I wondered what it would have sounded like if it had broken. I felt I'd never listened to things like that before, I'd always rolled into a ball inside when anything was damaged. I found myself staring at my mother's photograph and then, I'm still trying to remember why, I ran upstairs.

"Bread." I've had to stop here to think, because that was one of the words in the pamphlet. Bread is what they call money to buy drugs. I wonder if the pamphlet were drugged somehow, because when I think about it that was the effect it had. The evil of people!

"Daily prayer and lots of it," Sister Clare used to say to the people we were helping, and I've always remembered that advice. I don't think I feel drugged now, though. Perhaps I was when I went to the bathroom, although no doubt the words in the pamphlet were enough.

Our timetable was established a long time ago; I would run my father's bath after breakfast and when he'd finished, I would wash properly and brush my teeth. The bathroom would be full of steam and a warm smell I liked because it was my father's. I took off my clothes and then I began to squirm inside, remembering how my father had found me once standing on the toilet with no clothes on and trying to look in the shaving mirror, and he'd sat on the bath and beaten me. Then I regained control of myself, but while undressing I'd knocked the pamphlet into the bath. I had to grope for it through the steam, and then I saw that there were a few of my father's hairs around the inside of the bath, and I caught myself wondering where they'd come from. I want to cross that out, but at the same time I want to leave it to remind me what I'm capable of. Before God I don't usually have such thoughts. My father and I have always been just us.

Us again. All right, I'll explain and then I can get on. I feel guilty thinking of Mike and me as us, it seems disloyal. I don't know if I'm right, because I can hardly think of Mike and my father in the same way. But I keep thinking about it until my head hurts. I think my father feels something similar, and that's why he's begun hitting me again. I try to stop him, but he has a bad heart. That's all, and now I haven't much room in my diary. I washed and brushed my teeth, and when I came downstairs my father was waiting.

"Give that to me, please," he said.

Heaven help me, for a moment I didn't know what he meant and when I did I realized I was trying to hide the pamphlet behind my back. I blushed and apologized, and gave it to him.

"In heaven's name, what nonsense is this?" he said.

"Is it a poem? I think that's what it's meant to be." I hurried into the kitchen for no reason except so as not to have to look at him, because my face was burning and I was confused. I realized that I'd read the pamphlet through but couldn't remember having finished it, and a part of my mind knew what I'd read and was trying to tell me. My face is burning now.

It was worse to wait in the kitchen when the only sound in the house was the pages turning, and it was as bad to watch him frowning. I felt he was going to discover what I'd been reading before I did, and that terrified me as much as being caught that day in the bathroom. I tried to think of something to distract him.

As I did so he spoke, and when he saw me start his frown deepened. "Look at these colors," he said. "They're false. I ask you, are these the colors of God's earth?"

"Earth isn't a color," I said. I don't know why, because I knew it was a stupid thing to say. "Sorry," I said, and the pamphlet was making me crafty, because I said "Let me have it and I'll show you, some of the colors are beautiful."

"On no account," he said, and I began to draw into myself, because I knew that at any minute he would make the discovery I dreaded, and I still didn't know what it was. I realize now I said out loud "Oh, God, what have I done?"

"Done? What do you mean?" he said, and I'd reached such a pitch I almost cursed inside myself. "I mean I don't think we have enough vegetables for dinner for three," I said weakly.

"Be quiet now and let me look at this. There's no call for you to bring God into your housework."

"Will you excuse me then, while I go and see?" But I was equally terrified to leave him with the pamphlet or to stay; my head was pounding.

"Thy," he read. I remembered I'd read that word two or three times. "Is this supposed to be religious? If so it's a poor job," he said. He turned two pages, then he went rigid and raised his eyes to me.

"Come here," he said. That's what he said in the bathroom when I was little, and that's how I went to him, with my ribs hurting because I was breathing so fast. He gripped my shoulder and held up the page.

"Kingdom," he read and turned back. "Come, kingdom, thy. Thy kingdom come! Do you know what this filth is?" he shouted and a purple vein grew from beneath his hair. I couldn't speak, only shake my head. But of course I did know, because the first word in the pamphlet had been "Amen."

"Thy kingdom come! That's what they want today, isn't it? The devil's kingdom!" He swung me round to face him, hurting my shoulder. "And this is how they go about it! Was this your friend's idea? Did he send you this?" he shouted, his face still darkening, and I could only shake my head until my ears screamed.

"Name me one person who would send you this!" he shouted, and I managed to say "I don't know anyone. They could have got my name from anywhere." Then I gulped back a cry, because he'd pulled the covers back and was ripping out the pages.

"Thy" sailed by me, and I picked it up seeing only the colors, soft shades of yellow and lime. My father's face seemed to swell and loom over me, and I crumpled the page into his hand and closed my eyes. I heard his breath snarling and the rip of the paper, and I was thinking of the time he forbade me to see the boy next door again, because he wasn't a Catholic. I know it was for my own good, but then I lay sobbing in the garden, and when a butterfly settled near me I tore it like a wet scrap of paper. My father's destruction of the pamphlet seemed like that, and I sobbed before I could stop myself.

"Be quiet!" I felt him grab my shoulder. "Tell me before God, did you read this?" I opened my eyes and there on the floor I saw the word "hallowed," like pieces of jigsaw when you know they fit together by their color. I looked at him and couldn't speak, seeing the vein trembling on his skull.

"Hallowed is as hallowed does," I was thinking, anything to cover the slippery surface of my mind, because now I could see through it and there was my father on the floor, his heart burst. I was thinking that then there'd be just me and Mike to save me from despair, the worst sin, just us.

"Heaven help you, child!" my father shouted. "Don't think up lies! Did you read this filth?"

"In a way," I stammered. "I mean, I didn't read it, just looked at the colors. The art."

"Art! You call this art?" he shouted. I must have become crafty again, as I sometimes was when I was little, thinking I could tell when he'd softened. That, and the fact that the pamphlet had gone; the thoughts it was feeding me had gone; my muteness had gone, and although I was shaking I felt a tremendous relief. Everything seemed all right again. "Yes. Well, it is. In a way," I said.

"Who taught you that? Your friend?" he shouted, and knocked me across the room. I ran to my bedroom sobbing, and the sheet beneath the blanket was wet when I'd finished. I sat on my bed for an hour after that, thinking all that I've written down. It was then that I thought of writing it, because Sister Clare used to make the people write down their lives; she said it helped. I knew I could write it, if my father would speak to me.

"Father, please forgive me," I said when I went down. He was staring out into the garden. After a while he turned and nodded. "I forgive you," he said. "I know you didn't understand. But never do anything like that again unless you want to kill me." And I ran up to my room again, but this time I was smiling.

Our house feels peaceful now, and I feel somehow cleaner for having written all this down. I shall read it through now to see what effect it has, and perhaps Mike can read it when he's brought us back from Mass. No, on second thoughts, there are things in it he shouldn't know until after we're married. He can see it when it's properly finished. I'll have to rewrite it before I send it anywhere, if I do, because I know the effort of writing isn't meant to be visible. And it certainly is at the moment; every time I've hesitated at the beginning of a paragraph the ink's collected in my nib, and the words stand out from the rest. They look almost as if someone else had written them in.

Ash

"You go on ahead and see to things," Anthea had said. "I'll see you at the weekend." Remembering, Lloyd gnashed the gears as the house came into view, its bricks blushing in the sunset. Yes, he could see to things: one mistake in signing a hotel register and she doubted him. The removal men had left at last; the house was tranquil, subdued as the faded orange of the bricks, the grass of the garden disturbed only by a dent where a table had leaned its weight on its leg. The few notes he'd taken on the Cotswold dialect struggled to rise from the seat beside him. He was satisfied with them, but it was Anthea's project on folk-tales, Anthea whom Brichester University had commissioned to compile the book, Anthea's money which had claimed the larger part of the house, while he was just a temporarily redundant journalist. And Anthea who had insisted that they live together outside Brichester, of course. All right, he knew that the morality of sex was personal and therefore private: that was why she had run out past the hotel porter and his huge umbrella like a bedewed mushroom; but it wasn't sufficient reason. He kicked the car forward, toward the corner shop.

The shopkeeper's spring was rusty; he uncoiled laboriously upward behind the counter with a box of Kleenex. Dust lay on his crown of hair like ash on a fire in the morning. He and his customer turned to Lloyd like images mirrored on the plane of dust between them. "You'll be new," said the image behind the counter.

Perhaps he'd shown his ignorance of a local custom, Lloyd thought. He surveyed the bottles of disinfectant, crinkled packets of stockings, pegged protractors and set-squares, newspapers. "Have you cigarettes?"

"I don't know if we'd have your brand." But they had, Lloyd found, irritated then triumphant: he disliked affectation.

"And what's bringing you up here?"

"Well, cigarettes. Oh, down here, you mean?" The silent image had extracted a Kleenex and coughed red-eyed; the shop-bell rattled, muffled with dust, and the newcomers stood listening. Dear God, Lloyd thought, in a minute they'll all be crowding round like peasants from one of those Transylvanian villages at Shepperton. "I'm doing research into local customs," he said.

"That'll be nice," said the shopkeeper.

"Should be interesting, that," remarked one of the late-comers. Look, Lloyd thought, I'm as bored as you are. There wasn't one accent he recognized from the tape.

"You're at number 37 then, are you?" someone asked.

A Kleenex hung lolling out of the box. "You won't be living there alone?"

"Not for long." Even Anthea couldn't expect him to lie about that.

"It's a tragic house, is that." You're never Cotswold, Lloyd thought accusingly.

"I can remember the day she left him as clear as yesterday," the shopkeeper said.

"Aye, but he wouldn't lose his sleep over that, I reckon. If that woman thought she was badly done to she'd turn on you in the street. Anyone, mind you, and you didn't know her from Adam."

"He was as bad after she left, though, remember. We had to complain in the end. He left the next day."

"Well," Lloyd said, "I'll see you sometime." Muddy boots vacated their prints for him. The bell's tongue trembled, thick. He parked the car in the alley behind the street and walked back; as he glanced up the road which joined the street opposite his house the streetlamps opened

THE HEIGHT OF THE SCREAM

unblinking eyes and led his gaze to a gap of darkness. He'd already forgotten the shop; he scarcely thought he needed to make notes.

He set the recorder on the hall table by the telephone and hung up his coat. "Anthea?" he called, hurrying upstairs. How odd! he thought, halting. I must miss her more than I thought. For a second he'd been sure that she was hiding, ready to leap on him—but she would have considered that undignified. His fingers traced a splinter recessed in the banister.

Somewhere something was burning; the air was faintly acrid. He ran downstairs and threw open the door beneath the staircase. But beyond the rakes, the lawnmower brown with rust and brittle strands of grass, the beach of scattered coal, the furnace door hung loose and disclosed a cold hole. No smoke betrayed the kitchen; the cooker and refrigerator stood sharp on the red stone flags. He looked into the sitting-room. The furniture sat stolidly in the dim light from the street; the key-holes on the face of the Victorian clock were nostrils, unbreathing; on the mantelpiece a black marble hand rough and wrinkled with dust had been moved toward the door by a removal-man. Lloyd thought it ugly, but left it where it was; Anthea might find it interesting.

He wandered upstairs. At the bedroom door he knocked and entered. Now listen, he told himself furiously, twice is too much. It's Tuesday, only four days to the weekend. Against the brown wallpaper which soaked up the light the bed stood, almost puritanically white. He returned to the kitchen and began to beat an omelette. Later he would ring Anthea.

But her telephone purred complacently. Eventually he shrugged into the mirror and set down the receiver. He cleaned out the mouthpiece, which was clogged with dust or ash, and took notes and recorder to bed with him, distributing them on Anthea's side. When he found that he'd somehow erased the tape he swore bitterly; all he could hear was the faint muttering of a woman's voice, one that he didn't even recognize.

Anthea said: "I trust you're eating well? The University seems quite excited by the sample notes I gave them. Lonely without you, but only for three days by the time you read this. Ring me tonight to let me know you're surviving."

As he read the bacon charred. However, he hid it in bread and ate it while he reread Anthea's letter. The morning newspaper had arrived with the compliments of the corner shop. He supposed he would have to thank them, but it would be an effort: "Mrs. Jenner and Mrs. Wolsey gave a talk on Spain and showed slides at the Free Trade Hall; Mrs. Cooper won first prize in the Swiss roll competition." Thank heaven he was only an observer, and transient. Where they drew their folk-tales from he couldn't fathom. Certainly not from their imaginations, which must have starved to death decades ago.

In the hall a moth fluttered across from the sitting-room and came to rest on the mirror above the telephone. Grass was springing erect to conceal the dent in the lawn. The lampposts perspired. A moth, or something grey.

"Nice day," said the man at the first cottage. "Not so nice for the farmers," said his wife, and discussion ensued. Even if they could reach back to folk-tales, they weren't prepared to yield them up to Lloyd. He left the notebook and recorder in the car, near a Tudor church sheltering gargoyles with eroded faces, and began to climb a shattered path past wire-netting cages of clockwork hens. But in the askew hillside cottage, beneath a light-bulb which seemed sensitive to a personal gravity, all he could call forth was a ten-year-old pitchfork murder which he could have found in a dozen newspaper files. Perhaps his research had been discussed in a pub and rejected, or perhaps there was no more material to retrieve. So long as Anthea realized that he'd done his best.

Dabbing milk from his lips, he picked up the receiver and stared blankly at the blank wall. Moth and mirror had vanished. Surely he'd locked the front door. Yes, of course he had. He pushed open the sitting-room door and the furniture lit up with what light wasn't lost to the walls; over the mantelpiece hung only a rectangle of unreflecting wallpaper. If this is village pilfering it's another yardstick of their intelligence, Lloyd thought angrily. He crossed to the window to examine the fastenings; within the pane the furniture hung isolated in the darkness. He turned uneasily; he'd been brushed by the thought that now he couldn't see behind him. Not that it mattered. He peered into the bathroom; the mirror was still peeling with steam from his bath. The wings of the dressing-table mirror were closed across its face, and refused to give way. He shook at them and wrenched. Suddenly they sprang open, crashed back against the wall, and his helpless reflection exploded and collapsed into an avalanche of glass.

Anthea answered the phone on the third pulse. "How's the field trip?" she asked.

"Reasonably successful. But of course the recorder's broken down. I've taken it for repair."

"That's a pity. Can't be helped, I suppose. How are you managing generally?"

"Perfectly well. The house is in shape."

"I managed to get out of the Head of Philology's dinner date this time."

"Well, that's encouraging. Anthea? Are you still there?"

"Yes, I'm still here. Is someone there with you?"

"Not that I know of."

"It must be the operator. Anyway, we'd better not accumulate a phone bill just yet. Oh, Lloyd, if you're not having much success with the natives, I'll take over the difficult ones at the weekend. I'm missing you." She sounded a little surprised. "Ring me tomorrow," she said.

He unhooked the microphone from his ear and carried the tape-recorder upstairs. But his voice was louder than Anthea's, and the second time he played back their conversation he could hear only what he might have said. Besides, he must have omitted to erase; in the

ASH

background the anonymous woman's voice of last night muttered obsessively, sometimes coming close, almost shouting Anthea down, but still incomprehensible. He switched off the recorder and fell asleep.

Next morning he checked the doors and windows before breakfast. They hadn't betrayed him, and the only hint of activity in the house was a flight of scraps of ash which fluttered toward him as he opened the sitting-room door. On an impulse he descended into the cellar, but the only door other than that through which he'd entered was the door of the furnace. In any case, if anyone had entered through the cellar they would have been wary of the clatter of the scattered coal yet might well have tripped over one especially large piece just beneath the furnace door.

As he pried eggs loose from the pan he heard the click of the letterbox. A letter from Anthea, perhaps. He slid the eggs onto a plate and hurried into the hall. Before he reached the hall, however, an odd thought troubled him: he couldn't remember having heard the letter strike the mat. He peered at the sliver of light which was trying to slip beneath the door. But except for a few flurried flakes of ash which had drifted from the sitting-room, the hall was empty. Lloyd returned to the kitchen, catching at thoughts. Perhaps, on the point of delivering the morning paper, someone had realized that he'd shown no interest. Wait a minute, though; wasn't the paper a weekly? It might have been, but he couldn't find his copy in the house.

The day proved unsuccessful. Few cottages were roused by his knock, and those few offered only tales of someone else who'd seen a headless horseman. Late in the afternoon the recorder choked to death on a fragment of ash. Lloyd parked the car and walked back to the house. In the hall a light was extinguished—drew back, rather, as he overtook the reflection of the streetlamp. He wondered whether Anthea would drive down on Friday night or on Saturday morning.

Well, he could ask, he didn't have to seem too eager.

He twisted the key in the lock and turned the doorknob. Halfway, it tried to turn back beneath his fingers, as if on the other side a weak child were playing a feeble joke. Irritated, he wrenched the door open. He must remember to oil the mechanism.

Though the telephone was stubborn, he finally reached Anthea. "First of all, when are you coming down?" he asked.

"Hello?" she said.

"Hello. When are you coming down?"

"Who is this?" Anthea demanded.

Lloyd sneezed, and the ash retreated. "Well, it's not the Head of Philology," he said.

"Listen," Anthea said, her voice cold as the receiver. "I don't know who you are or what you want, but I don't believe a word of it. I obviously know Lloyd a great deal better than you do, which I suspect is not at all."

"Anthea?" Lloyd pleaded, beating off the ash which swarmed about his face like flies.

"Go to hell!" Anthea shouted, and was gone.

When he set the receiver down at last, cursing village telephone exchanges and village bigots, Lloyd realized that he had to know where the ash was coming from. He had never lit a fire; he'd thought that the removal-men had produced the ash in the sitting-room grate. But when he examined the grate he found no sign of a new fire; only the trail of restless ash toward the door and, lying palm down and crawling with ash near the grate, the ancient marble hand from the mantelpiece. He was sorry that it hadn't broken when it fell. After he'd searched the house twice for smoke, he persuaded himself to go to bed. At least the bedroom was free of ash, except for one shred which must have clung to his cheek and now had settled on the pillow. In the last muffled minute before sleep he thought he heard the dull clang of a metal door, distant enough to be outside the house.

ASH

He couldn't remember what the dream had been. Twice he had awakened, coughing away a glimpse of something dark that rolled toward him. When he returned from the bathroom, his hand came away black from the bedroom doorknob. He ate breakfast slowly, dovetailing thoughts. Then he made his way to the corner shop.

"Yes, once she left him he turned out to be as bad," the shopkeeper said, blotting an incontinent cup of tea with a newspaper. "No thought for others at all, he hadn't. Two days after she went he was burning things in the furnace. Her stuff, I suppose. We couldn't stand the smell, do you remember?"

"You're right there," said the newcomer, unannounced by the mute bell. "You and me and Tom went round and told him about it. He was sorry enough, I'll say that for him. Even if he did keep it burning half the night. And the next day, he'd gone."

"Yes," Lloyd said. "He would have."

"Sad," the newcomer said, stamping cracked mud from his colorless boots. "A sad house. You'll be all right, anyway. I see your friend's arrived."

Lloyd surged with relief, then with anxiety. "You mean she's up there waiting?"

"Waiting? No, I mean she's inside."

"Inside the house," Lloyd said dully, touching the only key to the house. "What did you see?"

"Nothing I shouldn't ought to have. The postman put a letter through the box, see, but she must have pushed it out by mistake, because she waited a bit and opened the door and took the letter in. Don't worry, I didn't see anything I shouldn't. Only her hand, and anyway she was wearing black gloves."

"I'm glad of that," Lloyd said, backing toward the door. But he had to be sure. "Thank you for the newspaper," he told the shopkeeper.

"No, no, don't think of it. I'll put you down for next week's if you like."

171

"I don't know if I'll be here that long," Lloyd said and emerged, breathing unevenly. Perhaps they'd delivered the copy he already had and at the last moment had realized—but he couldn't go in again to ask. He sat in the car, staring at the sun knifed by a Tudor gable, and finally drove around the village. No hotel, no rooms to let. In any case, he had to tell Anthea what he intended. But the only intact public telephone failed to reach her; the bell at her number was measured and relentless, and nobody else knew where she was. He could still drive back to Brichester and catch her before she left. It wouldn't take more than an hour. Then he imagined himself trying to explain. That was not the way to keep Anthea. He would wait for her outside the house.

In the afternoon he coaxed forth a folk-tale over the paralyzed tape-recorder. When he emerged from the cottage the sun was melting orange on the forested hills over which it was balanced. Anthea might be on her way. He drove fast; the tufted sun leapt, peered and fell back. Clouds of fire moved sluggishly in the windows of the house. Lloyd sat in the car at the end of the street opposite, and waited.

And when Anthea arrived, he would run across and tell her— what? Two stolen mirrors? No, he couldn't pretend he was playing detective. He took out the key and stared at it. The hand, the letter and the front door must have belonged to the next-door neighbor. He locked the car and entered the house.

In the kitchen he made coffee and set out another cup. He looked at his watch. Anthea must arrive soon. If she hadn't arrived by eleven he would sleep in the car. He stood up to make sure that all the lights were lit. The hall light blazed; the square of wall above the telephone was dull yet threatening; the dark scrap which hung from its corner must be torn wallpaper. The sitting-room furniture seemed darkened by the room, perhaps by dust. Or by ash; the floor was clean. Suddenly cold, Lloyd turned to leave, then whirled again. The marble hand was nowhere to be seen.

ASH

He began to hurry about the room, peering under chairs and into ill-defined corners. Then, in the cellar, the furnace door clanged.

Gripping the back of a chair, he strained his ears. At once he heard the soft dull exhalation of something thrown on a fire. Or perhaps it had been something charred and hollow cast out of the furnace. He moved through the cold intense light into the hall, and a car drew up outside.

It was Anthea, he knew. Almost he scampered to her. Almost, but he wasn't going to; he would deal with this himself. He inched open the cellar door and descended the first steps.

The light was on, but dim; ash clung to the bulb like insects on a rotting pear. The furnace door was shut; wings of shadow hung from the furnace, hiding the walls. At the bottom of the steps the floor and the coal were merged by darkness, but he could see fragments of coal coming alert with ash as the breeze of his descent brushed them. The garden implements were blurred in the corners. He hesitated on the last step; he should have left the cellar door open to draw in the light from the hall.

The cellar door opened.

He twisted about, teetering on the step. The door was opening stealthily; a bent strip of light probed into the cellar, throwing his stretched shadow across the coal, as far as the furnace door and one particularly large piece of coal. No, it wasn't a piece of coal; it was more like a charred football, rolling back and forth in a draft from the door, rolling at him as the ash rose swarming from the floor and the hall light went out.

Lloyd scrambled frantically up the steps, his nails catching at the stone. Something like brittle sand collected and piled on the back of his neck, on his arms. The dim choked light dragged him down, away from the black gap of the doorway. He reached the last three steps. The grey flakes were stinging his eyes, but he could make out that someone was hiding beyond the doorway, sneaking the shrivelled

173

marble hand around the door-frame and groping for the cellar switch.

At that moment the doorbell rang.

Purged of thought, Lloyd threw himself at whatever waited in the frame of darkness. There was nobody; he collided with the wall. Something fell to the floor by his feet. He kicked out and stumbled toward the front door. A soft mass gathered and hung in his path. He covered his face with one hand, choking, and clawed his way through; light fragments flew into his face like blind moths and settled on his cheeks. He threw open the front door and dragged it to behind him as Anthea began to speak.

When she saw his face, she ran to the car and helped him in. He gestured, coughing uncontrollably, and she drove through the flashing lines of streetlamps into the hills. She stopped the car far out in the massed dark. But Lloyd was brushing at his sleeves, his face, his hands, until blood began to trickle through the clinging flakes, and it was some time before he could speak. "One day I'll tell you what happened," he said at last, "but just now I want to be quiet."

"Where are we going?" she asked, subdued.

"Not back there. You're safe from that," he said. "To my flat. That's what I said. To my flat."

The Telephones

As Tim entered the pub the coin telephone rang once, an immediately realized wrong number. Briefly he thought of an assignation. He would have liked to have been telephoned among the businessmen behind their lunchtime tankards by a girl. He patted beads of sweat from his forehead and laid his hand for a moment on the bar, where its pattern of whorled ovals faded instantly from the pine. "I'm sorry, sir," the barmaid said. "I'm afraid I can't serve you."

"May I ask why not?"

"We're not allowed to serve anyone with long hair."

"I hardly think that's legal."

"Would you like to speak to the landlord?"

"I would, yes."

The landlord turned smiling, pulling hurriedly at his bow tie as if caught with an imperfectly wrapped gift. "I'm sorry, sir, I'm afraid it's a matter of policy."

"I don't think your license gives you that much leeway."

"There's a sign on the wall over there which entitles us to refuse admission."

Tim looked toward the sign and realized furiously that he need not have. Beneath it a businessman with an attaché case and a plate of ham rolls watched and grinned. "Yes, on reasonable grounds," Tim said.

"I'm sure you realize we have nothing against you personally. But if we served you we'd have all sorts of long-haired people coming in, causing a nuisance and taking drugs."

"I'm not one of your local trendies," Tim said. "I'm not likely to bring in hordes of ravening hash-heads."

"I'm sure you're not, sir. I'm very sorry."

"Suppose I go out and phone the police?"

"I'm afraid they'd laugh at you. They suggested that we instigate this ban."

"I see. Very well, I shall get in touch with my solicitor."

"As you wish, sir."

Tim turned to leave and halted. The businessman's grin was wider; it clamped on his tankard as beer poured down like foam from a factory outlet, it chewed a ham roll and an overlap of ham protruded from it like a ragged pressed tongue. Tim realized that his boots had also been slaughtered. He bent and pulling them off, kicked the boots toward the man. "Eat those as well," he said.

"You'd put anyone off their food with that hair of yours, wondering which you were."

Tim strode out. He reached the door and the telephone shrilled again, like a warning.

Emerging, he gasped. The businessman's complacent hatred had suffocated him like clinging fog. Tim's occasional telepathy was improving, whether thanks to or in spite of his efforts, although it functioned only for broad and often unpleasant concepts. In the pub invisible wet towels had seemed to drape his head. He glared at the front of the pub and tried to project an image of the businessman posturing in a ballerina's costume, but he could tell it wasn't taking; his telepathy seemed to be entirely one-way. At least it increased his sensitivity. He felt that was crucial, particularly nowadays.

He pulled off his socks and stuffed them into a waste-bin. A traffic warden frowned and looked away. Tim padded through the one o'clock crowds; on the pavement, hot and rough as sandpaper, toecaps nudged him; the crowd's thoughts drifted over him—happiness; an appointment, hurry, heart thumping and stomach sore; a hanged and mutilated murderer; depression; a bar full of perfumed men. If they were the crowd's, of course; he couldn't distinguish his own subconscious muttering. Suddenly he wanted to be somewhere he could allow his mind to reach out to beauty. Later he could phone Frank, who was a solicitor. He ran across a pedestrian crossing, black and white, burning and lukewarm, and caught a bus to the edge of Brichester. If society can't find a way to make you conform, he might have thought, it will crush your image of yourself. In fact he thought: just because I'm sensitive doesn't mean there's any doubt that I'm a man, I'll show you.

Beyond Brichester he began to walk up the Severnford road. There was a hospitable hotel several miles up, at the Berkeley intersection. For the first mile a pavement followed the road. Soil spilled from the grassy bank which bordered it, blackening Tim's soles and gritting warmly between his toes.

The hard blue sky was focused to display a sharp golden sun. Beneath, its light poured off the curves of cars, whose outlines wavered as they labored uphill over the bubbling tarmac. Dogs lolled from their windows, looking hopeless and hysterical as victims of a kidnapper; children were heaped in the back seats, scrambling over each other like a nest of spiders, staring at Tim. Exhaust fumes trickled through the grass and stained the sky. Nor do I need you, Tim thought, hopping to pull free a dry brown sliver of grass which had pierced his sole.

Ahead of him a girl in slacks trudged humped beneath a rucksack, buttocks and thumb protruding. Tim began to hurry, hobbling over gravel spilled from the driveway of a cottage. Perhaps he could offer to carry her rucksack. She was in danger. As he began to run, a fawn Mini drew close to her and stopped. The rear window was blocked by suitcases, perhaps of samples, but Tim saw a hand take her elbow as she climbed in beside the driver. Poor girl, Tim thought, and then: Frank would have taken her arm and her rucksack and escorted her.

He hurried on, trying to skim the pavement, which was hot as the stones of a fireplace.

Where the pavement disintegrated into brown earth and pebbles stood a telephone box. Tim called Frank's office, holding the callbox door open with one sole pressed against the glass, smooth and soothing as ice. But Frank was still at lunch. Tim consulted his watch; it was almost two o'clock. He stared along the pebbled vista, barbed with parched grass. Perhaps he should try to thumb a lift—the pub was more than an hour's walk ahead. Thumb a lift, poor girl. He stepped onto the baked cracked path, and the telephone rang.

When it had rung three times he picked up the receiver. "BRIchester 3109," he said.

"Who's that?" demanded a man's voice.

"This is a public callbox."

"I was expecting to find a boy there," the voice said despondently. "We were going to get together."

Tim leaned his head out of the box. Cars chased by; there was no house nor pedestrian in sight, nor anything against the sky except fields of taut bright grass. "There's nobody about, I'm afraid," he said.

"They never are when it comes to the point," the voice complained.

"He may be waiting where I can't see him. Maybe he's waiting for me to go. I tell you what; try again in five minutes."

"Wait," the voice said. "What are you doing at the moment?"

Tim's foot slipped from the pane; the door was closing lazily, inexorably. He kicked out and thrust it wide. "Just walking," he stammered.

"All on your own? You don't sound like a lonely boy. Do you drink alone?"

"Sometimes," Tim said.

"How awful. I know, you wait there and I'll come to you. You don't mind waiting for something worthwhile?"

"I must go. I'm sorry," Tim stammered. Explain, he thought. No need to be offensive. "I'm tired. I'm trying to thumb a lift," he said.

"You can give your thumb to the drivers," the voice said, "but keep the rest for me."

Tim slammed the receiver into place and fled. The pebbles struggled harshly underfoot like frightened insects; the grass whipped his ankles. Eventually he slowed, panting, his hair flopping wetly over his forehead. This can't have happened to me, he told himself. I'm a man.

He strode on, thumbing wildly. A jeep almost halted, until the driver glanced back at Tim's face and frowned in disappointment. A white Morris Minor paced him for a few seconds, then sped on. A breeze flowed between his fingers like water and ceased. He pressed forward, into the endless cushion of still air.

A few trees thrust from the border ahead, like cylinders of chocolate about to melt in the trembling distance. For a second Tim clenched; a tree could hide a man. Rubbish, he thought. You don't wait in ambush on a busy road like this. Someone would stop if they saw something wrong. Of course they would. If they saw a struggle. He glanced back over his ponderous outstretched arm at the headlong moist faces, intent on the bumper ahead. Besides, he thought, he wouldn't come after me when I reacted as I did. They're sensitive, everyone knows that. But his mind was shrinking away from a thought like a white-hot knife: if Tim were trapped he'd never know himself again. Vaguely he felt more afraid of the fear; to fear is to believe, to believe is to succumb. He stepped from the wrinkled earth to a grass path where insects dropped from grass-blades and squirmed underfoot.

He glanced at his watch. Half-past two, half a mile beyond the last time he'd looked. Perhaps if he stood in the path of a car, swore it was urgent— A white Morris Minor cruised by. That's the second, he thought. Suddenly he strained his eyes and made out the number. He hadn't noted the number of the first.

Then, around a tree ahead, he glimpsed the crimson corner of a telephone box. He stood still for a moment, then began to run. His feet slashed through the grass; emerging stones crushed his toes like hammers. He reached the box and wrenched open the door. There was no directory on the shelf. He slumped. The air from the box hung inert about him like the stale smoke in a train compartment. All at once he stared at the wall above the telephone. One glass frame displayed the number of a taxi-rank. He caught up the receiver. He opened his mouth and heard the voice.

"Teaser," it said. "You wouldn't admit to it, would you? You can't run fast. You can't tease and then run away."

The receiver fell like a noose and hung dangling in the suffocated box. Before it had stopped swinging Tim was five trees distant, sweating a liquid skin, heaving out gusts of harsh air. He felt something wrong with his mind, as if deep within a piece had jarred loose and were refusing to engage; as if, since he had tried to project his thoughts at the businessman, some function had been arrested. The world felt unreal.

Still fleeing, he twisted his head back over his shoulder. A sports car bright as a fairground carriage swung around a curve behind him. He leapt into the road, hands outstretched to push the car to a halt. The car drove at him, swerved across the road and a woman's voice screamed over the screaming wheels: "Get out of the way, you bloody pansy! Opt out if you want to but don't kill everyone else in the process!"

An image of a striking hand flew into his eyes. He stood watching the sports car shrink. He can't be in a car, Tim thought. He must be in a phone box. Perhaps the last one down the road. Or the next ahead, came the answer. Or he's phoning from wherever he lives. He could have found out the number of this box from the exchange, he could have deduced I'd decide to phone. A white Morris Minor passed on the other side of the road. Tim whirled. He didn't recognize the number-plate. But he could have changed it, he thought wildly. He hadn't thought to look at the driver.

For a moment Tim glanced back at the telephone box. He could phone the police. And tell them what? No, he thought, both he and I must hate the police. We're both persecuted. Momentarily he felt sympathetic. It was the man's right not to conform, after all. So long as he stayed away from Tim. He could have nothing to do with Tim.

A quarter of a mile further on Tim saw a figure striding toward him. The figure was precisely detailed as a manikin, yet the face eluded him. Instantly Tim realized how far he was from Brichester. His feet were raw as a racked throat. Between him and the figure stood a telephone box, blazing against banks of flowers, blossoms clustered like puffs of hot white smoke. Scents curled about Tim like pourings of stirred color; it occurred to him that this rich mixture would blot out any other perfume. He and the figure in the checked shirt had almost reached the telephone box. Tim stopped. The figure passed the box and strode toward him. The telephone rang.

Overwhelmingly relieved, Tim paced around the figure with no more than a glance. The threat had located itself. The insistent ringing faded behind him.

He thought: once I reach the Berkeley intersection I can get into the hotel. I can buy a meal if I have to; they're bound to provide that. Then I can ring for a taxi. If I can't get through on the public phone I'll say it's out of order; they must have a private phone somewhere. Phones do go out of order sometimes.

He froze. And phones do sometimes ring for a wrong number.

He looked back. The flowers hung exhausted into the sky; the figure had vanished. He had hardly glimpsed the face, but now he remembered that it had smiled. A casual greeting, perhaps, but now it crinkled into a significance which clung to the edge of Tim's mind. If the phone had rung innocently, if that was why the man had smiled— Once again he had the sense that the components of his mind were failing to engage. He plodded back toward the box, wading through the grass, staring blindly at the hectic cars. I didn't answer the ring. If it was him he'll try again. He knows I must be near. Shall I answer? My God, yes! he thought. Then I'll cut him off and ring the operator! She can tell me where he is, she can call a taxi!

He strode into the phone box, inhaling a sediment of scent. Flowers intruded on the panes like Victorian borders. Behind him in the grimy mirror, scribbled with relationships, the door closed. Immediately the phone rang.

Tim's fingers slipped from the receiver. As he captured it, he felt an indefinable movement in the depths of his mind, a meshing. "So you've decided to come round," the voice said.

"Come round where?" Almost Tim laughed, although his limbs trembled. "Where are you?" he said.

"You're still determined not to realize," the voice said. "I'm here. Here in the phone box."

Tim's eyes struggled. His gaze caught at the massed flowers, the empty fields, the long hot hard road. Then he met his own eyes in the mirror. His sly reflected mouth grinned.

He put out his hand to obscure his treacherous reflection, and touched not glass but flesh.

In the Shadows

The children were beginning to flood into the library when I saw the book. I'd written the tickets for the film show and the queue for them was squashing itself against the counter, pushing, elbowing, chattering. The branch librarian turned from her chat with a reader to glower. They were jostling for the first ticket, though they knew it wasn't a film show at all but only a strip of stills with a pompous script for one of them to read aloud, and though they must know as well as I did that long before the end they'd be loudly restless, when Sharon returned her book with an inadvertent crash on the counter. Its title lit up in my mind. PERFORMING SHADOWPLAYS, it said.

"Mrs. Sim," I said to the branch librarian (someone in the queue muttering Mississippi), "could I do a shadow show instead of the film? Maybe a ghost show, since it's nearly Hallowe'en? Nothing too disturbing, of course."

"So long as they don't disturb anyone else I don't care what you do."

Too many ideas were tumbling into my mind for me to bother about her tone. We used the far wall of the junior section for exhibitions of books and pictures, but we'd just taken the last one down and the wall was a blank white blackboard. Perfect, I thought, and I could use the film projector as the light source, use it to entertain the kids for once. I scribbled a GHOST SHOW notice and substituted it in the frame for the film show placard. Most of the queue cheered. Some of the old men dozing over newspapers in the main library looked up, frowning.

"I'm not coming for ghosts," Sharon said. "They're stupid." One or two agreed, but the others had crumpled their tickets within impregnable fists. "It starts in an hour so don't be late," I said. And I'd better get working on the props, I thought. I've lumbered myself there. But it's worth it. And at least I'm not stuck with my predecessor's choice of the city librarian's suggested children's shows.

I was cutting some of the cardboard backing from the exhibition into a shape I hoped would produce a turnip-face shadow, and the library doors were swinging to admit swathes of rain and the grumbling of balked traffic on the main road outside, and people were drumming their fingers on the counter as I tried not to cut within the outline, and the minute hand opposite me kept jerking two minutes ahead of the time it had been pretending it was. I looked up and saw Lorna and Diane watching me. "Come on now, you, out," I said.

Lorna gazed at me with blank dislike. "We'll be good," Diane said.

Then it'll be the first time, I thought. Even when they began simply by slouching and hiding their detested puberty beneath shapeless grey school uniforms, they'd always end by throwing books on the floor to make me chase them round the library and out. "What are you doing?" Lorna asked me.

"Cutting things ready for the show. These are to make shadows on that wall."

"Can we help?"

It was the first time I'd heard anything like enthusiasm from Lorna, but "Thanks," I said, "I think it'll be quicker if I do them."

"We can come to the show though, can't we?" Diane said.

"Are you quite sure you'll be good? Will you promise?"

"We'll be quiet," Lorna said. "We'll help you keep everybody quiet."

There was a scream of brakes outside, and another chopped-off scream. "Just keep your eye on those two," Mrs. Sim said loudly. "Yes, you two, you know what I'm talking about. We were always having trouble with them years ago, when I got this library. I used to take them home to their father every time. He was a docker and I'll tell you one thing," she called after the two girls, "he knew what to do with his muscles. No use you looking at me like that," she said to me. "It's all very well you feeling sorry for them, and I'm sure you would have then if you'd heard them scream, but you just prove to me that it did them any harm."

But I felt it was more important to make Debbie, who had just come in for her ticket, feel welcome. I was glad she'd come for a ticket, for it meant she was forgetting the death of her three-month-old sister several weeks ago, whose pram had fallen down the tower-block stairs. "They won't be real ghosts, will they?" she said.

"Wait and see." It looked as if my audience wouldn't be troubled by unbelievers, all of whom refused to let themselves be attracted by my notice. At least I wouldn't have to fight incredulity, I thought. Only honest criticism.

When I'd finished cutting out the turnip I gave in to my curiosity about the sound of brakes outside. "It was only a cat," one of the dissipating crowd told me, and there it was in the gutter, burst. I caught sight of Lorna and Diane slumped in the entrance to the alley next to the library. A foot behind them, the light from the street was sliced off clean by blackness. I thought sadly, they're probably as happy there as they can be now.

The show was due to begin at six. At five past nobody had arrived. I'd set up the projector on a table near the entrance foyer; drafts sneaked in when the doors swung. Orange light from the street leaked over the wall I would be using as a screen, but we had no curtains. I sat behind the counter, trying to flap a bat's wings without moving my thumbs which formed its head. "Perhaps we'll have some peace," Mrs. Sim said.

Even she was surprised a minute later when the kids came in, because we hadn't heard them coming. Diane was at the head of the line and Lorna trudged at the tail, and between them was an orderly schoolyard rank of seven younger children. I was glad to see Debbie among them. I smiled at any that looked at me, and one or two responded weakly. They took a chair each from the reading tables and sat down in a line facing the blank wall. I waited for them all to converge on me to talk as they always did. I waited for the holders of the remaining tickets to arrive.

Debbie was standing up. "Sit down and shut up. Remember what we told you," Lorna said.

I'd never seen her so enthusiastically involved in anything, let alone a role, but "It's all right," I called to Lorna. "Let her come."

"Don't interfere," Mrs. Sim said. "It's nice to see them behaving themselves for once. I think you'd better start."

"There's eleven kids still to come."

"It doesn't look as if they're coming. The ones you've got will be all the easier to control."

As I made for the junior section I felt a twinge of stage-fright. The kids I knew had suddenly merged into an aggressively impersonal entity: an audience. I'd forgotten my props and had to go back for them. I grabbed the cardboard box full of the cut-out figures and the bits I'd pruned from them, and threw it on the table beside the projector. Light slapped the wall in front of the children, and I snatched the shapes from the box and strode forward.

My tension was tightening. What made it worse was that I hadn't had time to prepare a story. I had to rely on whatever improvisation the props suggested. I sat in front of the wall, side on to the kids, and sent a bat flapping across the screen, my drooping fingers waving slowly. "It's Hallowe'en night," I said.

I had to watch what my hands were doing, which meant that I couldn't see the reactions of the audience, if any. Certainly I could hear none. I raised my hand shrouded with a handkerchief, shaking, wagging its head. I managed to summon forth a low hooting noise, suggestive of a quaking owl, to give it voice. I didn't know if it frightened the kids, but it didn't do anything for me, and I faded it out, blushing. .

As I picked up a skeleton puppet I sneaked a glance at the kids. Their heads were cut out of darkness by keen light. I couldn't see their faces. It was worse than the times I'd read them stories: then they had at least been visibly restless and I'd tried to adjust my pace and to anticipate the dull passages so I could paraphrase across them, but now it felt simply as if I were being drained by the silence. Their silence and their emotionless faces full of darkness were encouraging me to strain, and they were drinking up the efforts I made and giving nothing back. They were squeezing me dry. I wondered what on earth was the matter with them.

Nonsense, I thought, it's not with them at all. I'm just not reaching them. Try again. I lifted up the skeleton by the threads run through its palms. I hadn't had time to hinge its limbs, but at least it could dance, however stiffly. It dangled and jerked on the wall, skull nodding. This time I heard the kids stir audibly, but although I was looking at them I couldn't read their emotions, they were still masked by darkness. I glanced back at the skeleton and saw why they'd stirred.

When I'd grabbed the props from the box I must have bent them. I'd folded the skeleton's neck so badly that the skull was nodding forward at an angle, and because of the angle the shadow-skull looked as if it were dissolving. It was squashed and pulled down on one side, and it lolled as if its neck were broken: not funny at all. I pushed the skull back into place, but it flopped awry again. I hoped their stir had been of laughter, because for me it was as if blood had begun to spout in the midst of a Punch and Judy show; the skeleton looked altogether too dead.

Above the junior section the windows juddered, jangling faintly in their frame. Everyone, including me, looked up. A bus was revving throatily at the stop outside. I welcomed the distraction. I put down the skeleton and felt around beneath my chair for another prop. I was still fumbling when I heard them gasp. I turned and saw a face on the wall.

Though it was difficult to call it a face. It had a couple of eyes, one largely clogged by a tangle of something like web. Otherwise it had no features except the fragments that seemed to be peeling or sprouting from its surface. "I know what that is," I said, hurrying back to the projector. I'd seen that the draft through the foyer had toppled the box by the projector, and some of the prunings of cardboard had fallen into the beam. I swept the small tangled heap into the box.

The face stayed on the wall.

Adrenalin burned through me. I gazed about, looking for the source of the face. For a moment I suspected Lorna and Diane, but they were nowhere near the projector beam. Otherwise the space above the children's heads was empty of everything but light and the face, gazing out of the wall with its empty socket and its webbed eye.

Then the silence changed. Of course it wasn't silence, there was the sound of the throbbing bus which now was moving away, and that was the change I'd heard. When I looked at the wall the face had gone. Something outside, I thought with relief, a trick of the light from the bus. "I didn't make that one," I said, returning to my chair. "I wonder what it was."

And it was then, as the stupidity of my remark clunked home, that I realized that the tension which was sapping me wasn't mine at all, but theirs. I'd frightened them; that was why they were silent. They should have been responding audibly by now, favorably or not. "Well, that's enough ghosts," I said.

How could I round off the show reassuringly? I couldn't send them out into the night with terror behind their shoulders. "Those bats I showed you before," I said, remembering the idea I'd adapted from the book. "They were butterflies. See?" And I fluttered my hands against the wall. But somehow it wasn't a butterfly, it looked more like the feeble twitching of dying fingers.

It can't look like that to them, I thought. "And here's a dog," I said. His nose was my second and third fingers pressed together and held out straight, his eye was my first finger making a brow. His lower jaw was my little finger, which I tried to open and shut. But my straight fingers trembled uncontrollably and parted, and the dog's nose split open and gaped all the way back under the eye.

And their terror struck me as if the block of light had suddenly become solid. My mind had acknowledged their fear, but now I felt it: as if a swelling full of fear in my stomach had burst and flooded my whole body. I held myself still, not looking at anything, and the light levered its way into the side of my eye. I rummaged through my memories of the book, looking for a shadow that couldn't be frightening. I'd seen one somewhere. A pram. A pram, that's what I would make.

I remembered: clench the fingers of your left hand and press your thumb against the fist, bending back the thumb's tip; that's the pram and its handle. The kids were leaning forward to try to make out what I was doing. Hook the fingers of your right hand and let them overhang the other end of your left fist; there's the hood. One of the kids made a stifled sound. And your right thumb has only to peek over the fist and move about to be a baby. But I was having trouble with my baby, which seemed to be just a limbless object trying feebly to raise itself.

Still, I thought, they can see what it is. I was about to tell them anyway when I found myself gazing at the cut-out black oval that was Debbie's head, and realizing that I didn't have to. Because I'd remembered how her sister had died.

I think most of them knew why she was standing up, groping against the violent light, and those who didn't at least knew that something was badly wrong. The shape was peering facelessly over the side of the pram. It was flexing itself as if for a leap. Debbie's huge shadow was looming beside it, swaying. I pulled my hands apart and the baby fell from the wall, like a grub, and was lost in the darkness that carpeted the floor.

I ran to the projector and switched it off. I snatched at the switch for the overhead lights, whose illumination now looked thick and amber. "Well, that's it," I said and desperately, "I hope you enjoyed the show." They weren't crowding around me, pleading for more; they weren't even asking when the tickets for the next show would be ready. I couldn't blame them, but they were edging out of their chairs as if they couldn't believe they were really free, they were slamming the chairs back against the tables, they were running for the doors. But they hadn't reached the foyer when they halted, almost knocking down Debbie, who was staring beneath the last table.

By their faces it must be a spider, I thought. Lorna and Diane were tidying the replaced chairs. I crossed to the paralyzed group of children. They might have been miming fear. Perhaps they were, because all I could see from my side of the table was what might have been the shadow of a wiggling toe on the floor. Except that nobody was barefoot. I was squinting into the dimness when they saw me coming. The mime unfroze and they fled, almost knocking down an old woman in the foyer. There was nothing to be seen beneath the table. One of the kids must have been making the shadow. I thought wryly: that's justice, I suppose.

I returned to the counter, trying to fit the evening's events together. "You two were good for once," Mrs. Sim was saying to Lorna and Diane. "Just shows you can be when you try."

"Good? Not them two," the old woman shouted from the other counter. "You should have seen them before. Pushing children into that alley outside, they were. Her," she accused Diane, "she was telling them what would happen if her shadow touched them and the other one, she was back in the alley grabbing them and making them scream, pretending she was a shadow. Scared some of them off completely. Good my Aunt Fanny."

"But why should they do that?" I said, half knowing.

"To tell stories about you, that's why. Saying the man in the library showed her how to make shadows live. Saying you could do worse with yours if you wanted. They had a dead cat in the alley as well. Said she'd done that with her shadow."

"Get out," Mrs. Sim said, "or I'll call the police," and the old woman helped to chase them, snarling and brandishing her stick.

By the time I was able to leave the counter they'd gone, somewhere in the night with the swaying drizzle and the pasted litter and the peacock's-feather petrol. I wasn't looking for them; I shouldn't have known what to say. I was looking for the others. Eventually I saw Debbie and three others on the next block, waiting for their mothers beneath the awning of the Bingo hall. I had almost reached them before they saw me, but when they did they darted into the traffic, slipping on the wet tarmac, and stood on the other pavement until I'd gone back to the library. I haven't seen them since, nor the rest of the audience. They don't often use the library now, and never when I'm there.

When I reached the counter I saw a dark shape about the size of my thumb squirming across the floor behind Mrs. Sim. I trod on it and felt it give way with a slight crack and flatten softly. But when I looked there was nothing there.

Horror House of Blood

"Listen, I'm really sorry to bother you like this," the young man at the door said. "My name's David Lloyd and I'm a film director."

Marilyn drew back her foot, which she'd poised to kick should he try to stop the door. "You've been filming up the street," she said.

"Right, that's me. You've been watching us, right?"

"No, but you can't avoid being gossiped at in the shops round here. Anyway, come in, you're standing in a draft. I'm afraid you'll have to take us as you find us."

Lloyd surveyed the interior beyond the short entrance hall like an airlock: one large room reduced to an L by a partitioned-off kitchen; two settees surrounded by collages of Sunday newspaper sections; a man of about thirty with a chubby pink just-shaved face and a dressing-gown, rising to his feet and swinging up his hand; a dining area next to the kitchen, a table and chairs of plain pale wood; a staircase leading up the pale blue wall on Lloyd's right to a landing and a door. "Knockout," Lloyd said.

"I'm Frank Taylor and this is my wife Marilyn," the man said. "And you're a film director? Quiet on the set for Mr. Hitchcock, that sort of thing?"

"Right, that sort of thing. Not quite that big a name yet, maybe. In fact, that's what I want to talk to you about."

"If you're looking for extras I'm always telling Marilyn she should be in the movies. Go on, do 'Come up and see me sometime' for him. Well, maybe it's a bit early in the day. But you'd swear Mae West was in the room."

"Right on. It's not extras, actually, let me tell you what it is. This is my first film, right, and it just could be in line for a festival. I've got some money in it and so have some other people. We had budget problems but we thought we'd cracked them by shooting on location in the suburbs, right. Some friends of mine lived up your street here and we were using their house. But they got an offer in America and they just pissed off, sorry, you don't mind, good, they just pissed off after selling the house to these other people who won't let us film there. So zap, no film."

"All your work wasted," Marilyn said.

"A lot of people's six weeks wasted. I mean, you can understand that, Mr. Taylor, Frank, right on, call me Dave. So I don't have to tell you what's on my mind, you can see right through me. We're trying to duplicate the interior we were using and this is just knockout. Exactly the same. Not that you haven't done a lot with it, I mean you can tell it's your house and nobody else's. I'm just no good with words, you can tell that, right? But I want to believe I'm good with visuals. I really think I am. And by Christ I want those stairs."

"What were you thinking of doing with them?" Marilyn said.

"Can I show you?" Lloyd began to pace up the stairs, squinting through a rectangle of his fingers, swaying his head and fingers and body in slow complex syncopation. "It's just the suspense scenes we have to shoot. A lot of this film takes place on the stairs, it saves money and makes for claustrophobia. The paint's the wrong color but that's okay, we'll be shooting monochrome with a filter. Now here I am tracking up the stairs, I'm the camera, right, I'm swaying a bit toward the wall so it feels as if it's closing in, I'm tracking in on the door, it's almost filling the screen and slowly, slowly, it opens—"

Slowly the door opened.

"It doesn't do that," Marilyn said.

"Yes, it has been," Frank said. "Last week it did, I forgot to tell you. I'll have to fix it."

"Well, we'll have someone inside to move it when we're shooting," Lloyd said. "But that shows you the sort of thing we'll be doing. We won't damage anything, I mean we won't even touch anything. And three days at the outside to pack up and go. I don't know what else to say except, you know, I'd be incredibly grateful."

"I don't see why not, do you?" Frank said.

"Not really, I suppose," Marilyn said. "Only it's a pity you won't be here. Don't expect a technical analysis every night when you come home."

"I only wish we could pay you, I mean except for the electricity," Lloyd said. "That's why the rest of the people we tried wouldn't have us. Anyway, listen, Mrs. Taylor, we won't be asking for anything, even bring our own flasks of coffee. Maybe we can take you out to lunch one day. Make a change from the housework, I mean, we guys don't know what it is to work."

"The boutique where I worked has closed," Marilyn said. "I'm just straightening things before I apply for another job."

"Looks like you've given us a wardrobe mistress, Frank," Lloyd said. "See you tomorrow, Mrs. Taylor, on the set of *Horror House of Blood*. Look, that door's rehearsing again."

When Frank arrived home on Tuesday night he found Marilyn hugging herself on the front lawn. "Have they thrown you out?"

"No, I'm standing guard so you don't spoil their film. That, and I've seen all I can stand."

"Yesterday you were fascinated."

"With the mechanics of it. It's the people I can't bear."

"The cast or the characters?"

"I can't tell. Perhaps both. Your friend Lloyd is an insufferable pig and his wife, if that's what she is in real life, is so meek it's terrifying. I can't see the point, but I know I don't like being in there with it. I don't care if it is only a film, it isn't pleasant to have two strangers in your home goading each other to violence by being what they are, and you not knowing what's going to happen."

"I think we're being invited in," Frank said. "David, would you and your wife like a cup of tea?"

"Love one," Lloyd said. "My wife's making dinner for the crew so you must excuse her. Listen, Frank, I'm sorry to be in your way when you come home. We've had to wedge your bedroom door because it's not cued to open yet, and I moved the phone behind the settee."

"Don't worry about it. I tell you what, though, we wouldn't mind hearing what the film is about. Only it's been disturbing my wife a bit in the wrong way, hasn't it, Marilyn. Not understanding, if you see what I mean."

"Right on. We've only got one more scene to shoot, Mrs. Taylor, so we won't be in your way after tomorrow. I mean, you've been fantastic, but I know you've got things to do. Let me tell you about this scene. I'm the husband, right, and I'm cracking up because my wife's possessed by this thing. She keeps becoming a real maniac, you know, violent, lots of aggro. So I go upstairs to her with a knife in case I need it. Then I hear her calling out and she sounds okay, so I leave the knife on the stairs. I go in and you hear us talking. You're staring at this door, right, your bedroom door, it's hanging there, it's all you can see, you know something's going to happen, the voices stop and there's dead silence, everything's still and it's like waiting for a snake to strike. Then you see her eyes, right? Straight cut in to closeup, these absolutely mad eyes—"

"Sorry to interrupt," Frank said, "but if I understand what you're trying to do, wouldn't it be better to have it as a dinner scene? With her picking up a knife from the table and stabbing him, if that was your idea? I was just thinking that anyone who wouldn't accept the possession idea would go along with the wife losing her self-control. Right?"

"That's not bad," Lloyd said, peering between the treads of the stairs at the table. "That's good," gliding across the room and circling the table. "That's knockout!" zooming his face in on a knife. "Thing is, we've got the stairs now, and if we shifted to the table we'd have to reshoot some of the stuff in the can. And we could have done a lot with this fantastic low ceiling. Christ, what a film we could make if we had money."

"Yet you still expect it to be a success?" Marilyn said.

"I don't book films. It could make a second feature or it could make a festival where they like this sort of thing. It'll get me more work, that's where it's at. I'm sure you understand that, Frank."

When he'd left Marilyn pulled out the wedge from the bedroom door. She stood on the landing for some minutes, watching the hanging dormant wood and the immobile surrounding crack.

Marilyn was pulling out the dressing-table drawers and smiling at the hidden treasures in the corners—a cuff-link, two Christmas cards left over from ten months ago, a plastic pawn—when she heard Lloyd downstairs saying "Yes, that might do. Christ, perfect!" She heard the stairs creak as he padded upward. She tensed, preparing a cold smile in case he should open the door. Then she giggled and turning her back to the door, pulled up her skirt and mimed dressing. But the creaks receded. Curious and determined not to talk herself out of it, she opened the door.

They'd switched off their lamps. She had gone upstairs partly to rest her eyes and her brain, for each time they switched off the glare the room and stairs looked dim and unreal, like a fading photograph, and she resented having to spend energy in adjusting. Lloyd and his cameraman were sandwiching the continuity girl on the couch, passing the script back and forth and scribbling on it with marker pens. Lloyd's wife was staring out of the window at a woman cleaning her car. The continuity girl's eyes met Marilyn's through the gesticulations on the couch. Marilyn smiled in sympathy with her expression, then almost tripped on a knife on the stairs.

It was her little sharp kitchen knife, scratched and discolored but still clean, which she used for cutting vegetables. One day her mother had let her use it, and that was the day she'd started to learn cookery. She remembered the warmth of the kitchen and the windows blurring, her mother laughing as Marilyn prised the knife from her fingers and her silent eye-corner supervision as Marilyn chopped the carrots, the single wind-troubled rose that swelled and dwindled on the blurred window like a red stain, and the almost inaudible hum as the coffin slid into the crematorium. "Who put this here?" she demanded.

"I did. It's for this last scene," Lloyd said. "I'm sorry, we didn't hear you coming down."

"This is my knife."

"Yes, but I mean you don't use it, do you? Really? Right, sorry. I'll tell you what it is. You know in horror films knives always look brand new, like it was an advertising film for steel or something. We want something nastier than that, something that looks real, a bit rusty and jagged, you know. It really would be a help if we could use it. Critics might, I know you can't predict critics any more than audiences, but they might think it was imaginative. I mean, imaginative details can add up to a good review."

Lloyd backed out of the bedroom and down the stairs, his whole body focused on an attempt to snatch up the knife before his wife caught sight of it. As he descended slowly, groping with his foot for the next step, his body began to stoop toward his right hand as if a weight were dragging it down. Then his wife's hand flew out and had the knife. She reared above him and stabbed. "Don't poke with it!" Lloyd shouted, his back to the camera. "Slice, you stupid bitch, slice! Imagine slicing off lumps of flesh with it! Imagine chopping slices off my cock!"

He plodded to the bottom of the stairs, mopping his forehead. "Jesus," he said. "Right, let's do it for real."

"I'm sorry, you mustn't use that," Marilyn said. "It's very sharp and you might have an accident."

"Oh come on. It's not coming anywhere near me. We'll be filming all the spouting blood next week."

"I'm sorry," Marilyn said.

"Wait five minutes," Lloyd said to his crew, and hurried out. Marilyn glanced round at them, but they avoided her eyes. Only Lloyd's wife met them for a moment. On the stairs as she'd tried to master the knife Marilyn had seemed to see a tiny fear scuttling inside her eyes, trying to hide and at the same time trying to escape. Now her eyes were as clear and blank as her skin and her dazzling silver hair. Marilyn looked away and stared at herself in the mirror, at the wrinkles around her eyes and mouth that Frank said smiled when she smiled.

Less than five minutes later the telephone rang. It was Frank. "Look, what on earth's the problem?" he said. "They aren't going to kill each other just for a film."

"There's more to it than that," Marilyn said. "I don't want it in my house."

"I'd say that was a tribute to the film. Anyway, look, I was halfway through programming and it doesn't help to be interrupted. It's not as if they've just barged in, after all. I told them they could film and I don't think there's any reason to go back on that. And listen, he didn't have to go out to phone. For heaven's sake be a bit more hospitable."

When Lloyd returned he didn't look at her. "Go on and remember, make it real," he told his wife. As he replaced the knife on the stairs the lamps blazed and glinted dully on the blade. Marilyn felt as if she were in a bunker in the desert, but she restrained herself from making for the kitchen. An urge recurred to snatch the knife and return it to the kitchen, but instead she snorted at herself and sat in a chair against the mantelpiece. "You won't mind if I watch, will you," she said.

"Right on. See how it grabs you." Lloyd was ascending the stairs slowly, hesitantly, listening to an absent voice and nodding and smiling, his face turned slightly to the camera that loomed at his back.

He mimed planting the knife and the camera stooped to look at it. Marilyn heard the stairs creak long and deliberately beneath the camera's weight. They'd said it wasn't as heavy as it looked. She almost rose to her feet, then pressed her ankles together to restrain herself.

Lloyd had entered the bedroom. The camera was staring at the door. As it began to retreat, the cameraman's foot feeling for the edge of the stair, the stair emitting a prolonged throbbing creak, Marilyn heard Lloyd's voice beyond the door. "Let's see you do one good scene, right? I may not be Paul Newman but you sure as shit aren't Joanne Woodward. Now you grab that knife and cut great gobs of flesh out of me. Enjoy it, right?"

Slowly, slowly, the door opened. Lloyd emerged backwards like an insect from a hole, as if desperate for the moment at which he could turn and flee. One foot slipped on the edge of the staircase and his hand swung out, fingers frantic as the legs of an impaled spider. He slid his hand down the banister and then without warning ran down and made a grab for the knife.

His wife was quicker. She had the handle as he grasped the knife, and his fingers closed on the blade. His wife let go, and Marilyn cried out, for his hand came up with the blade still hanging from the folded cuts in his fingers. "Now then, real blood!" he shouted. "You felt it, right, like slicing butter! Go on, you stupid cow, you're over the shock, you're mad! Get the knife and slice, slice!" Then he fell back, his hand slithering down the wall in a trail of blood as she went to work on him.

"Get a sponge for the wall," Lloyd said to his wife, running water over his fingers. "That was knockout," he said. "Absolutely real."

As soon as Frank had closed the front door he said "I'm sorry. I shouldn't have left you to put up with them by yourself."

"I think I managed perfectly well," Marilyn said.

Later they massaged each other before making love. His arms sometimes grew tense at the computer keyboard, and she freed them. Her neck and shoulders felt like a single plate of metal now the day had accumulated, although she understated this, not wanting it to seem a reproachful symbol or a further turn in the knot of half-felt but unspoken argument. Suddenly, as he kneaded her shoulders, she was moist and wide. For a moment she felt betrayed by her body, then she knelt forward and speared herself on him. At first his movements were slow and caressing, but as they continued he raised his thighs from the bed and thrust as if to impale her helpless. He must have read the plea in her eyes not to turn her beneath him.

As they lay touching, their breath easing, they heard a creak on the stairs so loud as to be almost an explosion. Marilyn started, then ran to open the door. As she did so the top stair creaked back into shape. "It was the camera," she said. "All that weight, the stairs couldn't take it. Poor stairs." She hurried into the bathroom and wiped herself. When she lay down beside him again she said "Frank, did that door really open before they came?"

"Yes," he said slipping an arm beneath her neck and stroking her cheek.

"Really?"

"Yes, of course."

"Really?"

"No, damn it! I don't know why I bothered trying to reassure you. It's you who have to stay at home with it."

She propped herself above him. "But what am I supposed to be frightened of?" she said.

Next morning at breakfast she said "We haven't had a party for a while." Since Lloyd and his crew had left the house felt like a vacuum, and all her reservations about the house returned: its anonymity, its oppressiveness, the sense of being threatened by a kind of middle-class commune where the front door was open to everyone else and their trivia. It's near London, she told herself. That's important.

They managed to call the party for Saturday. Marilyn was surprised how many people were free. Perhaps they were trying to ignore the suburbs too, she thought. She showed the latest arrivals where to throw their coats on the bed. Someone was already vomiting in the bathroom. It's going to be a good party, she thought.

Some of Frank's colleagues had congregated in the kitchen around the makeshift bar. "Oh, that old sod," one said. "Have you seen him since he came back from holiday? He's got himself a hairpiece. Either that or he's been sticking his head in a dungheap."

Frank picked his way upstairs through guests sitting on the staircase. A few were perched on the side of the bath. "Listen, you can use our bedroom," he said. "There's room in there even with all the coats."

Marilyn passed a group of wives carefully poised on the edge of a settee, blowing out thin cones of smoke with a chorus of soft pops, and joined a poker game. "This is a hard school," one of the men said. "All right," Marilyn said, and won three pounds.

She went upstairs, patting her way among the heads and shoulders. She hadn't realized so many people would bring so many people. In the spare bedroom they were sitting shoulder to shoulder against the wall. Her and Frank's bedroom door was open, but the room was empty. She leaned into the spare room and said to whomever she was looking at "There's a room next door as well."

"Oh no, not me," the girl said. "Try someone else."

Descending the stairs was like groping her way down a strewn hill in a mist. There was a ceiling of tobacco-smoke halfway down. Marilyn coughed and nearly tripped, falling against the shoulders of a man who kneed the woman below him, and so on down the stairs. There were laughs and howls of protest.

"Listen, everyone," Frank said. "If we could shift some of you into our bedroom it would make things a good deal easier."

There was a silence. Then a friend of a friend said "If that's a joke it's in appalling taste. Can we have our coats, please."

When he'd gone, taking with him half-a-dozen others and any hint of an explanation, the party seemed to arrange itself more comfortably. Corks popped and conversation welled. The subject of the bedroom sank at once and seemed not worth the rescuing. Nobody entered the room except to retrieve coats.

Swaying upstairs after turning out the downstairs lights, Frank found Marilyn standing outside their bedroom. "Shall I carry you across the threshold?" he said, steadying himself against the doorframe.

She saw herself caught up and borne into the darkness. "No thanks, you only just managed it the first time," she said laughing, and groped beyond his shoulder for the bedroom light-switch. She felt her fingers almost touching the darkness. Then Frank sagged into the dark bedroom, taking her with him. A great gasp rushed into her, pummelling her chest. As she levered herself up from him she felt his body trembling. He was choking back laughter.

"Did you do that on purpose?" she demanded.

"Of course not," he said, roaring with laughter.

She lay in bed with darkness pressing on her open eyes. Just before she awoke the pressure of her eyelids built up a blaze of crimson. Then she was tiptoeing toward the bedroom. As she opened the door cautiously she leapt up from the bed, and her eyes were pools of blood.

On Sunday afternoon they walked in the nearby park. They walked until night and heavy rain began to fall. Marilyn ran to shelter beneath the awning of a deserted kiosk. The rain swung toward them, forcing water through their clothes, and then away. "I wish you hadn't hired out the house," she said.

"They had to get the film in the can somewhere."

"They had to what?" she said, peering at his lips.

"They had to make their film, right?"

At his last word she peered closer. His mind slipped out of synchronization, and his lips continued moving for a moment without words. "Oh come on," he said.

"It's not going to be the same."

"Don't tell me about it. You're capable of dealing with it yourself, you said so. If you don't need protecting, fair enough. It's a good job I didn't marry you for that, that's all."

She stared at his lips as he spoke. Because his shadow lay across her he couldn't see her eyes.

On Thursday afternoon he telephoned her. "I just thought you'd like to know that those notes I asked you to put in my trousers pocket last night aren't there."

"You're right. They were on the bedroom floor. You must have dropped them."

"Then it must have been the way you hung my trousers."

"Perhaps it was. I was just about to ring you, if we can talk about something else now. There's something here."

"Look, you don't want me to come home, do you? I've got two minutes to conference. Come up here if you must."

"Please don't disturb yourself. It's nothing I can't deal with."

"On your showing with those notes I'd tend to wonder."

"Well, I'll have to try to improve. I should be able to take care of my own house, shouldn't I. After all, my place is in the home."

"Not necessarily. Not without efficiency."

At the door of the conference room he turned and rang the switchboard. "If my wife calls, call me," he said. Later, as he drove home, a frown kept shadowing his vision. I mustn't expect too much of her, he thought. After all, I'm three years older. I shouldn't be upsetting her except as a last resort. That's not what I'm for.

He pulled down the garage door and hurried along the path through the gardens, which most resembled a few scraps of green velvet among which were stuck lamps like white-headed pins. As he neared the back door his fist, raised to knock, sank. Through the frosted-glass panel of the door he could see on the white walls of the kitchen great blurs of dull crimson. A crimson trickle had seeped beneath the door and down the step.

He was stooping and almost touching the trickle with his fingers, while his mind tried to prepare itself to enter the house, when a pale blur opened the back door. It was Marilyn. She looked almost as if she were sleepwalking. "Mind where you walk," she said. "There's broken glass."

Indeed there was, and some of it still bore fragments of the ketchup label. "Why?" Frank said. "Don't answer that, I'm being stupid."

"Perhaps you are," she said, opening a cupboard and removing a mop and sponges.

"I'll do that. You sit down."

"No. After all, it's my job."

He took her arm gently and having led her to the settee, poured her a whisky. When he'd finished cleaning the kitchen she hadn't touched the drink. He'd counted the labels as he cleared up: at least four bottles. It seemed odd to him that she should have bought so many simply in order to express her frustration.

"Why did you buy so much ketchup?" he said, trying to trivialize.

"It's better than real blood, isn't it?" she said and then smiled sadly at him and frowned, hesitating. "To try to get it over with," she said.

On Friday night he was smiling behind a bouquet. He was happy to be home, to be with Marilyn all weekend: perhaps they could talk. A dull crusted trail of crimson hung down the back step. Must clean that, he thought.

Marilyn was cooking, but she turned and hugged him when she saw the flowers. "We've got a vase somewhere. I'll find it," he said. He found it beneath the sink. As he straightened up he saw the handle of a knife protruding from the kitchen bin. It was the small knife Marilyn used for chopping vegetables, its blade broken.

"Did you break this today?" he said.

"Yes, I broke it."

"I'll buy you another tomorrow."

"No. No thanks, I don't want one."

He arranged the flowers in the glass vase and stood it on the table. As he did so he caught sight of his hand refracted through the water, his fingers broken and warped. He pulled his hand away and glimpsed the knife hanging from the fingers, which were cut half through. They felt cold from the metal and exposure to the air that wedged itself icily into the gashes, yet warm with the blood that pumped up. The raw flesh and nerves seemed to be tasting the metal, for the cold flavor somehow seeped into his brain without relating to his tongue.

He had time to dread moving his hand in case the fingers flopped back against the knuckles before the moment passed. She's infecting me, he thought. No, that's unfair, it's a hangover from the film. That's right, that was the knife David Lloyd was going to use in the film. I wonder what he did with it exactly. We'll have to wait and see the film. I hope it's soon. I'd like to see what he's made of our house. Although perhaps I'd better make sure it doesn't catch me in this sort of susceptible mood.

"Will you cut this for me?" Marilyn called.

She pointed to a French loaf on the bread-board. Suddenly he realized that she'd asked him to cut several things in the past few days: string, vegetables, meat. And the meals she'd made tended to involve little chopping and cutting. The only knives she used were the blunt saw-edged table knives. He frowned.

"I know it's my job," she said.

"Well, it is really."

"Perhaps I'll be better in a few days," she said. He saw her hands were shaking.

"Don't worry," he said. Her gaze sought his lips. He turned toward the bread-board, away from her, and tried to think of an approach to the subject that didn't sound like a cliché. There was no use in beginning with alienation. But he couldn't produce an opening, and while he was pondering he saw her reflected dimly in the glass doors of a cupboard. Her hands were calm. Turning suddenly, he said "It's tension, we'll crack it," and saw her swiftly begin trembling her hands in evidence. Well, he thought, she's saying she needs me to protect her. That's what I've been saying all along, but out loud.

"I know what the tension is," he said. "Now listen and don't argue. It wasn't the film, it was you working. I could see it building up. Now you've given up work you don't know what to do with yourself. I tell you what I'll do. I'll come home for lunch every day. Then you won't have any excuse to get bored with the house. I think you feel it's still a bit unfamiliar, more than I do. But it is your house, you know, Marilyn. More even than mine. It's yours and you're stuck with it."

She was staring at the kitchen bin. He reached out to make her look up at him, but didn't touch her; she might simply withdraw further. "Now look, you know I'm right," he said. "Just think a bit and you'll see I am."

He sat down on one of the settees. A wedge of light from the front window fell across him. He felt spotlighted, held on a stage by the light. He heard Marilyn stirring soup, the unhurried purr of a mower on a lawn, a group of boys bouncing a football toward the nearby field. He felt the tensions of the day begin to seep out of him. Everything was all right, he thought, essentially.

A tongue of newspaper thrust through the letterbox, clacking then plopping to the floor. Frank shifted on the settee; he'd get the paper in a minute. Then he heard Marilyn moving behind him, near the stairs. "It's all right, don't bother," he said. "I'll get it." He glanced around to smile. Marilyn was not behind him.

For a retarded moment, during which the light seemed to solidify about him, he had the irrational conviction that she was hiding below the back of the settee. He couldn't stop himself from looking to see. "I thought you'd come out of the kitchen," he called, picking up the newspaper. "Can't imagine why I'd think that."

He'd found an item in the newspaper that made him laugh and was rephrasing it in the terms he felt would amuse her most when his ears began to throb. His blood was thumping them like a shoulder against a door. All at once the sounds around him were snatched away, leaving him suspended in silence. He looked up, glaring. No, the sounds were there, but annoyingly muffled. He poked at his ears, swallowing. They felt as if a vacuum were pulling at them, he thought, and something was tugging at his nerves. He flapped the newspaper at himself angrily, tense, distracted. The light isolated him on its stage.

He'd smoothed out the paper again and was relaxing when he heard a vague muffled sound behind him, rolling down the stairs. More than anything else the muffled quality annoyed him, as if a projectionist had neglected to turn up the sound. What's she doing now? he thought irritably. He turned round, and saw Marilyn in the kitchen, quickly nipping hot plates. But as he turned back to his reading he realized the edge of his eye or of his mind had retained another glimpse, of a red shape coming to rest at the foot of the stairs.

What have we got that's red? he thought, folding a page over. Red? he thought, trying to concentrate on the editorial, denying himself the relief of turning to look. Red? We haven't *got* anything that's red, he thought. "For God's sake!" he shouted, flinging down the newspaper and striding to the stairs.

There was nothing. Marilyn had run from the kitchen and was staring at him. "It's all right, it's all right," he said, gesturing her away. "It's nothing." She was still staring at him. "Nothing!" he shouted, frowning at her. He started upstairs. "Just off to the loo," he called to placate her, a motive he didn't bother to conceal.

THE HEIGHT OF THE SCREAM

He was almost at the top when the bedroom door swung open. The top stair creaked loudly. As he stooped to examine it he felt a cold tickling sensation on his face, on his hands. He felt air cutting through his clothes, then through his flesh. Warmth leaked over his skin. He was still wondering what was happening when he felt his eyeballs part. He cried out and fell the length of the stairs.

At his cry Marilyn cried out too. She snatched the broken knife-blade from the bin and ran to the stairs. Frank was lying at the bottom. The shadow of a bruise was growing on his forehead, but he was otherwise unmarked. Heedless of the blood that filled the creases of her hand from her clumsy grip on the blade she stood over him, glaring defiantly up the stairs.

He regained consciousness minutes later, as she cradled him. She was about to help him to his feet when the bedroom door began to tremble. She grabbed the knife-blade from the pool of her blood, wondering if it were about to begin.